MW01701839

BLEED THROUGH

adriana
arrington

Adriana
Arrington

CURIOSITY
QUILLS PRESS
A Division of **Whampa, LLC**
P.O. Box 2160
Reston, VA 20195
Tel/Fax: 800-998-2509
http://curiosityquills.com

http://adrianaarrington.com

Cover Art by Eugene Teplitsky
http://eugeneteplitsky.deviantart.com

ISBN 978-1-62007-837-2 (ebook)
ISBN 978-1-62007-838-9 (paperback)

for my mother, who taught me a love of writing

and for my father, who passed me all those Dean Koontz and Stephen King novels on the side

1

MONDAY, AUGUST 25th

The screen door groaned and shuddered as Liam pushed against it. Warped by years of intense heat and rain, the flimsy metal frame no longer fit squarely in the doorjamb. He kicked at the bottom left corner and budged the door forward.

Come on, you piece of crap. Open!

An aluminum soda can, liberated from the dark corner of his bedroom closet, crinkled under his clenched fingers, and a thick textbook titled "Accounting Principles, Vol. 1" teetered between his elbow and stomach.

The creaking door summoned the family tomcat, RP, like a demon from hell. His claws scratched against the gray linoleum as he streaked through the living room and collided with Liam's left foot.

"He's gonna shred you to pieces," said Joshua. He stood next to the dining room windows that looked over the backyard. Afternoon sunshine filtered through gauzy curtains but didn't reach his pockmarked face. His uniform of black jeans and leather jacket swallowed the light around him. "Serves you right for leaving me."

Liam ignored the taunt and concentrated on not dropping his soda. After a few frenzied seconds spent trying to evade the worst of RP's nipping, he squeezed through the door and slammed it shut before the cat made his escape. He didn't begrudge the animal his freedom. Quite the contrary. But his mother would skewer him if he granted the fur ball's wish. She feared the cat would get hurt if he got loose, or worse yet, run away to the dense woods near their home.

"Maybe next time, pal."

RP glowered at him and swished his gray and black tail. The cat hated him. As a general rule, most cats did. They knew what he did when nobody watched. But RP held extra-special disdain for him; he understood the upheaval Liam caused by his mere presence.

Joshua remained in the dining room, frowning with such intensity Liam licked his lips in nervousness.

Acutely aware of their baleful glares, he turned and stepped onto the timeworn concrete patio, avoiding its many buckles and cracks. The Florida humidity clamped onto his body like an alligator snapping its jaws over fresh prey. He didn't mind. The intense afternoon heat was real; a sensation he could trust.

A rusted porch swing with dirty, flattened yellow pads groaned in protest when he plopped down on it. Twangy country music from a neighbor's house filtered through the air as he pushed off the ground with his right leg. The world rocked back and forth.

He placed the accounting textbook to his side and popped open the soda. It fizzed up to his lips as he raised the can and tilted it back, and he allowed the acidic sugar to flood his mouth. He swished the soda around each tooth—that's right, Mother Dearest, each and every tooth—reveling in its heavenly poison before chugging it.

With a half-hearted flick of his wrist, he flipped open his textbook and attempted to read the first page. He made it through two and a half sentences before the various accounting terms and principles became mere letters and sounds meshed together. How Isaac and his mother expected him to garner an ounce of excitement over starting community college was beyond him. Most days, he barely found the energy to function. But Isaac and his mother said the routine of school would be good for him, so off to school he went.

He rose from the squeaky swing and marched away from Isaac's house, leaving the accounting tome where it lay but holding onto his soda. His mother had turned to the gospel of health food and subjected her family to its ceaseless melody. As a result, high-fructose corn syrup had become even rarer than happiness in their home. Three days ago, he'd carried out some professional-grade smuggling to hide the carbonated contraband in his closet, and he had no intention of letting it go to waste.

The bell from the marina tolled in rhythm with his footsteps. Although he didn't want to live with his mother and stepfather, at least the locale offered some consolation. Not only was Isaac's house colonels' quarters, its backyard led to the Tyndall Air Force Base yacht club as well as a beach so often deserted it might as well have been private. Both were less than a quarter mile away. Still, Liam missed the small place he'd shared with his father in Ohio until six months ago. That had been home.

He picked his way through the pathetic excuse of a lawn that boasted more sandburs than grass. No backyard leading to a beach could be truly awful, though, especially one edged by an imposing live oak grove. The trees' gnarled limbs invited him to climb, their drooping branches like crooked fingers that whispered, "Come play." Sometimes Liam answered their call. Today, he wanted to be farther from the house. Farther from Joshua.

A salty breeze ruffled his red hair as he crossed the street and made his way past the shoppette and the yacht club. Closed on Mondays, the clubhouse sat dark and empty. Liam exhaled in relief. No red-nosed retirees would watch him today.

His shoes crunched over a gravel path that trickled out to the slender jetty, just beyond the marina's smaller dock. If he traveled any farther, he'd be in the ocean. The sun blazed over his head as he settled down on jagged, small rocks. He dipped his hand in the warm gulf water and swirled it around in circles.

A like-minded beast, the ocean hid its dangerous undercurrents beneath a smooth surface. Here, with only the waves as benevolent bystanders, he allowed his mind to wander wherever it wished.

His gaze caught on a run-down speedboat moored at the dock. Twenty years ago it'd probably shined a midnight blue, but years of ocean spray had lightened it to an anemic steel color. Though chipped and faded, its name, "Miss Behavin," still remained legible on the hull.

"Bet somebody loved you once. Seems you've fallen on hard times now. No worries, though, I'm not one to judge," he said.

His dad would've brought the old girl back to her former glory with twenty bucks and a six-pack of beer. He closed his eyes and reimagined the boat with a spanking new paint job, a metallic black that glinted in the sunlight, and a new, rumbling motor. Clad in a Denver Broncos T-shirt and cheap jeans, his father hung a fishing line over the side and sang along to classic rock, off-key as ever.

A booming voice shattered his imaginings.

"Don't threaten me, you sonuvabitch! You wanna ruin my life? I'll never let that happen!"

The sound of fists making contact with flesh carried over the water. Grunts of pain and exertion followed. Liam opened his eyes and searched for the commotion. Across the marina, two middle-aged men in civilian clothes fought on the weathered dock.

One, a tall, white guy with a flat face and snub nose, hammered on a shorter, stocky man. The victim's buzzed, blond hair ended above a spider tattoo on his neck.

"Cull, get your hands off me! Stop!" the smaller man yelled. Blood gushed from his broken nose.

The victim raised his hands above his head to stop the blows, but the taller man, Cull, sent him lurching to the wooden planks with a savage kick to the stomach.

With a face chillingly devoid of emotion, Cull methodically pounded on the man with the spider tattoo. The smack of flesh on flesh turned squelchy as Cull kicked and punched, punched and kicked. Soon, nothing but a bloody, tenderized husk remained of the smaller man.

Bile rose to Liam's throat as waves lapped at his feet, wetting the space between his toes and flip-flops. He felt like a coward for not interfering. In a perfect world, he'd be a Good Samaritan and rescue the smaller man. But in this world? He just hoped to avoid Cull's wrath. Cull, however, didn't seem the sort to ignore witnesses to a crime. The idea sent Liam's stomach lurching. His soda slipped from rigid fingers and clanged to the rocks below, spilling its precious caramel contents into the ocean.

The victim lay motionless on the dock. One last kick from Cull rocked his body to the side. His head lolled to the right, setting his vacant, glassy stare on Liam.

Cull stood straight and stretched his neck. Spattered with blood, his sage green T-shirt looked like a gory Jackson Pollack imitation. Heavy drops of rain darkened the shoulders of his shirt and plastered his short, dark hair against his skull. Cull flexed his knuckles while making a slow search of the marina, turning his body toward Liam but letting his beady gaze slide right over him, as if he wasn't there. Satisfied nobody saw his crime, Cull grabbed hold of his limp victim and tossed him onto the closest sailboat.

Sweat beaded on Liam's brow, and his pulse raced. Had Cull really not seen him?

The murderer boarded the boat, older but pristinely maintained with glittering cursive letters naming her "Freedom," and vanished below deck. Liam's instincts screamed at him to run, but he stayed put. He needed to know what happened next.

Cull reappeared with a white towel and jug. He poured water over deep crimson stains on the dock and mopped the area with the towel, which turned a sickly strawberry pink.

He held out his hand and looked at the sky. "Never been so happy for a rain storm," he said.

Then he and Freedom disappeared, evaporating into the air like a passing memory.

2

Liam looked up to the heavens. No clouds hovered above, nor did any drops of rain fall on his face.

Damn.

The whole scene was a figment of his imagination. The last time he'd had such a vivid hallucination had been right after his father died and right before his latest stint in a hospital. His knees buckled and he fell to the ground. Shards of broken oyster shells dug into his skin.

This couldn't happen. Hadn't his brain received the memo?

No relapses allowed.

He wanted to move out of Isaac's house, and soon. His probation deal, however, barred his independence until a psychologist deemed him "stable." Which, until five minutes ago, he'd believed he had nearly achieved.

His body shook with nerves as he brushed off his knees and stood. No use in ignoring facts. Dr. Jen needed to adjust the dosage on his meds. She always said medicating schizophrenia was a moving target. Its magic bullseye had apparently relocated. They'd have to search for it again.

Sweat trickled between his shoulder blades as he stumbled across the jetty. He kept his eyes trained on the ground as he passed the yacht club, and he refused to believe the tunnel vision that transformed Isaac's sandy backyard into the endless Sahara.

"Every insurmountable task can be broken down into smaller,

manageable ones. Don't worry about leaping when you can take a small step," Dr. Jen had told him last week.

Only 562 steps existed between Isaac's house and the jetty's end. He'd already taken fifty. Five hundred and twelve to go. With painstaking precision, he counted each step out loud. Around the three hundreds, his throat became so dry his tongue swelled. He kept counting.

Step 562 placed him directly behind the screen door. He yanked it open and made a beeline to the kitchen, where his pillbox lay on top of the ancient microwave. He twisted off the cap and shook out a small, yellow round tablet. After a short pause, he fished out two more. With trembling hands, he tossed the pills in his mouth and ran the faucet. Water spilled over his face as he leaned down and gulped. He heaved with exhaustion and slid down the cabinets, crumpling on the gray and white linoleum.

Joshua sat next to him. "Can't say I feel bad for you. Nasty things happen when you abandon me."

"I know."

Liam stared straight ahead in dreadful anticipation of more hallucinations. Although none came, and his muscles screamed to stretch, he didn't dare move. Motion might earn him unwanted attention. Moments turned into hours turned into days turned into years.

Silence reigned until a door slammed in the carport outside the kitchen. He summoned all the courage he possessed and moved his head to glance at the clock. 5:36 p.m. His mother and Tasha were home.

A surge of adrenaline-filled panic provided him with the strength to stand. If his mother discovered him like this, he'd be back in a clinic tonight. He lumbered into the living room and flopped onto the couch. The remote slipped out of his fumbling fingers twice, but he pressed the power button right as the front door banged open. Better to be semi-catatonic in front of the TV like a normal American.

"Liam!" Tasha cried with delight, running toward her older brother with arms wide. She threw all of her fifty pounds into a bear hug.

"Hey, baby girl." Extra medication had a tendency to make him slur words, so he focused on his pronunciation. Hopefully, he didn't overcompensate. His mother hated it when he sounded like a robot.

Tasha pulled back from her hug and dazzled Liam with a proud, toothless grin. "I lost another one at school!" she proclaimed, poking her tongue through the gap in her front teeth. Her corkscrew curls, pulled up into pigtails topped with gossamer butterflies, danced with each bounce she took.

"Tooth losing is *not* allowed!" he said in mock horror. "You must stop growing. Consider that an order, cadet!"

She covered her mouth with warm, brown hands and giggled.

How many more years before she discovered how screwed up he was? One? Two?

"Look what I made you." She dug in her pocket and retrieved a neon-orange looped bracelet. She dangled it near his chin. "Do you like it?"

"I love it." He took the plastic bracelet from her small hands and rolled it onto his wrist. With a theatrical flourish, he waved his arm in the air. She laughed again.

His mother, Allison, stood in the doorway and inspected her children's interaction. Her light-olive complexion looked paler than normal for this point in the summer. She hadn't spent much time outside this year. Under Liam's gaze, her narrow shoulders tightened and inched close to her ears.

"What'd you do today?" she asked.

"Relaxed. Like I was supposed to."

Allison clenched her teeth but didn't push further. She never discussed his health with Tasha near. By now, her covering-up skills almost surpassed his.

"Who's hungry?" She slung her knock-off Chanel purse onto the dining-room table and sank into the couch next to her children.

"I'm starving!" Tasha said.

Liam shook his head. His medication both suppressed his appetite and slowed his metabolism, making him gain weight even while he ate less. Yet another wonderful side effect.

"I am, too. Go cook me some dinner," Allison ordered in jest.

"What? I can't make dinner. I'm only five!" Tasha argued. "Liam should do it. He's a grown-up."

"Grown-up." Such a subjective term. While technically an adult at twenty-five, in reality, he enjoyed less freedom than a young teen.

Tasha hopped up and commenced her hungry dance, which involved rubbing her belly and sliding her feet backward in a herky-jerky moonwalk imitation. If a cuter dance existed in the universe, Liam had yet to see it. His little sister could ask him to do whatever she liked, including cooking, and he'd oblige.

"All right then. What do you want?" Liam asked. He knew not to look at his mother but did anyhow. The same worry lines and sour expression crossed her face now that accompanied any helpful proclamations on his part.

The front door creaked open once again. Isaac strode through it, wearing his standard Air Force blues. He lifted off his hat and tossed it at the light-oak hall tree. Because it was Isaac's hat, and he charmed whatever he touched, it found a home on a hook and hung there. The silver oak leaf insignia on his uniform declaring him a lieutenant colonel glinted off the late afternoon light.

Tasha skipped over to him and buried herself in his chest. A wide smile crossed Isaac's face before he bent down to kiss her forehead.

"How are my ladies today?" He tapped Tasha's nose and nodded at Allison.

"Great! Liam's gonna make us dinner!" Tasha said.

"Oh?" Isaac's carefree smile withered, and his dark-brown eyes narrowed.

Allison shifted on the couch.

If Liam was a better son, he'd try harder to get along with his stepfather. It shouldn't be so difficult. He could see why his mother loved the man. Isaac epitomized the definition of the total package. The outside of the box—dark-brown skin, tall, athletic build—matched the inside; a brilliant, caring, and analytical mind.

Still, Liam bristled with anger whenever near his stepfather. It stung that his mother had married somebody so opposite of his father, and by extension, him. He'd managed the rejection from afar. But now that he lived with the man who symbolized everything he never could be? Unbearable.

Isaac set a flat stare on Liam. "What's on the menu for tonight?"

"It's a surprise." He winked at Isaac. What did the man think? That Liam would serve up the old bitty who lived across the street? Although the idea *had* crossed his mind a few times—the woman wasn't even human anymore, so technically it wouldn't be cannibalism—he wouldn't offend his family's naïve sensibilities.

His stepfather's telltale signs of irritation bubbled up right on cue; the vein in his neck popped out and he rubbed his thumb on his palm.

Allison jumped to her feet. "Uhh, I've got leftovers in the fridge. Don't worry about it, Liam, I'll go heat them up."

Super. Reheated quinoa with a dash of "it's so healthy!" spinach. Old lady replica never sounded so tasty.

"Ready to start classes tomorrow?" Isaac asked.

Liam shrugged. "Only one way to find out."

Isaac's jaw tensed, and he darted a glance at Allison. They were always there, the subtle reminders of the requirements in place for Liam to live with them: take his medication, go to school, never, ever be alone with his little sister.

"I'm ready," Liam muttered. He stood with a slight stumble and gestured toward his room. "Don't worry about making me a serving of leftovers. I'm knocking off early tonight."

Nobody but Tasha argued with him.

"But I just got home!" His sister stomped her foot in petulance.

"I know, baby girl. And I'm sorry. But I've got to rest up for class tomorrow."

Tasha sighed. "Tomorrow?"

"Promise." He held up his fingers in a scout's honor sign.

He walked down the L-shaped hall to his room at the rear of the house. Unlike Tasha's matchy-match décor, his bedroom veered toward generic. A guest room before his unanticipated arrival, neither Allison nor he saw any sense in personalizing it. A navy bedspread covered his twin-sized bed, which rested on a simple metal frame. Soft light spread from a taupe lampshade atop a nondescript dresser. Although the bare walls practically screamed for a Picasso or de Kooning print, only one item graced them. Next to his nightstand, he'd pinned a picture of his father and him from Before. A five-pound bass dangled from his fingertips, and his father shot the camera a thumbs-up. They both smiled wide, unaware of the future and its miseries.

He kicked off his shoes and turned on Pearl Jam's "Ten" album. It had been his dad's favorite. Isaac also happened to hate it.

His mother's fancy handwriting proclaimed tomorrow the "First Day of Class!" on a calendar on his wall. Below, in a much smaller and constrained script, Isaac had written, "Dr. Jen appt. 0900."

Nine a.m. couldn't come fast enough. Liam set his alarm clock. His psychologist would help him unpack what he saw today and make sense of it all.

"You've got them worried," Joshua said. Perched on the edge of a denim-cushioned papasan, he picked at the rattan frame with dirty fingernails. He tapped his boots against the linoleum floor.

"I've got it covered," Liam said.

"The hell you do." Joshua yanked off a sliver of rattan and threw it at him. "Don't make me hurt you."

He took a step backward. "You can't hurt me."

The papasan frame creaked as Joshua leaned forward. "We both know that's not true."

Liam hung his head and avoided meeting Joshua's eyes.

"He knows what you saw. He's going to find you and kill you too."

Liam didn't have to ask who "he" was. "He" was the murderer. Cull.

Springs from the stiff bed poked his back as he eased onto it. "I know."

3

TUESDAY, AUGUST 26th

People always accused Liam of making poor decisions, but they could make some mighty odd choices themselves. Take Dr. Jen, for example. In all likelihood, she could decorate her tiny office however she liked. Nobody told her what color chair to buy, how to organize her desk, or what artwork to display. So when she chose to hang a print of Van Gogh's "Corridor in Saint-Paul Hospital" above her computer monitor, it left Liam scratching his head.

His chest constricted every time he looked at the print, which depicted a vast hallway of repeating golden arches that turned the color of corroded copper as they snaked away in the distance. The crimson floor, full of movement and sheen, resembled a canal of blood. Not even the hemorrhaging hallway in The Overlook Hotel frightened him more.

"You've got some shitty taste in art, Dr. Jen. Do you actually enjoy looking at that piece or do you like torturing your patients?" Liam gnawed his pinky nail down to the nub.

Dr. Jen turned her head and looked at the print. "I thought it might make a few patients feel better. Some of the most talented and revered people in history have had their struggles with mental health. Vincent Van Gogh was but one of those people. Knowing you're not alone is half the battle sometimes."

"Yeah, well, the other half is not being reminded you're one step away from a mental institution. Maybe next time you should pick out 'Sunflowers' or 'Starry Night.' Neither of those would make me want to stab you." He yanked at his earlobes.

"Let's examine this feeling further. What exactly about the painting disturbs you?" Dr. Jen pushed her thin, silver glasses back up to the bridge of her nose. Sapphire earrings flashed against her dark-beige skin.

He spit out his nail. "It makes me feel like a caged rat, waiting to be drowned."

She nodded, and her chestnut bun wiggled on top of her head. "You feel trapped at home."

"I need to move out today." He continued to stare at the print. Or maybe the print stared at him.

"I understand your desire for independence. And while you've made great strides toward your goal of moving out, I'm not sure you're ready yet." Dr. Jen smiled kindly to soften the blow of her words. She had a singular talent for telling the truth without hurting his feelings

"It doesn't matter if I'm ready. If I stay, somebody's gonna kill me." He squeezed the arms of his chair until his knuckles went white.

"Why would you think that?" Her hands lay over a notepad in her lap, still and tranquil.

"I saw a murder." He licked his lips. "A man beat the bloody hell out of a guy right before my eyes."

Dr. Jen leaned back. "When did this happen?"

"Yesterday."

"Were you alone at the time?"

"Yes."

She arched an eyebrow. "Have you reported it to the authorities?"

"No." Liam chewed his cheek, wishing he didn't have such an awful track record with reality. "You think I had a hallucination, don't you?"

She tapped her blue ballpoint pen on her notepad. "The more important question is what you think. Were there any signs it could be one?"

"Maybe." He scratched his scalp. "It seemed like the murderer, Cull, couldn't see me. Like I was invisible to him." He didn't mention Cull, and his boat, disappearing into thin air. "But it was so different than my usual hallucinations. The killer didn't threaten me. He didn't encourage me to hurt anybody. He didn't even acknowledge me."

"For now, let's table whether or not this event is real. Instead, I want to know why you're scared of a killer who can't see you."

He picked at the orange bracelet Tasha made him. "I just have a feeling."

The psychologist stood and adjusted her modest black skirt suit. "Feelings can be powerful." She reached over her desk and grabbed both golden-framed sides of the Van Gogh and lifted it off the wall. With a quick flip of her wrists, she turned the print backward, hiding its nasty hallway from view. "Emotions sometimes lie to us and make us want to behave in an unacceptable manner. How should you handle your fear?"

The office felt ten feet bigger without the print's overbearing presence. Liam slid his legs forward and relaxed his knees. "By distracting it. By remembering, there's more to life than being afraid. By engaging in activities I enjoy." He gave a sheepish shrug and looked to the side. "To be honest, I like to paint."

She chuckled. "Doesn't surprise me. You've certainly got a better command of tone and interpretation than I do." She sat back down and crossed her ankles. "Painting is a wonderful and safe avenue of self-expression. You can pour your frustrations and fears into artwork without repercussion."

He stifled a cough. Although Dr. Jen's sentiment was lovely, it wasn't true. There were always repercussions, even for hobbies as innocent as slopping paint on a canvas. He'd learned that lesson the first time he'd caught his mother sobbing over one of his more vivid portraits. Granted, he'd painted Joshua stabbing him in the neck. Maybe his mother had been right to cry. At any rate, Liam hid his artwork now. Any creations went straight under his bed, where they could offend only the dust bunnies.

"Are there other self-calming methods you could practice?" she asked.

None that worked, but he knew what his psychologist wanted to hear. "Reading," he said.

The wrinkles around Dr. Jen's mouth deepened as she grinned at her patient's progress. "My favorite pastime."

His lips, on their way to a fake smile, hitched mid-scowl when he noticed the edges on her face blurring as if she was a photo out of focus. He blinked. Instead of disappearing, the blurring became a fuzzy halo radiating from her entire body, a great flowing mass of whiteness that throbbed and pulsed like a living organism until it coalesced into an image of a woman who resembled her. Same facial structure with high cheekbones, same full-figured body build, but she wore a decade or two less of age on her face. The corners of her mouth turned down, and unshed tears brimmed in her eyes. The woman stood as motionless as a 3-D photograph.

He pointed a shaking finger at the apparition. "Can you see her?"

Dr. Jen tilted her head to the side. "See who?"

"There's a woman next to you. She looks like you. But she's stark white, like a ghost." Liam's heart jumped up into his throat.

Apparently immune to terrifying declarations from her patients, Dr. Jen didn't bother to glance around the room. She kept her laser-like focus on him. "Does she frighten you?"

"I'm not sure." The adrenaline thrumming through his veins would seem to indicate she did, but another emotion churned under the fear. Anticipation, maybe?

"Is she threatening either of us?"

"No... but she's connected to you. It's like you're projecting her from your body. Like you're conjuring her somehow." The longer the ghost woman ignored him, the easier it became to breathe again. His heart sunk back in his chest.

"Have you ever seen a projection like this before?" Dr. Jen scrawled an observation in her notepad.

He shook his head, scrutinizing the woman in white. "She's wearing a long dress, with horizontal stripes on it," he said.

The scratching of pen on paper stopped as Dr. Jen looked up.

"Her hair's up, like yours. But she also has on a thick, black headband. She has a tattoo on her wrist. An infinity symbol."

The pen fell from Dr. Jen's stiff fingers, bouncing off the carpet before landing at his feet. Her mouth hung open, and her hands trembled.

She whispered, "How do you know about her?"

He squirmed in his chair. He'd finally accomplished the unthinkable—he'd upset Dr. Jen. Deep down, he'd always known she would reject him at some point. He wouldn't have thought this hallucination would be the deal breaker, though.

Trying his best to be surreptitious, he glanced from his doctor to the doorway. "What do you mean? I'm only telling you what I see."

"Liam, for our relationship to work best, you shouldn't know about my personal life. Why did you investigate my past?" She placed a still shaking hand over her abdomen and grimaced.

"I didn't." He pushed up in his chair and tapped both feet against the carpet.

The air hung thick with her accusation and measured breathing. "We've never lied to each other before, Liam. It's what makes this work. Tell me why you researched me."

He fought back the scream building in his throat and jumped out of his seat. Unable to take the look on Dr. Jen's face, he closed his eyes and fumbled for the door handle. A sharp ringing in his ears overwhelmed all other sound as he jerked open the office door and walked out.

He'd never left an appointment with Dr. Jen before finishing his allotted time. These sessions kept him sane. She kept him sane. But he was no liar. She should know by now.

Eyes lowered to avoid any potential interactions, he scuffled through the waiting room. The receptionist slid back the glass partition separating her from patients, expecting him to stop and make his next appointment. He didn't. Instead, the weight of Dr. Jen's rejection propelled him forward as icy cold tentacles of fear spread through his chest. He pushed open the glass exit door and stepped into the muggy Florida morning. His mother's car, a run-down red Hyundai with one door faded pink, awaited him across the street. Like a convict escaping prison, he ran to it.

4

The Hyundai's noisy engine struggled to life. Liam shifted the car into reverse, zoomed through the parking lot and onto busy Highway 98. A woman driving a cherry-red convertible shot him the bird as he switched lanes and cut her off. He flipped one back. Generic hotels and billboards advertising mobile homes littered the side of the road.

Two new symptoms in two days didn't bode well. Despite his knotted stomach, he forced himself to breathe. How could Dr. Jen accuse him of manufacturing the vision? And who had that woman been, and why had she upset his psychologist so much?

The morning's unexpected turn left him with a sour taste in his mouth. He'd expected his session with Dr. Jen to prepare him for his first day of college. Instead, it'd only made him more anxious.

Gulf Coast State College loomed ahead, the start of his supposed road to recovery. He drove past the exit. One missed class wouldn't make a big difference.

Sorry, Mom. Valedictorian I ain't.

He crept over the Hathaway Bridge, still congested by crowds of tourists jamming in one last vacation before the end of summer. Minivans piled full of kids and haggard parents lined the bridge alongside him. Traffic didn't get any better as he turned onto Thomas Drive. He didn't mind—he had some time to kill.

Tacky beach attire stores and kitschy restaurants with blinking neon signs led the way to Diamond Bay Park. He turned into its packed lot and pulled into the one open spot. The engine clicked and moaned its way to sleep. He grabbed his backpack, which, along with the thick accounting textbook, contained a tattered copy of "The Catcher in the Rye." He'd take Dr. Jen's advice. Perhaps reading would calm him.

Despite heavy platinum clouds in the distance, throngs of people crowded the beach. He dodged through groups of kids throwing snow-white clumps of sand at each other in play, barely avoiding a missile some brat purposefully lobbed at him. Siblings and friends splashed in the clear water as Liam edged around sand castles sunburnt fathers built for diapered toddlers. Happiness, or a close approximation of it, shined everywhere. It made the absence of joy in his life all the more glaring.

If his father had still been around, he'd urge Liam to stop waiting for life to serve up a fun time and create his own entertainment. And the man would have a point. Since moving to Tyndall five months ago, Liam hadn't once gone to the beach with his mother or sister. The trip would never happen if he waited for an invitation. He needed to take the initiative and organize an outing. Tasha would like it. For that matter, so would he.

He kicked off his Adidas flip-flops and carried them as his feet sank into the warm sand. A bolt of lightning streaked in the distance. He closed his eyes with gratitude. Nobody with a brain would remain under the wide-open skies of the beach during a Florida thunderstorm. Dutiful parents proved him right when they gathered their children and belongings.

Thankful he'd have a few minutes of peace before the storm hit, he settled down on the sand. Though departing vacationers kicked sand in his face, he ignored the momentary discomfort. A little pain for a lot of solitude was a worthwhile trade. He flipped open his book and tried to let his mind wander into its alternate world.

The beach quieted except for the rolls of thunder booming closer and closer to the shore. A strong wind flipped back the pages of his novel, placing Liam chapters behind where he wanted to be. He ignored the oncoming storm and searched for the page he lost.

A pair of petite feet with toenails painted a turquoise blue parked themselves under the novel. A woman cleared her throat.

"Point made, troubled white boy. You'd rather get electrocuted than put down Holden Caulfield. Your life must be so tough."

He lowered his book and gazed upward. An Asian woman with shiny black hair cropped short against a round face stood over him. Her eyes, a brown so dark they were almost black, danced with mischief. She wore a gray tank top and jean cutoffs that accentuated her ample lower body. A ray of sunlight broke through the clouds and settled on her, making her tawny skin glow like an angel had kissed her.

Liam struggled a moment to find his voice. "Excuse me?"

"I don't know if you noticed, but a storm's coming. Pretty bad one, too." She spoke with a heavy Panhandle drawl and placed a hand on her hip in overplayed exasperation. "Why don't you pick up your poor, tortured soul and drive it on home so you can come publicly pout another time?"

"You're not a lifeguard, you can't tell me to leave." He snorted. "Besides, aren't you risking your life simply to lecture me?"

She cocked her head. "True. But it irritates me when people die for stupid reasons. Natural reasons, okay. I don't like it any, but that's how the universe works. Dying because you won't leave the beach when you should? Unacceptable."

"Why do you care about me? I'm a pathetic, white-boy loser." Giant raindrops speckled his paperback. In annoyance, he threw it into his backpack and stood, brushing sand off his shorts and legs.

She shrugged. "I was in my car getting ready to leave when I spotted you. I guess I've got a soft spot for wounded birds."

She didn't know the half of it.

"You can go home feeling saintly now. I'm leaving the beach in one tortured piece," he snapped.

The woman laughed and stuck out her hand. "Name's Mai Nguyen. Whom may I tell my family I saved today?"

Rain fell in a steady rhythm now, the grand deluge seconds away.

There seemed to be nobody on the beach but the two of them. He kept his hand to his side. "Liam Murphy."

"Well then, Liam, nice to meet you. And I will feel better knowing you went home and didn't die today." She held out her arms as if to usher him off the sand and back to the parking lot. He found himself complying, a smile teasing at the edge of his lips, until a shriek from the ocean whipped his head back to the waves pounding the beach.

5

A **middle-aged woman with a shock of red hair stood** waist deep in the swirling waves. She screamed out at the water, terror punctuating her words. "Somebody help! Please!" She pointed outward, where thirty or forty yards away, a pale, bald head crested out of a wave and then sunk again.

Liam streaked toward the woman, dropping his bag and flip-flops in the wet sand. Her distressed pleas sent goose bumps racing along his spine.

"Liam! Stop! What are you doing?" Mai yelled.

"I have to help that man! Can't you see he's drowning?"

Mai caught up to Liam and clasped his arm.

"There's nobody here but us," she said. Angry waves lapped against their feet.

He swallowed his rebuttal as he looked back out at the ocean. The man had disappeared.

Eyes full of confusion, Mai shook her head and placed her other hand on Liam's arm. "I don't see or hear anybody."

She was right. The woman had stopped screaming. In fact, she had stopped altogether. Not even footprints on the shore remained as evidence of her presence.

"Umm, right. Sorry. I thought I heard somebody," he mumbled.

She made eye contact and flashed a reassuring smile, keeping her hands on his arm. "Happens to the best of us."

Of course, it didn't. Not even remotely. He appreciated Mai's white lie anyway. Most people ran away from him, and nobody attempted to comfort him.

A bolt of lightning flashed in the sky, so close and bright the thunder cracked in his bones and blinded him temporarily.

"We have to leave. Now!" he yelled over the pouring rain. She nodded. He grabbed his Adidas slides and bag and ran back to the parking lot. Wet sand, kicked up by Mai sprinting alongside him, pelted his legs. Preoccupied with her proximity, Liam forgot to fish out his keys until he stood before the Hyundai, staring at it like it would magically open on its own.

"Still shaken up, aren't you?" She placed one hand on his shoulder before slipping his bag from his fingers, rummaging through it until she held up his keys in victory.

"Put the pointy end in the lock and turn." Mai smirked and motioned at his car.

Unsure whether he should be amused or irritated by her peculiar blend of sweet and sour, he swiped the keys from her hands. "Yeah, I know. Up until five minutes ago, I somehow managed to live without you bossing me around."

"Wonders never cease."

She waved goodbye before hopping into a Honda Civic three spaces over and, proving herself a royal nuisance, she flashed her lights until he jammed his keys in the lock and opened the door. Salty rainwater dripped over the seat and steering wheel as he eased into the car. Only after he slammed shut his door did she pull out of the parking lot, honking as she drove past.

That woman was a piece of work. Exactly what kind of work, he couldn't decide.

No matter how much Mai intrigued him, though, she couldn't take his mind off the drowning. The vision seemed as real as the one he'd seen at the yacht club. The woman had been as vivid as life, and the grief in her cries still echoed inside his head.

Why all the breakthrough symptoms? His brain had a distinct limit on how many times it could differentiate between hallucination and reality. If he didn't stop his precarious dance soon, he'd end up back in a hospital. The mere thought twisted his stomach.

He waited fifteen minutes to avoid the worst of the storm, and the hapless tourists driving through it, before turning on the car. The windshield wipers swished back and forth, clearing a direct path to the beach in front of him, where, once again, the woman with the red hair screamed and pointed out at the water. He gritted his teeth and backed out.

6

A**n hour later, Liam drove onto Eagle Drive. After** passing the turn for the yacht club, he pulled into Isaac's driveway. Parked underneath the carport, his stepfather's silver bike glinted against the afternoon light. His mother's SUV, however, was conspicuously absent.

Fantastic. It'd be only Isaac and him at home.

With a sigh of resignation, Liam swung his legs out of the Hyundai and walked toward the house, a squat rambler constructed of cinderblocks painted the same sickly yellow Van Gogh had selected for the hallway in "Corridor in Saint-Paul Hospital." Dr. Jen must share a design aesthetic with military-housing developers.

His throat constricted at the thought of his psychologist. What if she decided to drop him as a patient because of their disagreement?

He shuffled onto the porch and checked his phone for voicemails. Still none from Dr. Jen. Or anybody else. He was in no danger of winning any popularity contests.

The dissipated thunderstorm left the atmosphere damp and smothering. He turned the front door handle. As usual, Isaac had left the house unlocked. No matter how many times Liam begged him to implement better safety practices, he refused. Although base housing might not make for the largest accommodations, he believed they made some of the safest.

Of course, he'd change his mind if he knew a replica lived across the street from them.

His stepfather typically displayed better judgment, but Mrs. Channer was a shifty bugger. She camouflaged herself well as a past-her-expiration-date housewife. Most anybody would be fooled by her. But not Liam.

"Hello?" Liam glanced around the joint dining and living room. No sign of Isaac. He ventured farther in and peeked his head around the hallway corner. The faint sound of running water came from the master suite. Good. He'd spend the next few minutes in peace while Isaac took a shower.

The muscles in his lower back loosened just perceptibly before the stench of fresh-baked cookies snapped them taut again. Fear knotted Liam's stomach, but then his eyes caught on a fragrance plug-in. His mother insisted on using those nasty scents and must've switched in a new odor. He yanked it out of the wall, stomped into the kitchen, and tossed the disturbing fragrance into the trash.

Shirt pulled over his nose to protect it from the cookie stench, he collapsed onto the couch in the living room. A framed picture of his younger self stared at him from the top of a mahogany buffet. Taken before his troubles, or at least the ones obvious to everybody else, his smile overflowed with presumed bright prospects and blissful ignorance. He wore a crisp white *dobok* tied with his newly minted tae kwon do black belt.

On occasion, he caught his mother holding the photo. She grieved the loss of her son. What she didn't seem to understand was he shared her grief. He missed who he used to be more than she ever could. He longed to be the boy in the picture once again.

Isaac cleared his throat from the hallway. Liam roused himself from useless memories and nostalgia. No doubt Isaac thought him lost in the mazes of his mind. And he was, in a sense. But these mazes were on the sane side.

"How'd class go?" Isaac wore long basketball shorts and a sleeveless shirt emblazoned with "Northwestern University" on it. His biceps flexed as he leaned against the doorway and rubbed his hand over his closely shorn head.

"Uneventful," Liam lied. He sullenly tugged his shirt off his face.

As a JAG, Isaac knew how to interrogate an unwilling witness. "What did you think of the professor?"

As his father's son, Liam knew how to avoid answering a question. "She'll do."

Isaac's lips tightened, and he stayed mute, probably constructing his feelings into a non-threatening statement. Since Liam had come to live with them, Dr. Jen had worked with both Allison and him on cognitive behavioral therapy. To keep Liam as stable as possible, they aimed to keep the house calm and free of conflict.

That much they could all agree upon.

"Liam, you can do this. I know I don't have any idea how hard it is. But I do know you've got a strong will." He looked away as if the compliment pained him.

"Don't insult me, Isaac. You know I can't will myself better."

"I'm simply saying I believe in you." He held up a hand in frustration. "Not every comment I say to you is a criticism."

"Spare me. Do you even know what it's like? To have people judging you before they know who you really are?" Liam slapped the couch in emphasis and sat up straight. "The way you look at me, the way everybody looks at me, like I'm one step away from a mass-murder spree. It's exhausting."

"Are you seriously telling me I've never been subjected to people's prejudices?" Isaac barked a bitter laugh and rubbed the dark skin on his cheek before lifting his hand toward Liam. "I'm reduced to a stereotype every single day. You—even with a criminal record—can go into stores and mind your own business, and nobody will look at you twice. I go into the same store, and they've got more sights trained on me than a drone does on a Somalian terrorist."

Liam squeezed the bridge of his nose. Mired in the swamps of his mind, he didn't have the energy for sympathy, no matter how valid a point his stepfather made.

He gazed at Isaac, just long enough to be antagonizing, when it happened again.

A vague, white halo surrounded his stepfather. It withdrew from his body, taking its time to depart. The white mist swirled near his feet, amalgamating into a familiar figure. Liam blinked.

The shape had morphed into Tasha.

7

The ghostly Tasha was older, perhaps twenty or so. Her normally meticulous hair had fallen into a state of disrepair, gnarled into a huge tangle that hadn't seen a hint of care in months. Full of fear and pain, her eyes rounded into large Os. She drooled and gesticulated her fist in a violent tic.

Liam choked out loud as his greatest fear paraded in front of him. His sister was psychotic. She shared his illness.

This isn't real. Tasha is healthy. She won't get sick.

The brown, leather couch crinkled under his death grip. Dr. Jen counseled him to analyze his hallucinations. This particular one he understood well. His concern Tasha would end up like him was no deep, dark secret he had to unlock. So why did his mind conjure up this image?

Understanding spread through his brain like oil over a hot pan. He hadn't created this vision. It belonged to Isaac.

Damn.

So not only did he have to live with the man, but now he also had to see his inner thoughts?

The particles that made up schizophrenic Tasha dissolved, leaving the room silent with their absence.

"She won't end up like me," said Liam. He picked at a scab on his knee.

"What?" Isaac's eyes widened.

"Tasha. She's gonna be fine." He hoped with all his soul he told the truth. It wouldn't be fair if his illness also plagued Tasha. But then, schizophrenia didn't care about fair.

Isaac crossed his arms.

He dragged his feet across the floor. "The illness is on my father's side, as I'm sure Mom told you."

The set of Isaac's jaw and his sudden interest in the backyard suggested a deeper reason for his fears.

He smacked his forehead and snorted. "I can't believe it took me this long to put it together. There's a history on your side too, isn't there?"

The resounding silence of Isaac's answer told him all he needed to know. His stepfather continued to stare ahead, unwilling or unable to admit he might be capable of creating somebody like Liam.

"Well, this explains a lot. You don't hate me because I'm ill. You hate me because I'm a constant reminder of what might happen." He rose from the couch, stood in front of Isaac, and jabbed his finger in his stepfather's muscular chest. "So who was it? A long-forgotten aunt or uncle? Somebody left to rot on their own like Mom would've left me if the police hadn't called her?"

The muscles under Isaac's shirt rippled. "Step away from me, son."

"I'm not your son."

"Don't I know it." Isaac's lips compressed with instant regret.

Liam didn't mind. He fought lies all day long.

Isaac took a deep breath. "You can't blame your mother for what happened to you."

"Why not? She blames me for what I've done." Liam thumped his chest. "And she left me when I needed her most."

"Whatever you think, she didn't abandon you."

The air conditioner clanked on to combat the intense afternoon heat, and sunlight shone through the living room window, fading the navy and merlot hues of Isaac's Turkish rugs to anemic pastels.

"You weren't there for the beginning of my illness. You don't know." Liam grabbed his head and squeezed, red ringlets sprouting through his fingertips. "Instead of fearing what Tasha will become, you should fear how my Mom will handle it. Because let me tell you, she doesn't handle 'uncomfortable' situations well." He dropped his hands and jutted out his jaw. "Haven't you ever wondered why my mother lived half the country away from me?"

"Your father moved, and she stayed. That's all." Isaac didn't meet his gaze.

He laughed. "Dad thought the best treatment facility for schizophrenia was in Ohio, so he left the Air Force and moved us there. Only four years stood between him and retirement when he quit." Liam shook with rage and thrust four fingers in the air, waving them in Isaac's face. "To provide for me, he found a crappy job that met the clinic's health insurance requirements and worked there until he died. And Mom? She devoted one week a year to me. Poor thing would have to come and visit so Dad could get a break. Can you imagine the strain she must've felt?"

"You didn't want her near you." A vein on Isaac's forehead bulged.

"Ahh. So her story is I wanted to be abandoned?" Liam dipped his head in mock understanding. "Right, right. She never doubts what I tell her. Takes every word out of my mouth as gospel." He flipped his palms upward. "How can I possibly blame my mother for not helping me when I needed her most?"

Isaac leveled a hard stare at him. "It's not easy, you know. Living with somebody who's unpredictable. It can be scary."

"Pardon me if I can't summon up any pity." Liam sniffed. "It's pretty damn scary this side of schizophrenia too. Especially when your father dies and your mother leaves you to your own devices."

"You were in remission." A wise man, Isaac stood stiff like he thought moving one muscle might trigger a physical confrontation.

"Ever heard of a setback trigger?" Liam balled his fists. "Think having a state trooper stop by your house to tell you that your father is dead might cause one?"

Joshua appeared next to Isaac. "Hit him in the jaw," he urged Liam. "He's got it coming."

As if he heard Joshua's command, Isaac's nostrils flared. "Tasha will be home soon. I think it's best if you go out for a breath of fresh air."

Tick, tick, tick.

Liam inhaled and shoved aside Joshua's order. Even if Isaac was a prick, he spoke the truth. Tasha would be home soon. And Liam didn't want to scare her.

8

The marina loomed ahead. Parked boats, varying from modest motorboats to top-of-the-line sailboats, lined the parking lot next to it. Liam crossed the street and dropped by the base shoppette. The day required a soda.

He walked the aisles filled with basic needs such as bread, coffee, and boxed mac-n-cheese. His father had often taken him to shoppettes when he was younger, allowing him to grab a treat for good behavior. Maybe a Slim Jim, maybe a pack of sugary candy. Exactly the types of food his mother now forbid in her house. He grabbed a beverage from the refrigerated section and brought it to the counter.

"ID?" the bored cashier said.

Liam flashed his military ID card. The cashier bent forward to read it. After a moment, she looked up at him from under her bespectacled lenses. Maybe she hadn't ever seen a twenty-five-year-old dependent "child" before. Not many existed. Had to have special dispensation for it.

"Yep, that's me. Can I pay for this and be done with it?"

The woman grunted in reply and averted her gaze.

He contemplated peppering the cashier with questions so she had to interact with him but ultimately decided against the effort. Instead, he paid in silence, then strolled out of the shoppette and ambled by the yacht club. A few couples lingered on the clubhouse deck, chatting over early afternoon drinks. He hiked out to his usual perch at the tip of the jetty and avoided looking at the dock. The day had been trying enough without witnessing a murder.

A small fish skipped over the water as he popped open the lid of his soda. Much as he didn't like Isaac, he disliked fighting with him even more. What unsettled him most, though, was Tasha's apparition.

Could he possibly see into Isaac's mind? Into Dr. Jen's mind?

The visions were probably new and improved hallucinations. But the part of Liam's brain that clung to the hope he was better, that his illness was mostly in remission, insisted the scenes were real. Unbidden, his eyes trailed over the rippling waves to the dock.

Water sparkled in the empty slip adjacent to the murder scene. Perhaps Cull had docked Freedom elsewhere. Liam scanned the marina and found plenty of Black Pearls and a Serenity or two, but no Freedom.

He walked back up the jetty and reached the dock. He stepped tentatively onto the wooden slats, bleached gray by years of sunshine and salt water. A swift gust of wind pushed against his back, sending him stumbling fully onto the dock. The marina bell tolled as another blast of wind shoved him forward. He flexed his quadriceps and grounded his feet before taking small, choppy steps toward the scene of the crime.

No evidence of a murder lingered. No dried blood stains. No fresh gashes in the wood. No splintered boards. Nothing.

Liam dropped to his knees and grabbed hold of the dock with his left hand as he leaned over to his right and hung his body over the lapping water. Crusty barnacles adhered to the piling next to the empty slip. Not a spatter of blood tarnished them. He breathed out, relief and despair washing over him in equal measures. His head dangled below the dock. And then it occurred to him.

Look up.

So he did. No rusty bloodstains darkened the wood. Instead, his eyes caught on a large, sealed plastic baggie fastened with duct tape to the underside of the pier. He reached over and grabbed hold of the baggie and ripped off the duct tape. He swung the baggie above the dock and froze when it landed in his lap.

Due in part to his general disdain for mind-altering narcotics—he could summon up an alternate reality on his own, thank you very much—he'd never dabbled in drugs. Still, he was certain that's what lay in his lap now. Hundreds of smaller bags containing a powdery, white substance filled the plastic baggie. He cast a furtive glance at the clubhouse. The patrons checked their phones and smoked cigarettes. None so much as acknowledged his existence.

Liam opened the plastic bag, retrieved one of the smaller packets, and flicked it with his fingertips. Its white contents looked an awful lot like cocaine.

Curious whether the powder would shimmer in the sun, he held it above his head. Instead of focusing on the drugs, however, his eyes fixed on a white sailboat like the one from his vision. Except this one sailed directly toward him.

The murderer, Cull, leaned forward on Freedom's bow. Unlike last time, he looked directly at Liam, boring a hole in his eyes with a hard and unyielding stare.

9

Liam had no time to question whether or not the sailboat and Cull were real. He scrambled to his feet, dropped the large, plastic baggie, and sprinted back to land. Winded by the time he arrived at the clubhouse, he spared a glance back at the marina. Freedom already floated in her slip. Her skipper hopped onto the dock and grabbed the bag of drugs. Cull then hefted it onto the boat's deck without letting Liam out of his sight.

A gust of wind flapped a piece of plastic peeking between Liam's knuckles. With a sinking sensation, he unclutched his fist and groaned. He'd forgotten to leave behind the small pack of drugs.

Shit.

A few yacht club members gave him the side-eye as he ran past. He briefly considered asking them for help, but what could he say?

A dealer just caught me stealing his drugs! Help!

Cursing the extra pounds he'd gained, he fled back to Isaac's house. By the time he crossed the street and hit the sandy backyard, his hamstrings and lungs burned with exertion. He stashed the cocaine in his pocket and looked backward.

Cull chased him, of course, and closed the gap between them at a terrifying rate.

His heart pounded and his head throbbed, but Liam continued to drag his feet through the sand. He barely gulped down enough oxygen to keep his lungs working. Then he realized he'd forgotten to count. He had no idea how many steps remained until he reached Isaac's back door.

If he'd thought it hard to breathe before, now it felt impossible. Had he reached the four hundreds? Or closer to home, somewhere in the five hundreds? Dark spots swam in his vision as he struggled forward. He swung his arms in the air like he swam freestyle, hoping the motion would move him faster. It didn't.

The dark spots in his eyes turned to clouds that obscured his mother, head bowed behind the kitchen window. He panted for breath.

Liam tried to yell for her attention, but his plea came out a haggard, pathetic whisper. He stopped running and doubled over. With the last of his dwindling energy, he looked up and from the bottom of his chest, screamed, "Help!"

Startled by her son's yelling, Allison looked up in surprise. Her face fell as she spotted him. At first, she hesitated. Then she disappeared from view, and moments later, the screen door banged open.

"Liam?" Allison held a clear glass plate in her hand, dripping sudsy water on the concrete patio.

Exhausted, he dropped to his knees and spat on a brown patch of grass. He turned his head.

Cull was gone.

The dish crashed onto the concrete patio and shattered into a thousand slivered pieces. Allison half ran, half tiptoed through the glass shrapnel to her son and wrapped her arms around him. "Liam! What's wrong?"

Shielded in his mother's embrace, he regained his composure before breaking away. "A wasp chased me. I'm allergic, remember?"

"Of course. Let's get you inside before it comes back." She surveyed the backyard for the imaginary insect. It wasn't the first time he'd sent her looking for objects that didn't exist.

The two stood and picked their steps carefully to avoid the broken plate. Joshua waited behind the living room window. Smoke from his cigarette trailed his pointer and middle fingers, which he mimicked slicing across his neck. Liam looked away and focused on his little sister. Hands full of the family cat, she kept the screen door ajar by leaning her small back against it. RP hissed his typical greeting as Liam entered the house.

"Stop being so mean and nasty, Roly Poly!" said Tasha. Though her words were harsh, she cradled the animal in an affectionate hug. Too kind to know when to give up on a useless case, she continued to think she could domesticate him.

Allison led Liam to the couch and felt his forehead as he crumpled onto it. All the commotion must've alerted Isaac, who strode into the room and frowned.

"What happened?" he asked.

Tasha hopped on her toes and jostled the cat in her arms. "Liam got chased by a wasp!"

"Is that so?" Isaac's mouth twitched.

"Yep. But Liam is faster and stronger than any old bug. So he's fine."

Liam smiled at his sister. Only she could think he was fine.

Unsatisfied with his imprisonment, RP wrestled for his freedom and leapt out of Tasha's hands. The cat swept his long tail around him as he huddled under the dining room table. No doubt he'd stay there until dinner so he could nibble on Liam's toes. Furry little bastard.

"Sorry to be so dramatic." His chest still rose and fell in rapid waves.

"You sure you didn't get bitten?" Allison inspected his arms and legs for any telltale welts.

"Positive. I repel all living creatures, including insects." He meant it as a joke, but Tasha alone laughed. "It's a lot of excitement for me, though, so I'm going to unwind in my room."

He tried to ignore the relief in Isaac's eyes.

Despite minor protestations from his mother and rather more vocal ones from his sister, he made his way to his room and shut the door. He checked his phone, left on the dresser in his haste to leave the house earlier, and found a voicemail from Dr. Jen.

"Liam, I'm sorry about how our last session ended. I think it might be best if you come back in, and we can discuss how you're feeling. Please text me and let me know if you can come to my office tomorrow morning at nine."

Tears of relief welled in his eyes. He hadn't scared off his psychologist. He texted Dr. Jen a simple "yes" before sagging to the cool floor.

"What were you thinking, dumbass? Trying to attract more attention?" said Joshua. He punctuated each sentence with a thrust of the cigarette in his hand. "What made you fancy yourself some private dick that could poke around in other people's business?"

"I needed to know. If the vision was real or not."

Joshua scoffed. "Did you satisfy your curiosity?"

Quite the opposite. It couldn't be a coincidence that the same man from his vision was a drug dealer. Liam slid his hand into his pocket and pulled out the small bag of white powder. His dresser drawer creaked as he opened it and crammed the packet beneath a few rumpled pairs of boxers. Nobody would look there but him.

Joshua tapped on the metal blinds drawn tight. "You need to see what you've started," he said. "Open these."

"No." Liam never opened his blinds. Nosy neighbors like Mrs. Channer didn't deserve to ogle his room.

"You're going to want to see this," Joshua insisted.

Relenting, Liam crawled over to the edge of his room. With his forefinger and thumb, he separated two blinds from one another, the metal crinkling in complaint. At first, his search uncovered only the afternoon sun beating down on the sickly yellow lawn. But, as he peered around, he found him.

Cull stood behind a tree a few feet beyond the property line. He squinted at Isaac's house, flexing his fists open and shut. Liam yanked his fingers away from the blinds.

Joshua squatted down to eye level with him. "I told you he'd find you."

10

WEDNESDAY, AUGUST 27th

Liam tapped his fingernails on the chair and traced large circles on the brown carpet with his shoes. Dr. Jen's apparition had appeared next to her at the very start of the session and stayed there ever since. Though he tried ignoring it, his peripheral vision kept catching on the ghostly woman's dark infinity tattoo.

"So, the murderer saw you this time." Dr. Jen rested her chin on her fist.

Eyes glued to the invisible circles he'd drawn, Liam leaned back. "Yes."

"Did he threaten you?"

"He would've killed me if he caught me. But I got home just in time. He ran away when he saw my mother."

The black leather on her chair creased as she leaned into it. "Do you think it might not be a coincidence he disappeared when others might've seen him?"

He rolled out his bottom lip. Of course, he'd considered the possibility. The little baggie of drugs was real enough, though. He could bring it to Dr. Jen as proof, but then he'd have to admit he'd stolen cocaine. That didn't look great on a number of fronts.

"Maybe."

"Regardless, you're quite concerned, aren't you?"

He fought a dry mouth and cracked open his lips. "My life is in serious danger. Cull's watching me. Waiting for me."

"I'd like to suggest Cull is a proxy for your emotions." She laced her fingers together. "What you're feeling is natural. You're nearing your goal of independence, but a part of you is scared to achieve it and is self-sabotaging your efforts. I don't think your symptoms are progressing; rather, they're simply evolving."

He chewed on the thought. While the idea of being free to do what he wanted, when he wanted, appealed to him after having his every move scrutinized and analyzed for years, it also frightened him. Isaac and his mother weren't the only ones who didn't trust his judgment. He would make mistakes, and lots of them, while on his own.

If he could forget about the packet of drugs, Dr. Jen's theory made sense.

For the first time since entering the office, he lifted his face. Time was almost up. A digital clock glowed 9:43 in green LED letters. Above the clock, a new print had replaced the previous one.

"I see you took down the awful Van Gogh." He gestured at the new print in its place, a neutral and pleasing piece featuring baby loggerhead turtles hatching and waddling out to the ocean. The sea sparkled blue in the print and beckoned the vibrant green turtles to its warm waters.

"Nobody's gonna stab you for that one. Except maybe the art police."

She smiled. "It's not the most original print in the world, but it'll suffice for the time being. I shouldn't have had that Van Gogh in my office." She arched her perfectly shaped eyebrows. "Even psychologists experience lapses in judgment."

The inside of his cheek stung as he gnawed on it. Dr. Jen expected him to cop to researching her. He wouldn't lie, but he wouldn't risk losing her, either.

"I'm sorry for what I said yesterday. May we discuss it later?"

When honesty wasn't an option, procrastination was usually a helpful crutch.

She gazed at him with a pensive expression. "All right. But I'd like to talk about it in the near future."

The vision next to her intensified. Instead of remaining white, the stripes on the dress turned pink and blue. The projection's skin deepened from death white to the same dark beige of Dr. Jen's skin. Her eyes resembled small pools of inky blackness, and he couldn't distinguish where her iris separated from her cornea.

He dipped his head and attempted to look properly chastened. "So next appointment in two days?"

"Two days," she agreed.

He cracked his knuckles. Two days could be a long time.

11

Large drops of rain spattered across the Hyundai's windshield. The wipers strained against the downpour, unable to keep pace with the storm. Liam hunched over the steering wheel and sighed a breath of relief as he pulled off Highway 98 and onto the Gulf Coast State College campus. He parked in lot D and grabbed his backpack, holding it over his head before dashing to the library.

He shouldered his way through wet students milling around the atrium. The close contact made his mouth itch. In general, people meant interacting. Interacting meant judgment. And judgment didn't put his mind in a great place. At the best, he hoped others would find him quirky. At the worst, he'd scare them.

He hoped to avoid the worst.

Near the rear of the building, he found a row of empty computer workstations. He plunked down at one and flung the rainwater off his hands. Grateful for his newly minted GCSC identity, he logged into the school's network. Time for some research.

Although he'd prefer to use the family computer at home, Isaac prevented that option. His stepfather monitored any electronic devices he accessed. His use of the family computer particularly concerned Isaac. He checked every evening which websites Liam had visited, which terms he'd searched. So when Liam didn't want his stepfather breathing down his neck, he had to utilize technology someplace else. Like the library. Preferably one not on base.

Thank God for community college.

Perhaps school wouldn't be so bad after all. He wasn't up to class yet, but he could honestly tell his mother he'd been at GCSC today. Maybe after a few more trips to the library, he could sit through a lecture.

He typed in "murder at Tyndall AFB yacht club" and browsed through the disappointing results. No matching hits. He looked for missing person reports in the news. Still nothing.

In growing frustration, he searched, "drowning at Panama City Beach." He sifted through the hits, looking for one describing what he'd seen, and clicked on a promising death announcement. A tingling sensation ran up his spine.

The red-haired woman from the beach stared back at him from the monitor. The article described her as the widow of one Allen Smith, who had drowned on July eighteenth of the previous year. She had watched from shore as her husband drowned, unable to swim and assist him. Liam traced the woman's picture on the screen.

"Well, that's a little uncanny," a low, feminine voice said from beside him.

He jumped in his seat. A beautiful, young woman read the internet article over his shoulder. His brain fought for a moment to recognize her.

Mai. The woman from Diamond Bay Park.

"Sounds exactly like what you described at the beach." She wrinkled her nose. "Are you one of those obsessive types who reads about events and then reenacts them?"

Only in his dreams.

"I'm doing research for a class," Liam said.

"Hmm. And which class is that?" Mai crossed her arms in front of her chest. She wore a red tank and cutoff jeans. A gold crucifix adorned her neck and glinted off the fluorescent lights. Her flip-flops exposed toes painted a deep crimson.

"Why do you care?"

"You're different, Liam Murphy, and different intrigues me." She pulled out the chair next to him, turned it around, straddled it, and crisscrossed her arms over the backrest. "Why don't you try telling me the truth? I'm an open-minded gal."

"I've found people tend to be a little less open-minded than they profess."

"Ohh, a philosopher. I like that, too." Mai's cheeks dimpled when she smiled.

In a desperate bid to redirect the conversation, he resorted to rudeness. "What are you doing here?"

"You're not the only person in Panama City who attends college. I'm studying for a class. Can't you tell?" She winked at him. It took him aback. Had anybody ever winked at him? Not like a "my meds are making me tic-y so I'm blinking unevenly in your general direction" wink, but a real honest-to-goodness, flirty wink?

Mai dug into her backpack, a ratty black utilitarian bag bearing the scars of years of abuse. She pulled out the same Chemistry 101 textbook nestled in his bag and waved it in the air.

"Thrilling, right? But it fulfills a required course, so I'm taking it."

After a brief deliberation, he gambled on conversation. "I'm signed up for the same class."

She glanced at her watch, a slim, silver Citizen. "Funny. Class starts in three minutes. Doesn't look like you plan on attending."

"I'm more of a 'show up for the tests' kind of student."

"Ahh. So intent on being important you turn out mediocre?" She held out her hand, forestalling the rebuttal on his lips. "Not that being mediocre is wrong. It's actually a goal of mine. I'm aiming for perfectly average. Average looks, average intellect, average job. I'm going to prove to my older sister I can be perfectly average and perfectly happy at the same time."

"I'm not sure you're doing a particularly good job of hitting your target." Liam's brow dotted with perspiration.

"Excuse me?" Mai placed her hands on her hips.

"You're rather north of average, in my opinion."

"Well, Liam Murphy. Was that a compliment?" She leaned forward, a playful look glinting in her eyes.

Struck dumb by the flirtatious discussion, he sat open-mouthed.

"Not so quick on the comebacks, are you? I don't mind. In fact, I've been searching for an average guy for a while. The overachievers require too much maintenance for my taste. And the one lowlife I dated taught me some terrible lessons I never need to relearn." She looked him up and down. "Just when I'd decided Average Joes don't exist, you up and materialize."

Toes curled and leg muscles tensed, he fought the urge to laugh at the absurdity of her statement. His compass pointed as far from average as Mai's, albeit in the opposite direction. Still, he wracked his brains for something "normal" to say.

The computer monitor next to his workstation crashed to the ground, scattering both his thoughts and pieces of electronic equipment across the floor. A dishwater-blonde woman sat on the now-cleared desk with her hands clamped onto the back of a man who stripped off her clothes. She moaned with pleasure as she pulled at his jeans and wiggled them down.

Liam jumped out of his seat and backed away. "Mind getting a room?" he yelled.

And people thought he lacked self-control.

"What's wrong?" Mai asked. She scoured the space behind Liam, searching for the target of his scolding. "Who needs to get a room?"

As abruptly as they'd materialized, the couple disappeared. Rooted to the floor, Liam searched the air for any trace of what he'd witnessed. Nothing remained but an awkward silence. Again.

He dry washed his hands. "Nobody. I was messing around."

"No, you saw somebody. Like the other day." She swung her leg over the chair and stepped close to him. "And by the sounds of it, that somebody engaged in some rather naughty behavior." She flashed a wicked grin.

"You're gonna think I'm lying." He meant it to sound lighthearted, but it came out raw and blistered.

"No, I'm not. Try me."

No use in putting off the inevitable. Mai would judge him sooner or later.

"A man and a woman were right next to us, having... relations."

"Right there?" Mai pointed to the empty desk.

"Yep. In their ecstasy, they shoved the monitor crashing to the floor."

She sidestepped Liam and inspected the desk. Unlike all of the other workstations, no monitor lay on it. She knelt down and raked the floor with her hands.

"Aha! Look what I found." She held up a small metal shard. "Nifty little gift you've got there. It's like free porno," she muttered.

His jaw dropped. Mai hadn't even flinched at his revelation. She took what he said at face value. It'd been a while, a long while, since anybody had. And to top it off, she admired his "gift."

He ran his hand through his hair. He didn't want to draw out Mai's condemnation any longer. Rejection hurt more after any type of friendship emerged. "This is the first time I've seen that particular type of image. Usually they're not as fun."

She grimaced. "Like the drowning at the beach?"

"Along those lines."

"I'd prefer watching the make-out session as well. Much more enjoyable than death." She peered around the library. "So—who'd you see in the image?"

"I don't know," he said.

But he did. Because the librarian walked by, her hands full of books ready to be returned to shelves. A few seconds earlier, they'd been full of something else entirely. He jerked his head toward her and fake coughed.

"There she is," he whispered.

"What?!?" Mai giggled. "Way to go, Miss Librarian. I'm guessing after-hours in this place are a little more exciting than most people know."

He wagged his eyebrows. "Apparently."

"Well, you're chock full of surprises, Mr. Murphy. I'm glad we're in class together." Mai slid her hand down the back pocket of her shorts and smiled.

"Me, too."

12

The Hyundai hummed along as Liam drove to an all-day breakfast restaurant. Out of the corner of his eye, he shot a glance at Mai, still not believing she thought him trustworthy enough to get in his car. She'd insisted he owed her lunch "somewhere average" after all the excitement in the library caused her to skip class.

She tapped on the cheap plastic console. "So, when did these visions of yours start?"

"A couple of days ago." These *particular* hallucinations were quite new.

Popping open the glove compartment, she snooped through its contents and sighed when she found only paperwork. "What could be bringing them on? Stress in your life? New medication?"

"I'm on some heavy-duty medication. But I've been on it for years." Liam held his breath and waited for her to ask why he took it.

She didn't.

"Sometimes our bodies acclimate to medication. Maybe this is how yours has adjusted to your prescription. It's opened some avenue in your mind most people can't reach." She waved her hands in front of her like she consulted a crystal ball.

His stomach clenched. The idea had crossed his mind. He hated his medicine. Besides the weight he'd gained because of it, his pills also lowered his already pitiful internal motivation. To top it off, the medicine had damaged his eyesight. He also ran the risk of developing dyskinesia, which meant his mouth would contort involuntarily for the rest of his life. All in all, fun stuff.

But his pills kept him sane. Or so he thought. Were his schizophrenia symptoms truly worse than seeing people murdered or dying? The make-out session made him uncomfortable but wasn't so horrid. The ones where people died? Gut-wrenching. And what about all the ghostly projections he'd seen?

"Could be," he said.

Mai lifted her left foot onto the seat and rested her elbow on her knee. "So what do all of your visions have in common?"

"They were all intense. Like events you remember for the rest of your life."

"So they're all forms of memories. Memories with incredibly high emotional values associated with them." She stared ahead in deep concentration. "Can you think of any connection between you and these visions?"

Other than my delusional mind?

"No."

"I've got a theory, but it's kind of wacky." She snapped her fingers. "Wanna hear it?"

"Of course." He tamped down the butterflies in his stomach.

She shifted in her seat to face him and held up both her hands in a stop-the-press motion. "What if you're seeing ghosts?"

He exhaled. "Not a bad idea. Except the librarian is still alive and kicking, and, as far as I can tell, the woman from the beach is, too."

"True." She pursed her lips. "What else could it be?"

"Got me. Wish I could figure it out—it's not cool wondering whether I'll see some new awful vision every time I go somewhere."

After quiet contemplation, she pulled on his arm. "I've got a plan." Her touch lit his nerves on fire. "Turn right at the next light. We're going to run a little test."

He obliged and turned onto a small road that led past dumpy homes with broken windows and sagging roofs. At the end of the street, a wrought iron gate swung out from red brick pillars. A painted wooden sign attached to each pillar announced they entered "Peaceful Meadows Cemetery." As they rolled through the gates, a grassy field replaced the pavement. Car tracks led to a parking area.

"We decided I don't see ghosts." Half doubting his earlier resolve, he wiped clammy hands on the steering wheel.

"I know. But what if we're looking at it all wrong? I think you see memories all right, but not memories from people. It's the land's memory."

"Say what?"

"You heard me. What if they're imprints of memories? Like if a location could remember events?"

It sounded impossible to him, but then...

"Wouldn't the memories replay all day in that scenario?" He'd visited the yacht club multiple times, but he'd witnessed Cull beat a man to death only once.

Mai scrunched her forehead. "Maybe the episodes are attached to time."

She had a point. It'd been around 4:30 when he'd seen the murder. His trip to the marina the following day had taken place earlier in the afternoon.

"It's possible."

"I knew it!" She punched the air with her fist. "Call me Sherlock Nguyen."

She patted herself on the shoulder, prouder than even a peacock could manage. Somehow she pulled it off without being obnoxious. "This place has got to be full of traumatic memories. Don't you think you'd remember the day you buried somebody you love?"

Liam imagined he would. He hadn't attended his father's funeral because he'd been in the throes of a psychotic breakdown.

"So what's your plan? Walk through the cemetery until I see some grief-stricken images? You're a bottle of fun, Mai."

"Okay, so it does sound kinda terrible. Still, it'll help us figure out what's going on in that ginger head of yours." She pointed to a massive live oak tree draped with Spanish moss. "Park under there."

He shook his head in resignation and followed her orders. She waited for him to open her door and grasped his still clammy hand as she stepped out. Her warm palm steadied and inflamed his nerves all at once.

Seemingly ancient trees stood guard throughout the cemetery. Spanish moss, which drooped from their thick branches, protected row after row of modest gray headstones from the pitiless Florida sun.

"Shall we?" She gestured at the footpath beaten into the grass ahead of them.

A large crow swooped by his head and landed on the Hyundai's red roof. It cocked its head to the side and stared straight at Liam. When the bird opened its mouth and cawed, a blast of frigid air hurtled toward his face. An unnatural chill smacked his cheeks, snaked down his neck, and wrapped around his heart.

He sneaked a glance at Mai. Either she didn't see the bird, or it didn't exist. Smart money bet on the latter option.

Nice try, asshole. But I'm keeping my crazy bottled up today.

"After you," he said.

Mai led him to a small mausoleum long-ago overtaken by mildew. An angel sat atop the structure, one hand uplifted to the heavens while the other wiped away a frozen tear. A hot breeze clanged the mausoleum's rusted iron gate against the stained marble. "Hazel Johnson" was engraved above its entrance.

Mai bit her lip. "This one bothers me. At some point, this mausoleum stood grand and dignified. Now it's as sad and lonely as the meanest gravestone. Maybe even more so. Time doesn't take pity on any of us. Even those loved greatly during life."

"Who says anybody loved Hazel Johnson?"

Mai considered his question. "Nobody. I assumed so because of her impressive resting place. The mausoleum must've cost a pretty penny back in its day."

"So whoever buried her had money. Doesn't mean they loved her." His cheeks tightened, and he wrinkled his nose.

She stayed speechless, analyzing his face like she could read his frown lines the way a palm reader divines hands.

"Sorry, I don't mean to be argumentative." He looked away and waited for her to release his hand.

She didn't.

"No, you're right. I made an assumption based on some wobbly preconceptions. Let's keep moving," she said.

The pair walked on, their feet whispering through the grass. The sun blazed a brilliant orange, slicing through the shade and no doubt scorching Liam's fair skin, particularly prone to burning because of his medicine.

Then, like Mai predicted, it happened.

13

A **shrill keening pierced through the early afternoon** breeze, so loud Liam dropped Mai's hand and covered his ears.

"Are you hearing an imprint?" She winced at the expression on his face.

He nodded. To his right, a small child rocked next to a headstone. She clutched the hem of her pink dress, stained brown by newly tossed soil.

"Daddy!" she screamed. She pawed at the headstone as if she could raise her father back to life if she tried hard enough.

A middle-aged woman grasped the girl in her arms and held her tight. She said, "Let it all out, baby. It's okay to cry. I miss him, too." Large tears welled in the woman's hazel eyes and glittered down her face.

"Do you see them?" Liam wrung his hands together before pointing to the bereaved child and parent.

"No." Mai's tone had cooled, and all playfulness had disappeared from her voice. "You were right. This is a terrible idea. I can't believe I asked you to do this."

Sick to his stomach, he dropped his arms to his side. "Let's go."

She slipped her hand in his again, holding it just tight enough to keep him tethered to reality.

He had the audacity to believe they'd make it back to his car in peace, and he'd witnessed the worst of it.

As usual, he was wrong.

A wail to his right joined the little girl's sobbing, followed by screams from the graveyard's entrance, like a delayed refrain from Hell's choir. And then the quiet cries of hundreds of people poured into the afternoon air, merging together until their sobs of despair more closely resembled the thunder of a waterfall than human voices lifted in grief. Liam stumbled and fell to the ground, pressing his hands hard over his ears.

"No!" he yelled.

Distantly, he felt Mai pulling at his arms, trying to drag him to the car. He waved her off and rolled into a fetal position. The cries continued.

Clawing at any chance to make the wailing stop, he hummed a tune. The effort made the grieving voices grow louder. Long spools of clear spittle dribbled down his face and seeped into the cemetery's grounds.

He reached deep inside his memories to a time when he'd been happy. To the time when he and his father threw footballs in their backyard. Maybe, just maybe, a happy memory would override these sorrowful ones.

It didn't.

He steeled himself and opened his eyes. If the images demanded to be seen, he'd see them.

People packed the graveyard. All intent in their own misery and grief, none of them looked at him.

Nearby, an elderly lady patted the crest of a tombstone, stoic in her grief. If only the rest of the mourners acted more like her, and less like the twenty-something man who screamed while beating his black-suited chest. A young woman next to him sobbed quietly, burying her face in petite, trembling hands.

Liam blinked ten times.

The physical manifestations of broken hearts disappeared, and silence kissed his ears. Empty now save for its slowly rotting occupants, the graveyard seemed to breathe a sigh of relief along with him.

He rose to his feet and staggered to the car. His hand fumbled with the driver's side door before opening it, and he collapsed into the seat.

Mai hovered over him. “How may I help you?” she asked.

“Give me a sec.” He closed his eyes and held up a limp hand.

His mind couldn’t handle the graveyard’s memories. Mai’s simple act of treating him like a normal person, an average person, had ballooned his ego to such an extent he thought he could handle testing his psyche. He should’ve known better.

Humiliated she’d seen him drooling, he wiped his chin on his shirt and practiced the meditation breathing he’d learned in counseling.

When his heart rate returned to normal, he opened his eyes. She sat in the passenger seat, gloriously beautiful. Her eyelashes fluttered the bottom of her bangs as she looked back at him.

“I’m a jerk,” she said.

“Not even remotely. We should’ve thought our plan through a bit more, is all.”

She fiddled with the seatbelt buckle. “It’s not a game for you, is it? I hadn’t realized how hard it would be to see the visions you do.”

Relief coursed through his body as he lowered his head to the steering wheel. Mai sympathized with him. For the last ten years, nobody but his father had attempted to understand him or his world. And since his father had died, his world had become a very, very lonely place.

After allowing him several minutes of recovery, she placed a feather light hand on his shoulder. His heart stuttered.

“I could go for a little coffee,” he said.

“I could go for a lot,” she said.

He laughed. “Then let’s get out of here.”

14

The restaurant was dead except for a retiree who sat a few tables away. He wore a baseball cap embossed with "Vietnam Vet" in gold letters and a button-down, short-sleeved white shirt. He held up a newspaper and scanned the day's events from bespectacled eyes set deep on a wrinkled face.

Mai dropped the sticky plastic menu and waved her hands at him. "You've stared at that old man since we sat down. You got a thing for geezers?"

He shook his head. "I feel bad for him. He's lonely."

"Now I'm going to be the argumentative one. How do you know he's lonely? Just because he's by himself doesn't make him so."

No, but the vision attached to him did. Wrapped in a white halo, a woman in her early twenties sat next to the veteran. She chatted soundlessly with berry-red lips, and her dark-brown eyes sparkled. Her platinum-blonde hair, parted in the middle, swung over a psychedelic floral print shirt.

While Liam didn't blame the man for living in the past—he'd done more than his fair share of the same—his recent friendship with Mai proved the present could be wonderful, too. "Excuse me," he said.

Mai's eyes widened as he stood and made his way over to the old man.

"I'm sorry to bother you, sir," he began, fighting the urge to run back to his table and avoid speaking with a stranger, "but I wanted to thank you for your service. My dad was a vet also, so I know the sacrifices you made."

The old man lowered his paper and smiled at Liam, eyes crinkling with delight. He said, "Thank you, son. You can't know how much your gratitude means." The apparition next to him faded.

"It's the least I can do. Have a nice afternoon," said Liam. He dipped his head before returning to his table.

Mai's lips parted slightly. "Wow. I've never seen someone do that before. Is that a common occurrence for you?"

"Not really." Out of the corner of his eye he saw the older man still smiling. "I think it's a habit I'm going to pick up, though."

She set an unreadable gaze on him like she could figure out what made him tick. Before she succeeded, he asked, "What are you getting?"

"My favorite. Chocolate-chip pancakes and bacon. What about you?" She picked up a steaming mug of coffee.

"I'll stick with coffee. I'm not hungry."

She smirked. "I suppose if I doused my coffee with as much creamer and sugar as you, I wouldn't be hungry either. Your bastardized brew is like a meal all its own."

"We can't all be badasses like you and drink our coffee straight black. Some of us are more delicate than others." He pretended to hold his mug like a porcelain teacup, pinching his thumb and forefinger around its handle and holding up his other three fingers ostentatiously.

Mai didn't laugh. She wrapped her hand around his. "Anyone who can see what you do and still function isn't delicate. You're stronger than you give yourself credit."

What she didn't know was sometimes he didn't "function." That his mental health was more fragile than a dandelion in a hurricane.

He smiled and lowered the mug. "Thanks for thinking so."

"So graveyards aren't your favorite place." She squeezed his hand. "Most people would agree with you."

A fuzzy white fringe appeared around Mai's body. Beads of sweat popped out on the nape of his neck, and he tried not to cringe as the white mass took its form.

Unlike with Dr. Jen, Isaac, or the old man across the room, this image didn't form a 3-D shape. Sepia toned and crinkled like an old photograph, the flat projection revealed a Vietnamese man dressed in army fatigues. He stood in dense vegetation and grasped a revolver. With haunted eyes, he glared straight ahead under a battered helmet. He couldn't have been older than twenty-one or twenty-two.

"What about you, Mai? What do you think about graveyards?" He tried to keep his voice steady and neutral.

She pulled away her hand. "Before today, I kinda had a fetish for them. I know it's weird. The graveyard we visited? That's my place of serenity. Or at least it used to be. After what it did to you, I won't ever think of it the same way."

"There's no other reason graveyards call to you?"

She raised an eyebrow. "You do realize how creepy that question is, right?"

"Sorry. It appears I haven't fully recovered from my earlier episode." He picked up his coffee again and slurped it, eager to occupy his mouth so he stopped frightening Mai.

She took a deep breath. "You're right, though. I've got my reasons. I visit graveyards so I don't forget about a long-term goal of mine."

"Most of us will end up in a cemetery without reminding ourselves."

"Very funny." She rolled her eyes. "In all seriousness, though, after graduation, I intend to restore neglected cemeteries, specifically those for soldiers killed in action."

He tugged at his ear. "Wow. Heavy. What's driving you?"

"Though I never knew him, my grandfather. He died fighting for the Army of the Republic of Viet Nam in the sixties. He didn't serve on the wrong side of the war, but he did end up on the losing side." She touched the corner of her mouth before continuing. "Over the years, the Vietnamese government hasn't been overly concerned with maintaining enemy combatants' graves. Relatives have sent us pictures of the cemetery where my grandfather is buried." She rolled her shoulders and picked at her shirt. "To say it's neglected would be an understatement. Even the small headstone above his grave is broken in half. It's disrespectful. Everybody, or at least almost everybody, deserves a decent resting place, winning side of the war or not."

Now that he understood her projection, Liam nodded. Perhaps if these visions didn't unhinge him, he'd appreciate the insights they brought. But their cost, the unspooling of the thin thread of his sanity, was too high. "I'm sorry," he said.

She flexed her jaw muscles. "I am, too. One day, I'm going to remedy the situation. I owe it to him, and I owe it to my *bà nội*—my grandmother."

"Those sound like some lofty aspirations for a girl pretending to be mediocre." His spoon clinked against the side of his mug as he stirred his coffee.

She touched the crucifix on her neck and looked into the distance. "You caught me. Promise you won't tell anybody my secret."

"I won't if you won't."

Her dimples made another welcome appearance. "Deal. And now that I've told you a little about my family, why don't you share some information about yours?"

"I've got a little sister named Tasha. She's full of joy and energy and laughter." All the qualities schizophrenia had stolen from him. He unconsciously picked at his bracelet.

Mai regarded his wrist. "Now I understand the rubber-band jewelry. I thought neon orange fell a little out of your fashion zone. You ever take it off?"

"Never." He made a quick slicing motion with his hand.

"Doting older brother fits you well." She tapped the table. "Tasha is lucky to have you."

The life-sized photograph of her grandfather faded.

Breathing became easier. "I'm the lucky one. She makes living with my mom and stepfather bearable."

Mai twisted her mouth to the side. "So your folks aren't great?"

"My dad was an amazing man. The best person I ever knew."

"Knew?" She leaned forward and wrinkled her forehead.

Liam swallowed the lump in his throat. "He died earlier this year."

"I'm so sorry." She placed her hand over her heart.

"My father was, and still is, my hero. You'll never meet a tougher guy, physically or emotionally. Generous to a fault, he dedicated his life to serving others. Especially me." He concentrated on the torn, pink sugar packet on the table. "Dad survived two tours in Afghanistan. I thought of him as indestructible and kinda figured he'd outlive me. But you know what did him in?" He raised his face to meet Mai's and let out a half laugh, half groan. "A rainstorm and slippery leaves on a road in Ohio, half a mile from our house."

Her eyes stayed glued to his. She sat, silent, waiting for him to continue.

"I didn't take his passing very well, so my mother insisted I move in with her and my stepfather for a while." He left out the tidbit about his living arrangement being a requirement for his probation.

"So I gather your stepfather's a prick?"

"Not really. But I'm a constant reminder of what was, and he's a constant reminder of what is." He shrugged. "As a result, we can't stand each other."

"Sounds like it hasn't been the best year for you." She reached out and tucked an unruly lock of hair behind his ear.

He cursed his Irish skin as his face flushed. "It hasn't. But I've got a feeling life's about to improve."

A corner of her lips hitched up. "I like your optimism."

She held his gaze for a loaded moment before looking at her watch and sighing. "What I don't like is the service here. I haven't placed my order yet, and my next class starts in twenty minutes. I hate to cut this short, but do you mind dropping me back off at campus?"

"Of course." Liam took out a five and left it on the table to pay for their coffee.

Mai stood and looped her arm through his. "Don't think this gets you out of our date. You still owe me."

Our date.

And just like that, the memories from the cemetery faded to gray.

15

Y**ou're home later than I expected," Allison said.**

Liam closed the front door and locked it. "Traffic."

He walked into the kitchen and opened a cabinet, browsing for an edible snack. His appetite had returned on the ride home. A lone candy bar, hidden behind Styrofoam-like crackers and negative-calorie protein powders, revealed itself in the upper back corner. The wrapper crinkled as he tore it open and stuffed the chocolate in his mouth.

His mother eyed him disapprovingly. She said, "Sugar isn't good for your health."

So the hell what?

"I know." He doubted his anti-psychotic medicine worked any wonders on his liver either. But the only comment she made about his pills was "take it."

"Enjoying the day off?" he asked.

His mother had reduced her workload after he'd come to live with her. She'd stopped working Wednesdays, opening up her schedule to run all the errands that piled up during the week. The maneuverings ensured Liam and Tasha were never alone together.

Long, brown hair pulled up into a haphazard ponytail, Allison held up a bottle of disinfectant and paper towels. "It's a regular party in here. I bleached the bathrooms until they cried uncle, and the kitchen is up next." She stopped for a beat. "Isaac called. He forgot his lunch.

Mind bringing it to him?"

She always looked for ways to get the men in her life to interact, refusing to admit the less communicating the two did, the better.

Perched atop the stove, Joshua cracked his knuckles and popped his neck. "It's amazing what your mother will do to separate us. One of these days I'm gonna give the meddlesome woman what she deserves."

Liam ran his finger along his earlobe. "Okay."

A whoosh of cold air prickled his skin as his mother pulled a blue, vinyl lunch bag out of the fridge and tossed it to him. "Thanks, honey," she said. "If you could bike there, it'd help me out. I might need the car. Besides, exercise is a natural mood booster."

Exercise would help him about as much as air helped a fish, but he kept his mouth shut. A long bike ride gave him an excuse to stay out of the house longer. Joshua was in a mood.

With an awkward and halting touch, Allison laid her palm in his and passed him a twenty.

"Treat yourself to a healthy lunch. No burgers!" She waved her pointer finger in the air for emphasis.

He uttered "thanks" over his shoulder as he made his way to the front door. Departures worked better if he left the house immediately after Joshua learned of his plans.

A gray, drawstring bag hung from the hall tree. He plucked it off its hook and stuffed Isaac's lunch into the bag. The noise alerted RP to a possible departure, and he shot out like an Olympic sprinter from the kitchen and rubbed against Liam's legs.

The cat deserved a little alone time. And if he got lost in the process, all the better. Liam sneaked a glance toward the kitchen. Preoccupied with the countertops, his mother wouldn't notice if he let RP out.

He cracked open the door. "Don't kill too many birds."

The tomcat's whiskers quivered before he dashed out. He hightailed it to his outside refuge—a large bush behind the carport. The stupid animal longed for freedom but never truly enjoyed the rare occasions when he found it.

A callused hand grabbed his neck with a vise-like grip as he lifted his foot to walk out the door.

"You really wanna leave me alone with your mother?" Joshua asked. His nails dug into Liam's Adam's apple.

"You can't hurt her." Liam's stomach turned with sour bile.

"Are you trying to convince me or yourself?" asked Joshua.

"Let me go, you stupid bastard!" He swatted away Joshua's hand and hurtled toward his bicycle. It had been his father's, once upon a time. The salty humidity had done a number on the already well-worn Schwinn, its brown paint now barely discernible from the rust overtaking the frame. He hefted the drawstring sack onto his back, hopped on the bike, and sped down the driveway.

Across the street, Mrs. Channer looked up from her gardening and stared at him without smiling. He sneered in response. They had their routine down pat.

He pedaled up Eagle Drive, took a right onto Beacon Beach Drive, and glided onto the bike path that ran parallel to the road. Dense woods teeming with insects framed either side of the long street. Other than passing cars and rambling armadillos, he was alone.

Sweat rolled down his forehead and stung his eyes. His drenched Pearl Jam T-shirt clung to his midsection, accentuating the pounds medicine had added to his frame, and the drawstring bag on his back adhered to his shirt like glue.

He glanced behind to ensure no runners or bikers followed him, eased his pace, and sat up straight. The sun beat down on his head and burned his neck. He raised both arms shoulder height and closed his eyes, letting the humid breeze push him along.

Unable to maintain his balance for long, Liam gripped the handlebars again and prepared to enjoy the solitude of the next few miles.

Instead, a high-pitched bark sliced at his eardrums. It came from behind, on the path empty mere seconds ago. The hair on his neck stood on end as the barking turned to howls of pain. He jammed on the bike's brakes and planted his right foot on the cracked sidewalk. Wishing he could ignore the dog's pleas for help, he turned his head toward the commotion.

A blond teenaged boy clenched a leather leash in his hands and jerked it high into the air, hanging a scrawny Yorkshire Terrier above the pavement from its collar. The dog made a few pathetic choking noises before the kid dropped it to the ground and planted a hard kick in its side. The terrier keened in pain.

"Stop!" Liam yelled. He flung down his bike and sprinted toward the animal abuser, balling his hands into fists ready to punch.

The teen ignored Liam and spit on the dog, heedless of the freight train rushing at him.

Liam pulled back his right fist and pounded it forward with as much force as he could gather. Instead of smacking flesh, his closed hand whistled through the air. His feet stumbled with the momentum of the missed hit, and he fought to keep from sprawling onto the pavement. Confused, he swung his head to the right and left, searching for the teen and his dog.

They had disappeared.

He pulled his sweaty shirt away from his chest and fought a wave of nausea. No way was this a hallucination. It had to be another imprint, like the drowning and the mourners at the cemetery.

Repulsed by his hope that a kid had beaten his pet to death, he willed down the bile creeping up his throat and walked back to his bike.

The handlebars shook from his trembling hands as he rode away from the scene of the crime. This latest memory tortured him worse than the cemetery. The dog had been helpless, completely undeserving of the beating. As the sole witness to the terrier's abuse, Liam longed to serve up to the teen a dose of his own medicine. But how would he excuse thrashing the kid?

Don't worry, everybody—I can see the past! I'm meting out some vigilante justice.

Isaac wouldn't believe him, nor, for that matter, would his mother. Liam would have to let these visions haunt him. Unwelcome or not, the secrets belonged to him alone.

The scene replayed in his mind a hundred times before Beacon Beach Road dead-ended at Suwanee Avenue, where the heavy traffic surrounding the heart of Tyndall AFB's administrative area forced Liam to concentrate on navigating. Dr. Jen always said menial tasks helped clear his mind.

He arrived at the joint Base Exchange and Commissary, a boxy building that housed both a general merchandise and grocery store, and glided to a stop near the entrance. He didn't bother with the kickstand, as it had rusted through weeks ago, and let the Schwinn fall to the concrete. Isaac would have to wait for his meal.

Though the food court separating the BX and Commissary was small, it would suffice for lunch. His options consisted of either a sandwich shop or a Tex-Mex fast food restaurant. He settled for a couple of tacos.

His already suppressed appetite had shrunk even more after witnessing an innocent animal getting beaten to death. Nevertheless, he pressed through his meal. His mother would ask what he ate, and he didn't want to lie. Not about unimportant matters, at any rate.

He nibbled on the tacos, chewing chicken and tomatoes until his teeth ground together. After each bite, he rewarded himself with a long slurp of soda. Soon enough, he finished his drink but still had one and a half tacos remaining on his plate. He picked up his paper cup and shook it, stabbing his straw through mounds of ice in a futile attempt to uncover more syrupy liquid.

A young airman dressed in fatigues walked past him, holding the hand of a little boy who looked to be around two or three. The son's pudgy hand encircled the airman's ring finger, and his feet worked double time to keep up with his father's longer stride. Liam tried to ignore the pang of grief the pair caused him.

The drink's plastic lid cracked as he opened it. He fished out a few pieces of ice and crunched down on them. Though he always missed his father, the BX accentuated the feeling. It didn't matter that he'd never been to this particular Exchange with his father. BXs were roughly the same the world over, and he'd visited many of them with his dad. Full of nostalgia, their generic military atmosphere comforted him. A BX felt like home. Or at least how he fantasized home felt Before. Before his schizophrenia, Before his mother's abandonment, Before his father's death.

He crumpled up his trash and threw it in a black waste receptacle before making his way to the BX entrance. After flashing his ID card at the customer-greeting desk attendant, he wandered over to the men's department. Racks of T-shirts with brand names splashed across them stood row upon row. None interested him. The threadbare Pearl Jam T-shirt he wore still fit fine and hadn't seemed to bother Mai any.

The heavy scent of leather and wood lured him to the fragrance department. He held up a dark blue bottle in the shape of a man's torso, glanced around and, satisfied nobody watched, sprayed it in the air. He inhaled the scent and stepped through the invisible cloud. As the tiny particles of cologne settled on his skin, he wondered what Mai would think of it. Would it turn her on?

His cheeks burned with a sudden rush of blood. The mere thought of the woman got him all hot and bothered. But men his age behaved this way when they liked a woman, right? Mai would be proud of his "average" emotions.

Though the cologne was pricey, he made a mental note of its name. His mother would likely be so thrilled he expressed an interest in personal hygiene she'd buy it for him no matter the cost.

Unable to procrastinate any further, Liam resigned himself to visiting his stepfather. The oppressive afternoon heat rammed into him as he exited the BX and picked up his bike. He darted through traffic until he came to a beige building proclaiming itself the "Base Support Center." Along with a number of other departments, it housed the JAG offices and like most other buildings on base, conformed to the peculiar nondescript blandness of military architecture. He leaned his bike against the side of the entrance. A river of sweat slid down his hand as he wiped his brow. Isaac would no doubt be pleased to see him in his current sweaty condition.

At least he smelled nice.

He walked up the wide steps to the entrance and swung open the doors, welcoming the blast of air-conditioning on his skin. He gulped in the cool air as he walked down the hallway, lined on the left with small, square offices and on the right with beige cubicles. The patter of rapid typing and buzzing of phones filled the air. Between a brief break in cubicles stood a large copy machine, humming as it spit out dozens of warm papers. The young airman standing next to it tightened her lips when she saw him but didn't demand he stop. His presence here was nothing new.

A bronze nameplate engraved with "Lt Col Northman" shined next to an open door frame. Isaac sat in a black leather rolling chair, not unlike Dr. Jen's. Cradling a white phone to his ear, he put his pointer finger against his lips and motioned Liam into his office. Liam plunked down on the chair opposite Isaac's and tried to get comfortable on its cheap blue fabric.

Awards and plaques from various posts around the world—Turkey, Germany, California—decorated the white wall behind Isaac. Liam's eyes stuck on the plaque from Lackland AFB. Isaac had been stationed there when he met Allison. It also happened to be the station where Liam's symptoms had first spiraled out of control.

Captain America's accolades didn't stop with the military. He'd also received numerous awards and commendations from various civil rights organizations during his law school years. One award in particular captured Liam's attention. Gold letters set against a black plaque read, "The Organization for Mental Health Rights recognizes Isaac Northman for his steadfast and relentless support." Below hung a picture of his stepfather, younger and happier, shaking the hand of some muckety-muck.

Isaac caught him staring at the award and frowned.

"Andre, let me phone you back in five minutes. An unexpected appointment just popped up. Yes, thank you, I appreciate it." Isaac placed the phone in its cradle and regarded Liam. His Air Force blues, starched to perfection, crinkled when he leaned back.

"Allison send you with my lunch?" he said.

"You know it." Liam swung the bag to Isaac, who caught it with his left hand. His stepfather "forgot" his lunch on a fairly frequent basis, so they'd developed a certain rhythm for these encounters. At times, he considered telling Isaac he possessed other skills besides fetching ham sandwiches. That, however, would require a real conversation. He'd rather keep biking to Isaac's office than have a heart-to-heart with the man.

"You look hot. Want a drink?" Isaac asked.

A small white refrigerator vibrated in the corner. No doubt Isaac cheated on his mother's strict soda ban while at the office.

"Nah. I'm not thirsty."

Isaac nodded a curt dismissal. "See you at home, then."

Glad to complete their interaction, Liam rose and waved a desultory goodbye. He savored the last few paces of air-conditioned relief before stepping out of the building.

The bright sunlight temporarily blinded him, and he shielded his face with his hands. Once his eyes adjusted, he dropped his arms. Despite the heat, his body froze for a long moment.

There, smoking on the steps, awaited the murderer from the yacht club.

16

Fancy meeting you here," Cull said. His black polo shirt and khakis marked him as one of the many civvies who worked on base. He took a long drag on his cigarette and blew smoke out of the corner of his mouth.

Liam kept mum and hurried toward his bike. Dr. Jen had advised him not to engage new hallucinations. And if the man was real, Liam doubted he wanted to share a friendly conversation. He swung a leg over his bike and jerked the seat upright.

Cull stepped in front of him and blocked his path.

"What's the rush, man? We've got business to conduct." Cull took the cigarette stub out of his mouth and ground it onto the handlebar. Flecks of ash sprayed over Liam's legs. One ember sizzled on his knee.

"I don't want any trouble. All I want is to go home," Liam said.

Cull wagged his finger. "If you didn't want trouble, you shouldn't have stolen from me."

His pulse raced. "I don't know what you're talking about."

"You think I'm dumb? I saw you take some of my product. As a favor to Colonel Northman, I'll let you off easy, but you still owe me. And this little indulgence of yours is going to cost you $150. My theft surcharge is a hefty one. I'm sure you understand."

"I'm not giving you any money, Cull." He kicked one of the spokes on his bike and dug his other heel in the ground.

The killer froze. "So we're on a first-name basis now, huh? You think I'm gonna let you off easy 'cause you figured out who I am?"

"No. You're going to let me off easy because I saw what you did. I'll tell the police about it." Liam forced himself to meet Cull's eyes. Hallucination or not, he wasn't in the mood to be bullied.

A harsh laugh erupted from Cull's mouth. "'What I did?' You don't know the first thing about me. Your empty accusations don't scare me." He placed his face directly in front of Liam's. His breath stank of stale tobacco and coffee.

Eager to put some distance between them, Liam walked his bike backward.

"Not so fast." Cull grabbed hold of the bike and stopped the backward progression. He glanced around to check for witnesses. After he confirmed no bystanders watched his actions, he jerked Liam's face up toward his.

Blood poured down Cull's lips, forming a crimson cloud that swirled around his body. It morphed into the shape of a man whose red-stained eyes stared lifelessly ahead. With a gasp, Liam realized he looked at himself.

"What's the matter, son? Looks like you've seen a ghost. Keep your mouth shut or maybe you'll become one yourself. I'll be expecting payment soon. Make it $200 for the disrespect."

With a harsh snort, Cull shoved him away. Liam lost his balance and crashed over to the side. The bike landed hard on him. Concrete scraped the side of his face, and a back tooth wiggled loosely from the impact.

His former restraint evaporated. If Cull wanted a fight, he'd give him one. He kicked off his bike and jumped to a crouch.

The only battle to be had, however, was with himself. Cull had disappeared.

17

Allison switched off the vacuum to the sound of her cell phone ringing. She dashed over to her purse and rummaged through its interior until her hand folded around the buzzing device. The caller ID read "Callaway Realtors." Thank heavens. She needed a diversion from cleaning.

"Allison Northman, how may I help you?"

"Hey, Allison, it's me, Lexi. Listen, I've got a promising lead for you." Lexi's voice held the deep, gravelly tone of a lifelong smoker. "A couple called wanting to tour the property on Hugh Drive. They're already in love with it from internet searches."

"Who wouldn't be? Bayou front and recently renovated? Of course they love it," Allison said. If her family's issues didn't consume her every waking moment, she'd fantasize about buying the place herself.

"It gets better. Did I mention they're planning to pay in cash? Slam-dunk client. Since you haven't been in the office much lately, I thought I'd throw this opportunity your way. You deserve a break."

Butterflies collided in Allison' stomach. The house on Hugh Drive boasted one of the higher price points to go on the market lately. It'd be a great sale. "You're the best, Lexi. When does the couple want to see the house?"

"Saturday morning. You up for it?"

"Most definitely. Thanks, Lexi. I appreciate you thinking of me."

"I got your back, girl. I'll e-mail you the details. Call me after you make the sale." Lexi hung up, and the dial tone replaced her voice.

With the prospect of a big sale on the horizon, Allison buzzed around the house, tidying up Tasha's toys. Her daughter left a trail of pink and glitter in her wake. A smile snuck up her face. Tasha's innocence and sweetness soothed her soul like a balm of joy. They counteracted the daily reality of living with Liam.

She paused her housework frenzy long enough to select "Black" by Pearl Jam from her playlist and blare it from the living room speakers. Though one of her favorite songs, she didn't play it often because it reminded her of Sean and a time when life had been simpler. Happier. From before schizophrenia entered their lives like an avalanche of horrors.

She hummed under her breath and entered Tasha and Liam's bathroom. No drops of water dotted the tub. Liam hadn't showered today. He hadn't yesterday, either. She tried to brush away her concern that his lack of personal hygiene indicated a relapse might be imminent. Liam had never enjoyed bathing, even as a small child. One skipped shower didn't mean much. He'd work up a sweat biking to Isaac's office. If he didn't take a shower after returning, she'd allow herself to worry then.

A shadow passed by the frosted bathroom window. Shortly after, the doorbell rang. Allison wiped her hands on her jean shorts and walked out to the foyer.

She opened the front door and tried not to grimace at Sara Channer's glossy red smile. When they'd first met, her grin had come off as genuine. Now it looked as fake as the rest of her. Her perfectly coiffed hair shined a blonde rarely, if ever, seen in nature and much too young for her years. Sara wore a tennis outfit meant for a twenty-year-old without leathery, sun-spotted skin.

"I wanted to stop by and say hi," Sara said. "It's been a while since we last chatted."

If by a while you mean since you learned my son has schizophrenia, then yes, it has.

Allison cleared her throat. "Would you like to come in?"

"Only if I'm not imposing." Sara didn't wait for an answer before she walked into the house. She glanced around at the minimalist aesthetic, which mostly reflected Isaac's preferences. Allison had given the bulk of her belongings to Sean when he moved to Ohio with Liam.

"Spotless and beautiful as usual." A note of disbelieving admiration tinged her voice and reminded Allison of the first time the woman had visited. "You've done such a lovely job on the décor. It's not what I expected," she'd said.

Why exactly Sara hadn't expected a tasteful interior, Allison could never decide. Was it a slam against her African-American husband? Was it because she had previously been the wife of an enlisted man? Either way, it had cut short any endearment the backhanded compliment had meant to impart.

Allison resisted the urge to roll her eyes. "Thanks. Would you like some tea or coffee?"

"No, thank you." She waved her hand. "I can't stay long, just a quick check to see how you're doing."

What she really meant was she wanted to be gone before Liam returned home. She wouldn't have come over if she hadn't seen him leave on his bike.

"We're doing great." Allison pulled out a chair for her.

She compressed her thin lips into a tight smile and sat. Sara had perfected the art of passive-aggressive sympathy. One little twitch of her lips broadcasted a patronizing "I know you're lying, but I'll go along with your fib so we both feel better" vibe.

"How's work going? Tough time to be a realtor."

Allison coughed. "Yes, but I've got a great prospect for this weekend. Potentially my biggest sale of the year."

Another passive-aggressive smile. Sara tapped her nails on the table. "And Tasha, she's enjoying school this year?"

"She loves it. Her teacher, Mrs. Grist, is absolutely wonderful. Best teacher we could've asked for."

Sara nodded inattentively and patted down her hair like she

suspected a few strands had the audacity to free themselves from whatever product she used to tame them. As far as Allison could tell, none had.

Sara allowed a lull in the conversation, probably hoping Allison would confide in her about Liam.

Instead, Allison asked, "How are you and Allen doing?"

The question caught her off guard. She blinked and temporarily lost her glossy composure. "Oh, fine. He's been TDY to Barksdale for a few days now. Gets home tonight. I've cooked up a storm all day." She didn't meet Allison's eyes.

Both women knew how Allen had occupied himself while away. In fact, all the officers' wives knew. Quite a few of the enlisted wives, too. Allen flaunted his infidelities and spent his days satisfying himself and ignoring Sara.

Allison inhaled. Wrapped up in Liam's issues, she sometimes forgot other people had their own little hells to wade through. Sara could be petty, but her poor behavior didn't excuse more rudeness. And even though today was her first visit since learning of Liam's diagnosis, that was one more visit than most of Allison's friends had paid her. Some avoided her because they didn't know what to say, others because her son scared them. Most shunned her due to a mixture of both fears. As a result, she was almost as lonely as Sara.

"When do your kids come home for break?" Allison asked.

"They've both got fall break in mid-October. Ainsley will be driving herself home from Auburn. I'm a little worried about the distance."

Allison tried not to feel jealous about the mundane concerns Sara held for her children. If only her biggest worry for Liam revolved around his long drive home from college.

A loud clanking noise resonated from the carport. Sara jolted upright. Her eyes shot to the front door and opened wide as Liam burst in.

He looked a hot mess. His red, curly hair stuck to his forehead with sweat, and his legs and arms oozed blood. When Liam laid eyes on Sara, he stopped midstride. Shit. He had some ongoing delusion about the woman that made him act bizarrely whenever she was near.

"Liam, won't you say hi to Sara? She's come over for a quick visit."

Nose wrinkled in disgust, he glared at Sara before stomping off to his bedroom.

The dining room chair scratched over the linoleum as Sara pushed it out and stood. She ran a shaking hand down the buttons on her tennis shirt. "I don't want to be a nuisance, so I'll get going now."

"You're not a nuisance. Feel free to stay a little..." Allison didn't get a chance to finish her farewell. The front door slammed behind her neighbor's hasty retreat.

She sat alone at the table, staring out the back window at the ocean. Whatever high she'd felt after her conversation with Lexi fizzled into anxiety. She waited a long time to hear the shower start from the hallway bathroom.

It never did.

18

THURSDAY, AUGUST 28th

If Liam didn't take his mind off yesterday's incident, fear might strangle him. He'd taken Dr. Jen's advice and broken out his oils as a distraction tool. His mother's disapproving scrutiny prevented him from painting at home, so he now sat between the baseball and softball fields at Gulf Coast State College, trying to ignore the fire ant mound to his left and the heap of goose droppings to his right.

He should've worn his baseball cap. The sun's late morning rays focused into a single laser beam pointed straight at his face. He squinted against the intense sunshine and bemoaned his painting conditions. Besides the oversaturated light, his canvas lay directly on a crusty, brown patch of grass. Dirt stained the corners of his work in progress, and occasional gusts of wind threatened to flip it over.

Thick layers of paint glistened on the canvas. He didn't use a brush, preferring instead a palette knife's sharper edge. While most people would call his style abstract, he thought of it as extreme impressionism. In high school, he'd fancied himself an artist in the vein of Van Gogh, Degas, and Cezanne, with a touch of Kandinsky. His teacher, though, had fancied him more the serial killer type and held a conference with his parents to discuss the "disturbing" themes he gravitated toward. A sudden end to his formal art education had followed shortly thereafter.

Unwilling to give up the one activity he enjoyed, Liam had begun to paint in private. Or, like today, in extreme public. Sometimes the two could be unnervingly similar.

Both the tone and color in his latest creation deviated from his norm. Broad, fluid strokes of tomato red and warm amber combined into a loose circle dominating the canvas. Smaller ovals of scarlet and mustard yellow broke through the sphere and smatterings of turquoise fringed its edge. A few licks of obsidian black streaked through the work.

A voice called out from near the baseball field. "Liam? Is that you?"

Stiff blades of grass prickled Liam's elbow as he leaned against it to face his guest.

Mai.

Smarter than him, she wore a white ball cap. Her dark hair peeked out below the hat, outlining the delicate contours of her face, and her lilac sundress swished in the breeze as she walked to his impromptu workstation.

"You're an artist?" She sidestepped the tubes of oil paint scattered around his large canvas backpack and leaned over to inspect his work in progress.

Struck with an immediate case of cotton mouth, he stared blankly at her, waiting for her to shy away from his painting or to ask why he sat in the middle of a field. She didn't.

Instead, she whistled long and low. "That's one big ball of desire you've created, Mr. Murphy."

"You think so?"

"I know so. You've got it bad for someone." She settled on the dirt next to him, her knee touching his.

Sweat rolled down his throat.

"What I can't figure out are the bits of black you've integrated into the piece. Like you consider desire toxic," she said.

"It's not the desire I consider toxic." Liam bit his lip. How did Mai always manage to make him share more than he intended?

She hovered her pointer finger above the canvas, tracing the swirling circle. Then she paused and met his eyes. “If I don’t focus too closely, the circle resembles a face.”

“Almost.”

“The turquoise is an interesting addition. It’s the same shade of nail polish I wore when we met on the beach.”

A seagull squawked overhead.

“You’re talented, Liam. It’s a beautiful piece.”

A warm flush crawled up his neck, spreading onto his ears until the tips glowed as red as cherries. “I paint what I see.”

She took off her hat and fanned her face with it. “I’m inclined to take that as a compliment. Would it kill you to be more overt with your flattery?”

He laughed. “Maybe if I had an ounce of the confidence you have.”

“It’s less a matter of confidence and more one of directness.” She shot a breath of air up to her bangs, fluttering her dark tresses against her forehead.

A lone fire ant had ventured away from his colony and crawled toward her sandaled toes. Liam kicked out his foot and stomped it. “You don’t want me to be direct. I’ve got a habit of scaring people.”

She tsked. “There’s nothing scary about you. Well, maybe your habit of skipping class is frightening. But I’ll convert you to a mediocre student yet.”

Black paint oozed out of a tube before he could twist on its cap. “Some people aren’t redeemable.”

Mai dropped her head back and sighed. “Here we go with the Holden Caulfield drama again. Everyone’s got issues, Liam. There’s good in you, just like there’s good in me.”

If only. “Despite what you might think, I don’t choose to be difficult. Much as I’d like a rosy view of the world, I could never believe it. This,” he gestured at the ebony streaks on his canvas, “is my reality. A darkness lives in me.” He pulled away from Mai and wrapped his arms around his legs.

A groan of frustration escaped her lips before she scrunched up her cap and threw it at him. The white pellet of cotton hit him square in the chest before crumpling to the dirt. She placed her face inches from his and let loose.

"All right, so I'll admit you face some challenges I can't imagine. What with the drowning and mourners, you've got some funky stuff to deal with. But that doesn't mean you don't deserve love."

He hugged his knees tighter. "Easy for you to say. You hardly know me."

A look of disbelief crossed her face. "You think if I knew you better I'd find you unlovable?"

"That seems to be the normal reaction."

Mai sensed she'd struck a raw nerve and placed a timid hand on his knee. "Then I guess I'm not like 'normal' people. I like you. And I'm not one to abandon somebody when life gets difficult." She waved her hands in the air. "Pfft! There goes my goal of mediocrity."

Liam's muscles loosened, and his jaw unclenched. He strung the moment out as long as he dared. People didn't often admit to liking him. When she started picking at the burnt grass, he ended his silence. "I'd never dream of getting in the way of your life's ambition. By all means, keep shooting for average."

She said, "It's too late to backtrack. You're like all of my other friends, trying to press your agenda of achieve-ism on me."

"So we're just friends?" He held his breath and waited for her answer.

She shot him a mischievous look. "Who's full of confidence now?"

"What can I say? You're a positive influence." He brushed off Mai's cap and placed it over her shiny black hair. "I think you dropped something."

A smile cracked her face. "Don't think you can redirect me by being a smartass. That's my routine."

"I would never dream of stealing your social tactics." He held up his hands in surrender. "Between dragging me to a cemetery and lecturing me about how I should feel, you've set the bar so high I could never hope to top it."

Though her dimples begged to be touched as she rolled back and laughed, he kept his hands to himself.

"Regardless of my social faux pas, you still owe me a date. Don't think I forgot about it."

He sincerely hoped she hadn't.

Mai looked at her watch and scowled. "I need to head to class. Lunch tomorrow?"

"Tomorrow." Liam's heart thudded against his chest.

"See you then." She reached out and brushed his cheek. After flashing another fabulous smile, she jogged across the field back to the campus buildings, her sundress rippling with each stride. Too soon, he was alone in the field again.

With nothing left to do but take Mai's advice, he picked up his palette knife and squeezed a gob of garnet oil paint onto it. He pressed the knife over one of the black streaks, hoping to transform it into a deep red. The onyx bled through the wet paint, determined to make its presence known. Much as Mai would like to erase the darkness, it remained.

Careful not to smudge his artwork, he lifted it from the patchy soil and stashed his oils and other belongings into his backpack. If he stayed out much longer, Isaac and Allison would begin to worry. Besides, nothing could top the few minutes he'd spent with Mai. He wouldn't chance witnessing another imprint and ruin the day. An afternoon with Joshua was preferable to whatever horrors awaited him outside.

19

FRIDAY, AUGUST 29th

Friday morning and his therapy appointment hadn't come fast enough. Liam had spent Thursday afternoon huddled in his room, wishing he could relive his quick visit with Mai. Instead, he'd obsessed about his new visions. The imprint of the dog beating had been bad. The interaction with Cull had been worse. Jumpy and irritable, he'd half expected the murderer to show up at his front door. His mother hadn't helped by allowing Mrs. Channer inside the house Wednesday afternoon. No doubt she'd bugged his room and most likely the living room too.

Unfortunately, matters hadn't improved any when he'd entered Dr. Jen's office. Her projection, in its now customary spot, hovered next to the psychologist in vivid color and detail, taunting him to mention its presence.

He sniffed. "We need to try some different medication. The stuff I'm taking isn't working anymore."

"I agree you're having some breakthrough symptoms. Let's bump up the dosage for the next week and see if you feel some relief." Dr. Jen adjusted her silver-rimmed glasses.

"No, this prescription… it's making me see visions. The medicine is the problem."

"We've gone through this before, Liam. You need to be on this prescription. It helps stabilize you. I know it's not perfect, but it's the most potent ammo we've got against your illness."

He flicked his fingernails. Why couldn't Dr. Jen admit he might be right? His medication had a long list of unsavory side effects, many of which might not be exposed until he'd used the drug for years. Would it be so hard to tack on "may reveal the past" to that list?

"What if they're not hallucinations? What if what I'm seeing are real memories, and I'm witness to a murder? Cull sure seems to think I'm a danger."

She reached for her notepad. "The murderer is talking to you now?"

"He's threatening me. Telling me to keep my mouth shut." He omitted the part about accidentally stealing Cull's cocaine and owing the man a huge sum of money.

"Could he be symbolic of how you feel society is muzzling you? More specifically, do you feel talking about your illness is taboo?"

"No! It's not symbolic. It's actually happening!" he yelled. He jumped out of his seat and paced between his psychologist's desk and the office door. "I'm telling you, it's different. The visions I'm seeing have happened. They're memories. And then there are the projections. I see people's griefs, their concerns, their desires. I don't want to see any of those feelings. I've got enough of my own."

She clicked on her pen and tapped it against her notepad. "Is it possible you're transposing your own fears onto others?"

Tiny crimson stars flooded his vision. For the first time in months, he didn't wish away his anger, and instead, allowed it to guide him. Keeping secrets had gotten him nowhere. "Two sessions ago, you asked why I researched you. I didn't. The woman I described to you? She's here right now. You're projecting her. She's as much a burden to you as Joshua is to me. All I know about her is she makes you sad."

The corners of Dr. Jen's eyes wrinkled as she frowned. "This isn't funny, Liam."

"No, it's not. Don't you get it? I don't want to see her. I don't want to know about your personal life. We've made significant progress together these past few months, and I want to continue doing so. I wouldn't endanger our relationship by researching you."

Silence.

Then, she leaned back. "Where else do you see these images?"

"Everywhere." He waved his hands in the air. "At school. At home. Outside. Everywhere."

She pulled at her hair, which she wore down in soft, rolling waves today. "All right. Let's try some other medication. I must tell you, however, I'm hesitant about this plan. Your records indicate previous attempts with other prescriptions weren't as successful for you. But I'm willing to give it a shot. We'll have to make an appointment with your psychiatrist to get the new prescription, but she's out of town until Monday. May we schedule an emergency session with an alternate doctor today?"

"No. I'll wait until Monday." He hated meeting new doctors.

"Are you sure that's a wise decision?"

He shot her an exasperated look. "Didn't you just try to convince me to stay on my current meds?"

She pursed her lips. "Point made. I'll agree to your plan if you double your dosage until Monday."

"Deal."

20

The college library bustled with quiet energy. Liam avoided the hanky-panky workstation because it seemed a breach of privacy to peek into the librarian's love life. Besides, he was no peeping Tom. If he wanted to see porn, he'd go home and browse the Internet like any other twenty-five-year-old.

Students occupied all of the seats with a decent view of the entrance, but he had a trick or two up his sleeve for just such occasions. Next to the front door sat a pimply-faced kid probably still sniffing seventeen. He wore ear buds and swayed in time to a song. Liam planted his feet next to the scrawny kid's chair and glared at him.

Standing and staring shouldn't be scary.

But he'd learned from all his time in psychiatric wards that it most certainly was. The kid jumped a few inches out of his chair when he sensed Liam's presence. With eyes as wide as saucers, he gathered his laptop and books and tripped over his feet in a hasty escape.

Liam pulled out the chair and sighed as he sat down. The chances of Mai arriving this early to the library were slim. They had chemistry class now. She wouldn't skip it because two missed classes in one week didn't lead to mediocrity. It led to failure. He'd headed down that path so many times he knew it by heart. Still, when his watch hit fifteen minutes after class had started and she didn't show, he sagged against his chair.

Time continued to trickle by, slowed by his yearning to see Mai. He checked his watch for the hundredth time and yawned. Sleep had eluded him since his confrontation with Cull. One big knot of worry, his stomach twisted and churned. Much as he'd like a nap, his body wouldn't cooperate and allow him rest. He laced his hands over his face and closed his eyes anyway. Pretend sleep beat no sleep.

The background noise of quiet murmurings and occasional bursts of stifled laughter comforted him. Here, he could manage life. Even better, Cull couldn't threaten him, Isaac couldn't nag him, and Joshua couldn't follow him.

The day got even better when Mai arrived with footsteps so soft he didn't hear her approach. He did, however, smell her perfume—spicy with floral undertones and possibly the best scent ever.

She thought she roused him with a gentle poke. "Class is as easy to sleep in as the library, you know."

He moved his hands away from his face. "I'm working my way up to it."

"Right. Well, for today, I need you to work your way up to driving me to lunch. I'm starving. And you owe me a date."

She tapped her foot on the floor. Her toenails shimmered a crimson red.

Mai's wish was his command.

The neon lights of the nearest buffet restaurant flashed on and off as they pulled into its parking lot.

"Are you sure this is where you want to eat?" Liam asked.

"It's not fine cuisine, but it won't leave you huddled over the toilet all night either. Plus, the menu is easy on a college kid's piggybank." Mai rubbed her thumb and fingers together in the universal sign for money.

Despite Mai's lukewarm endorsement of the joint, he bet E. coli maintained a permanent residency there. Still, he appreciated her effort to keep costs down. Weeks of saving had filled his wallet, but mostly with an optical illusion. Twenty-nine dollar bills looked like more than they were. Isaac and his mother parceled out his allowance at a miserly rate because therapists had told them many people struggling with mental illness self-medicate with drugs.

No amount of anticipation, however, had prepared them for a free stash of coke at the yacht club behind their house. Sometimes, life was a real bitch.

"Let the feast begin. But don't come crying to me when you're worshipping at the porcelain throne tonight." He walked over to the passenger's side and opened the door to the sound of her laughter.

She leaned against his hand as she stood. "Don't tell me you're a snob, Liam."

He slammed the door shut behind her. "Nah, more like a general malcontent. You'll see."

Their feet crunched over the gravel parking lot, and she shot him a flirtatious glance. "You don't fool me. There's a big, soft teddy bear under this crusty exterior of yours. I think most people would be surprised at what goes on in your head."

"Most definitely." He grabbed hold of the silver fish head doubling as a handle for the restaurant's door and yanked it open. The scent of boiled crabs and reheated fish hung heavy in the air.

"I may have overstated this place's safety rating. Stay away from the shrimp," she whispered out of the corner of her mouth.

"Done." He wouldn't touch the rubbery, pathetic looking sea insects even under duress from Joshua.

After piling his plate high with safe-looking carbohydrates, he joined Mai. She'd zipped through the sneeze bars and had already selected a table near the exit. He inspected her meal as he sat down. The adventuresome sort, she'd plopped a tasting of every item from the buffet onto her plate. Save the shrimp, of course.

Steam rose from a biscuit as she sliced it open and slathered butter over it. "I've thought about your painting since I saw it yesterday. Where'd you end up hanging it?"

"Nowhere. I don't display my artwork."

She squeezed her biscuit shut and gave him the stink eye. "Not acceptable. I demand my portrait be exhibited. How else will I become known as the modern-day Mona Lisa?"

The knot festering in his stomach relaxed. Mai's magical presence calmed his soul more than any medication ever could. "I'll find a place for it," he lied.

"You better. Now, tell me, have you seen any more memory imprints?" She left her biscuit to soak up the golden juice of butter and twirled her fork in a mound of fettuccini.

He'd debated how much to tell her about what he saw. He didn't want to burden her with his issues, but he needed the help of an objective, third party to parse through his interactions with Cull.

"I have. A very dark one."

"Dark as in drowning dark?"

"Worse." He picked at a thick fry, crumbling its edge between his thumb and forefinger. "I saw a man beat someone to death."

Her fork clattered onto the white laminate table, spattering flecks of pasta over it. "What?"

Liam met her eyes. "I'll spare you the gory details. I wish I'd never seen it."

"I'm sorry you did." She covered his hand with hers.

Tension slithered back into his body. "Me too. Now I'm stuck wondering if I should report the killing. What do I tell the cops? 'I see visions?'" A nervous chuckle escaped his lips.

"There's got to be proof at the murder scene. Call in an anonymous tip."

"There's no sign of a struggle." He shook his head. "I checked it out."

She withdrew her hand from his and narrowed her eyes. "You investigated a murder scene on your own?"

"I needed to know if what I saw really happened." He pushed his plate forward, appetite now gone.

"I suppose I can understand your point of view. But you need to be careful. What if the murderer saw you?"

He rubbed his temple and wondered if a term for "I told you so" after the fact existed. "Then I'd be sitting across the table from you, asking what you think I should do next..."

Her mouth dropped open. She ran her tongue across her teeth and tugged at the ends of her hair. "You're kidding. The murderer saw you at the scene of his crime?"

"Yeah. I went there looking for clues, but discovered a big, plastic bag of cocaine instead. The killer saw me find it."

"Hold on." She held up her hands. "Are you telling me the murderer is also a drug dealer? And he's aware you know of both illicit activities?"

"He can't possibly know I saw a memory imprint of him committing murder. He's focused on the drugs."

"How do you know?" A muscle in her jaw twitched, and she crossed her arms.

He scratched at his cheek and grimaced. "Because he told me."

She gasped. The look on her face rapid cycled from shock to anger to alarm. "What? Where? At the dock?"

"No, he cornered me at my stepfather's office." He cleared his throat and looked at the empty table next to them.

"This keeps getting better and better. The guy works with your stepdad?"

Is that a note of disbelief in her voice?

"I'm not sure. I've never seen him there before, but that doesn't mean much."

"Talk about unbelievable coincidences. Honestly, Liam, if I didn't know better, I'd say you made this all up." She uncrossed her arms and stabbed at a piece of white fish. The overcooked flesh broke into several pieces and scattered across her plate as she flung down her fork.

"What about your stepdad? Would he know the guy?"

Liam shrugged. "Probably. But he wouldn't believe me if I told him about the murder."

"Why not?"

Besides being the most unreliable witness in the history of unreliable witnesses?

"I have a bit of an unfortunate 'Chicken Little' syndrome trailing me."

The crucifix on her throat disappeared as she clasped it in her fingers and tugged on it. "You're in a tight spot, Liam."

Finally. Somebody had enough sense to agree with him.

He wiped his sweaty palms on his shorts. "There's more. The killer demands I pay him $200 for some drugs I accidentally took."

"I'm not even going to ask how you 'accidentally' took some drugs." She dropped her head forward and rubbed the back of her neck. "Do you have the cash?"

"No. I can't pay him."

The table jolted as she slapped her hands on it, silverware and plates clinking from the impact.

"The situation has moved beyond our capabilities. I stand by my first suggestion. You've got to call in an anonymous tip. If the police find the drugs, they also might find signs of the murder."

He bit the inside of his cheek. "All right. But I've got to make the call from here. I don't want them to track it back to my house."

"Excellent idea. You need to be cautious." She picked at some suspicious-looking fish sticks on her plate. "You've accomplished the unimaginable. I'm too worried to eat regular food. I require chocolate." She pushed out from the table and glowered at him. "I'll be back in a sec."

Despite his worries, Liam took the opportunity to admire her cutoff jeans and what filled them out. The woman certainly knew how to wear a pair of shorts. His thoughts wandered into slightly dangerous territory and distracted him so much that at first he didn't notice his new visitor.

21

Typical Mai," a woman said. She startled Liam out of his pleasant trance and sat next to him, scowling.

"You're a friend?" A deep blush blossomed across his cheeks. He had no illusions about what a letch he must've looked like while ogling Mai.

She didn't offer her hand, nor did she answer his question. "I'm Thanh. And I suppose you must be the new project, Liam."

"Mai mentioned me?" He sounded more pathetic than he liked.

"Unfortunately."

Where Mai was nicely rounded, Thanh was all bones and angles. What his father would've called angry skinny.

Thanh leaned back into the orange booth, crunching its crackled plastic coating. "You don't have an ounce of sense, do you?"

"Maybe an ounce, but not much more."

She rolled her eyes. "Here you've got a woman like Mai interested in a... man... like you, and you bring her here? I don't care if she's enlisted you on her way to achieving mediocrity. You ought to know better."

Of course he knew better, but he had the minor problem of not being able to afford another restaurant. The ancient booth creaked under his shifting weight.

"I'm going to save Mai some heartache this time around. You're not good enough for her, nor will you ever be. The mere fact you agreed to bring her here tells me you're not ready for her. Don't let her silly campaign for normalcy fool you."

His mouth went dry. Thanh spoke the truth. He'd hurt Mai.

A plate loaded with treats banged down on the table. "Thanh! How'd you find me?" asked Mai. She shot an apprehensive glance at Liam and mouthed "sorry" with a shake of her head. Whether the "sorry" referred to Thanh and her manners or to finishing their conversation later, he wasn't sure.

"Are you kidding? I looked for the nearest, grossest place I could find. Bingo!" Thanh smiled and shook her head. "How can you stand to eat this crap?"

"I consider it a character-building experience." Mai nudged her plate to the middle of the table. She looked knowingly at Thanh. "Don't play. You know you want some."

"Only because you've completely ruined my taste buds." Thanh leaned over the plate, broke off a chunk of chocolate chip cookie, and popped it in her mouth. "Terrible," she said after swallowing.

Mai laughed. "So you don't want any more?" She shielded the plate with her shoulder and took a bite out of a lemon bar, but not before Thanh sneaked a stealthy hand across the table and retrieved the rest of the cookie.

If he'd been a braver man, he would've tried to grab a piece of brownie from the shared plate. But if he stuck his hand anywhere near it, he risked a swat from either woman. No lemon bar, spoonful of pudding, or chocolate cake justified the injury he'd earn if he dared disrupt their routine.

After they'd polished off the last of the desserts, Mai pointed her chin toward Liam. "By the look on his face, I'd wager you gave him your typical speech?"

Thanh threw an exasperated hand in the air. "I refuse to accept this ordinary charade of yours. You're one of the kindest, most thoughtful, intelligent people I know. Why is that so hard for you to admit?"

"I refuse to be miserable in a so-called pursuit of happiness. You've seen what it's done to my sister. So she's at the top of her class at Yale. It doesn't matter because she hates her life. It won't get better for her when she graduates either. She'll be so intent on being at the top of her field she'll never be happy. I measure success by happiness, not credentials."

"Fine. But don't settle for less than you deserve." Thanh's eyes flicked at Liam.

"Everybody deserves happiness. And how they achieve happiness is up to them." Mai patted her clenched lips with a balled up paper napkin.

"All right, all right. Enough of this conversation. Let's talk about something else. How are your applications coming?" Thanh said.

A wave of lightheadedness hit Liam, and he grasped the edge of the table. "What applications?"

"To colleges where I can finish my BA. Twelve more credits until I'm done with my associate's and can transfer." Mai looked at him questioningly. "What's your plan?"

He needed a plan other than moving out of his mother's house and maintaining stability? "Same as yours, of course. Where are you applying?"

"A couple of different places. UF, Miami. One or two spots up north."

"Mai is trying to break my heart." Thanh held her hand on her chest. "We made a pact long ago that the two of us would end up as Gators at the University of Florida. But now she's entertaining the idea of leaving the great sunshine state and going to school in Virginia.

"Have you seen some of the Spring Breakers from that state? They look downright depressed when they get here in March, all pale and anemic." She looked down her nose at him. "Sort of like you, really. Anyhow, she's got her eye on some small college specializing in historic preservation."

Thanh sighed. "Historic preservation, Liam. Can you imagine a mere college major separating us?"

He ignored her question. White fringe had appeared around Mai once again. He watched as it formed the same battered photograph of her grandfather he'd seen in the diner.

"I suppose a historic preservation major makes sense. It'll certainly help you achieve your goal of restoring your grandfather's grave," he said.

Thanh froze. "You told him?" A hint of accusation and jealousy crept through her voice.

Mai looked off to the side. "Liam's not as normal as you think."

"Apparently not." Thanh eyeballed the two of them like a prison guard scrutinized new convicts. She tapped her watch. "It's time to get back to campus. I'll give you a ride, Mai." She picked up her handbag before standing and tapping her foot.

Ice cubes sloshed together in Liam's drink as Mai slid out from the booth. "We're nowhere near finished with our conversation. Meet me after class?" she asked.

"Can't today. But I'll give you a call."

"Not without my number." Mai scribbled down her contact info on a napkin and let it float down to his lap. "Don't make me worry about you."

"Never." Liam gave his best attempt at a disarming smile.

The ladies waved as they walked out of the restaurant, arm in arm. Thanh shot him a level look over her shoulder before she let the door swing shut.

He'd seen that look plenty of times before.

She didn't trust him. Nor did she like him.

Join the freaking club.

He settled the bill, which exhausted his paltry funds, then drove around until he found the nearest pay phone, a more difficult task than he'd imagined. Nobody used payphones but criminals anymore. He finally found one behind the parking lot of a fast food joint. A sticky substance clung to the receiver as he picked it up and dialed.

"9-1-1, what's your emergency?" a crisp voice said.

"I've got information regarding narcotics on Tyndall AFB. A drug dealer is storing cocaine under one of the docks at the base marina." He plunged his finger down on the payphone's metal switch, and the dial tone cut off the dispatcher's next question.

He'd done his part. If the memory imprint really had revealed the past, the Air Force Security Forces would find evidence of murder.

22

By the time Liam arrived home, flashes of green and red dotted the marina. Security Forces had acted on his anonymous tip. An unfamiliar sensation of gratification rolled over him. For the first time in his life, the authorities had believed him.

He parked under the carport and ambled down the slight hill that led to the yacht club. A Security Forces sedan parked sideways in the road, blocking the marina from traffic. Liam bypassed the blockade by staying on the sandy lawn. A loud whistle stopped his progress.

"Sir, the marina is closed. You need to leave the premises," a Security Force specialist barked at him. She held one hand out in caution and placed the other on a holstered gun. Security Forces didn't screw around.

He took a few more steps forward. "I live up the hill and wanted to check out what all the commotion was about." He craned his neck to the side and saw both docks in the marina boiling with Security Forces activity.

"I'm not at liberty to discuss the investigation. Turn around. Now." She tapped her gun for emphasis.

He held up his hands. "Got it. Guess my daily trip to the shoppette for a soda will have to wait."

The specialist didn't laugh and set a steely gaze on him he'd bet didn't waver until he reached Isaac's house. The clicking of a hot engine recently turned off echoed from the carport. Allison was home.

"Mom?" he called as he walked through the back door.

Nobody answered. RP stepped out from under the dining room table in a languorous fashion, stretching his back paws and then front. A light-green object dangled between his fangs. Liam leaned over for a better view. An anole's limp reptilian head hung from one end of RP's mouth and its long, slender tail from the other.

Liam wrinkled his nose. "Gross."

The cat shook the lizard but didn't attempt to run past Liam into the oppressive afternoon heat. He must've had his fill on Wednesday. The family hadn't noticed him missing until the evening when he'd scratched at the back door to be let inside. Liam had played dumb about the animal's escape, but Allison and Isaac had known better.

Black and gray furry tail wrapped around him like a shield, RP stared at Liam. Atypically, he didn't growl or hiss.

"You must've found a nice lady friend outside and worked out some of your demons." Liam tipped his head down. "You're welcome."

RP flicked his tail in response. The anole stayed clamped in his jaws.

The hum of the ancient air conditioner buzzed through the house as Liam made a quick circuit looking for his mother. Tasha's room, full of pink and purple, radiated cheer even in her absence. Whereas mere mortals sloughed skin, she shed shimmery bits and pieces of positive energy like pixie dust. Whatever she touched glowed with warmth.

Unable to find his mother indoors, he resorted to peeking through the front door's peephole. Allison sat on the rusted yellow patio sofa. Lost in thought, she stared out toward the street. He reached for the handle to open the door but stopped cold when he saw his mother had a visitor.

His breath hitched. Allison held the hand of a young boy, perhaps ten or so. The child leaned against her, chatting with a smile on his face, maybe about his day at school. He wore a blue, button-up shirt and bright-white new sneakers. Neatly trimmed auburn hair fell above his ears and eyebrows.

Liam's legs gave a little, and he had to clutch the door to keep from falling. He looked at a memory of himself. As he had been Before. Or at least how his mother had seen him.

Allison smiled as she swung, her eyes set on the distant horizon and not her imagined son. Little Liam giggled at some whispered joke. He was happy and lovable. And sane.

The projection, laced with more nostalgia and longing than a Norman Rockwell painting, sucker-punched him in the gut. He sank to his knees and leaned his head against the wall. He'd grown accustomed to the idea his mother had always kept her emotional distance. But that wasn't true. Not so long ago, he'd adored her. Just as his father had. And his mother had, in turn, adored both of them. They'd all loved each other once upon a time.

"It's no wonder you feel sick. Your stupid memory is so sweet it's cloying." Joshua appeared next to Liam. He lounged lazily next to the front door and twirled a toothpick between his two front teeth. "Your mother used to think you were so perfect. But even then, I lived inside you. Remember?"

"No, I don't. You're a liar." Although he had an increasingly difficult time recalling life before Joshua, he did remember it'd been happy. Even if his tie to the past had loosened, his mother's sharp memory made it clear. He'd been good once.

"You were never good, Liam Murphy," Joshua said.

"Shut up." A tear glided over the stubble he'd neglected to shave in the morning.

Life hurt less when he didn't remember.

Joshua sat up straight and reared back with his fist, aiming straight for Liam's mouth. He didn't like backtalk. Muscles tensed, Liam braced for the impact.

And then, a miracle happened.

From under the dining room table, RP hissed, arched his tail in the air, and lowered his head to the ground in an attack stance. He sprang forward and barreled toward Joshua.

Shocked by the cat's attack, Joshua dropped his toothpick. "What the hell?" he screamed.

RP sank his teeth into Joshua's ankle and twisted to the side.

Joshua howled, booted the cat off his leg with a hard kick, and then evaporated. RP crashed into the door next to Liam.

Out of sheer habit, Liam shied away from the animal and kept a leery eye on him. "Did you just protect me?"

Already recovered from his collision, the cat licked his lips in response. The two looked at each other, waiting for the other to pounce.

The front door creaked open.

"Liam?" Allison said. She must've heard the commotion RP caused while chasing off Joshua. "Are you okay?"

Huddled in the corner, he inched his hand out to the cat. When RP didn't bite, he rubbed the top of his head. "Yep. Making friends with the cat."

His mother stood in the doorframe, open wide to the outside. A few wisps of her braided hair had escaped, and due to the humidity, now curled around her face. She wore a black pantsuit that complimented her trim figure. Though she trained a neutral expression on her face, her eyes opened wide in astonishment.

"He's letting you touch him?"

"Guess so."

The bonding moment ended when RP stretched and sauntered away. Liam took his cue and stood as well.

Allison stared at him, wordless and sad, most likely trying to reconcile the memory of her perfect son with the crumpled, exhausted version in front of her. If he had any spare emotional energy, he'd sympathize with her.

"I'm sorry I ended up like this." He waved a hand at his disheveled appearance. "It's not how I wanted life to turn out either."

Tears sprung to her eyes. "I know. I'm sorry I haven't been a better mother to you. I guess neither one of us received training for this."

Liam nodded and lifted a hand out to his mother. She grasped it and brought it close to her face so her now falling teardrops wet his palm.

Throat thick with stifled emotion, he retrieved his hand from his sobbing mother and backed away. "I'll be in my room until dinner."

"All right." She eased a shaking hand into her pocket.

It wasn't all right, though, and it hadn't been for a long, long time.

23

Tasha scratched her knife over the white plate, doing her best to cut the pork chop into a bite-sized portion. But no six-year-old possessed the strength to properly slice through pork this tough. Allison favored cooking meat until she burned all life and flavor out of it. The scent of charred flesh wafted over the oval oak dinner table.

"So then Alex pushed me and took my bubbles away," Tasha complained. She'd been delivering a blow-by-blow account of her interaction with some little punk who liked to pester her at daycare.

"Did you shove him back?" Liam asked. He jammed a dried-out puck of meat into his mouth.

Allison and Isaac's faces fell.

Oh, right. His mother and stepfather only approved shoving imaginary people.

Isaac wiped his hands on a napkin. "What I think your brother meant to say, sweetie, is that it's not okay for Alex to push you."

"I know. I didn't let him. I told the teacher about it," Tasha said.

While Isaac and Allison shared a worried glance, Tasha shot Liam a wink and pushed her right hand in front of her, just perceptibly.

He winked back.

"How was work, Isaac?" Liam asked. According to Dr. Jen, *engagement* was a cardinal sign of mental health. So engage he would.

"Rather subpar. We're working through some personnel issues." Isaac tapped his golden wedding band.

Now Liam didn't have to pretend to be engaged. "Is somebody at work exhibiting signs of aggression?" Belatedly, he realized his voice held too much excitement.

"No." Isaac frowned. "One of our paralegals is acting erratically, showing up for work late, leaving early. I might have to fire him."

The cheap fork in Liam's hand bent as he gripped it tight. "What does he look like?"

If possible, Isaac's frown deepened. "Why do you ask?"

He fidgeted in his seat. "Thought maybe I'd seen him around."

"You have no reason to know him." Isaac's shoulders tensed. Liam had a special way of worrying him.

The tension summoned Joshua. He hunched over Isaac; mere millimeters separated their faces. "Change the topic, dumbass. You're freaking him out."

Liam imagined throwing his plate, still loaded with kale salad and sliced beets, at Joshua's head. Blood red beets slid down his face and left a crimson trail down the contours of his neck.

"Go ahead, do it." Joshua's beady eyes bored into Liam's.

With a restraint Dr. Jen would cheer, Liam scratched his cheek. He said, "So what was the deal down at the yacht club?"

"Word has it Security Forces scoured the docks and marina for drugs. Anonymous tip." Allison tugged on her braid. "Looks like they came up empty, though. All the cruisers left, and the marina is open for business again. Probably some idiot wanting attention."

His previous feeling of satisfaction, still new and uninvestigated, shattered. "Security Forces didn't find anything?"

Isaac crossed his arms. "What did you expect them to find?"

The two men locked eyes.

"Nothing. Just seems like an awful lot of activity for an empty tip."

Isaac's forehead wrinkled in suspicion.

"Stellar job at redirecting his attention," Joshua said. "Are you going to tell him next you kill puppies for fun?"

"What's the plan for tomorrow, Mom?" Liam gagged down a kale leaf.

She blinked. Normally, he couldn't care less about their schedule.

Yes, notice this, me on my best behavior. I'm getting better, see?

"I've got an important showing in the morning, but I'll be back by late afternoon. Isaac will be here with Tasha and you," she said.

He smiled. "Hey, Isaac, how about we take an old-fashioned, family bike ride in the morning?" Whatever bonus points he'd scored during the conversation zeroed out. He knew better than to ask in front of Tasha, but scheduling any type of activity with his younger sister required extraordinary, and sometimes unsavory, measures.

Another frown from Isaac. Quite the workout he gave his lower chin tonight. "We'll see."

Joshua paced behind Isaac. "I'm gonna give him something real to worry about."

A knife, long, serrated, and sharp, glinted in Joshua's hands. He lunged toward Isaac, aiming for his broad back.

A low rumble from under the table, followed in quick succession by a hair-raising hiss, caught his family off guard. RP charged Joshua once again, who screamed in rage before disappearing. His knife clattered to the floor, unnoticed by the rest of the family. RP skidded into the kitchen, hackles up and eyes wide.

"What's the matter with RP?" asked Tasha. She went to stand, but Isaac placed a firm hand on her arm and kept her seated.

"There's no telling, baby girl. We brought that cat in from the wild, but the wild still lives in him. It's best to leave him be when he acts squirrelly." Allison peered into the kitchen, unnerved by the cat's actions despite her composed explanation. Under the low light of the chandelier, she caught Isaac's eye and shrugged.

They had no idea.

The meal ended in a familiar uneasy silence, which Liam hoped Tasha was too young to notice. He helped with the dishes—more engagement!—then begged off for the night. On the way to his room, he passed Tasha on the couch. Cross-legged, she peeled stickers from a princess book and transferred them to her collectibles album. To streamline the process, she'd stuck a number of the sparkly stickers on her nose and cheeks. She grabbed one from her face and adhered it to the proper spot in her album.

"Good night, Liam," she sang out. She blew a kiss and giggled when he caught it and smashed it on his nose. Just as a smile crept up his face, motion in his peripheral vision caught his attention.

Cull stood by the back door, towering over Tasha. Covered in blood, his little sister fought for breath underneath the killer's tight chokehold. Cull held a gun in his hand and waved it across the room.

Liam gasped and turned his head to the couch, where Tasha continued to organize her album, oblivious to any peril. Empty space replaced the vision when he darted his eyes again to the back door.

Terrified of the image he'd seen, Liam bolted to his room. RP trotted behind and indolently settled onto the papasan after Liam closed his door. Typically, Joshua sat in the papasan. But as long as RP curled up in it, Joshua wouldn't come near.

"It's not real, it's not real, it's not real," he muttered. But no matter how many times he repeated the mantra, his pulse refused to slow.

The image was simply that. An idea. Nothing more. His mind threw together random hallucinations to confuse him. Tasha was safe.

In a last-bid effort to redirect his thoughts, he dared to ruffle RP's fur. The cat tilted his head to the side as Liam worked the soft skin behind his ears. A purr as loud as a Harley Davidson motor rumbled from RP's chest.

"What's with the protective detail?"

With a large yawn, RP rolled over to his back and bared his belly. Five days ago, this simple act of trust would've been unthinkable. Somehow, the cat had warmed up to him.

The animal's transformation showed changes weren't always bad. Sometimes, they were beneficial.

Like his latest decision. He was done with medicine.

Despite what Dr. Jen thought, Liam didn't have a choice in the matter. He couldn't bear the weight of his family's secret burdens.

Strangers' projections proved difficult enough to process, but the mental cost of watching his mother wish for a version of him that didn't exist anymore? Torture.

If that memory had been the worst of the visions, though, he might have been able to live with them. The final, crushing blow had been Cull threatening Tasha. Liam couldn't bear to see his sister hurt, even with imagined injuries. Whatever tricks his mind may play on him while psychotic had to be better.

24

SATURDAY, AUGUST 30th

The morning started as a typical Saturday. Allison sold houses to families happier than hers, Isaac read the newspaper while keeping an eye on Liam, and Tasha tuned into her favorite TV program, a cartoon about rainbow-vomiting unicorns or some such adorable nonsense.

Most mornings, Liam picked at his cereal, a healthy oat and nut concoction his mother had created. Not today. He'd eaten all but the dregs due to his stronger than usual appetite.

"Liam, come over here! You've got to see what Sissy is doing!" Tasha shrieked from the couch.

Isaac snapped the newspaper low. "Who's Sissy?"

"My friend," said Tasha. "She's sitting right next to me. She's making the silliest faces!"

The newspaper tumbled to the floor as Isaac stood. "There's nobody in this room but the three of us," he said.

"Well, I knew you wouldn't be able to see her, Daddy, so I called for Liam. He can see people the rest of us can't."

Isaac curled his arms over his head and shot Liam a malevolent glare like he'd purposely spread his psychological cancer to Tasha.

For a few awkward moments, only the high-pitched voices from

Tasha's cartoon kept the family room from becoming deathly silent. But Liam refused to allow his baby sister to feel like a freak. He pushed out from the table and strode over to the couch.

Tasha had a visitor, all right. Sissy wasn't the one keeping her company, though. Arms crossed behind his head, Joshua smirked in the seat next to her.

"Hey, look at that. Your sister is just as batshit crazy as you are."

Sweat beaded on Liam's brow. He pointed at empty air and laughed. "Is silly string coming out of her nose?"

"Yes!" giggled Tasha. She held up her pastel-green teddy bear and rubbed it all over "Sissy's" face.

"Now it's on Teddy!" She dissolved into laughter and rolled on her side.

"Then it's time for Sissy to go home. She's made a big enough mess." He made a show of jumping in the air before landing on the couch and rooting his butt around the seat for emphasis.

"Is she gone?" Isaac whispered.

"Completely!" Tasha snuggled against Liam. Her tight curls fell around his shoulder, and she placed her teddy bear in his arms. "You're even funnier than Sissy."

"Of course I am."

He sat on the couch with his sister as long as he dared. Like a stone statue behind them, Isaac stood frozen in shock and dismay. Fear rolled off him in waves. Finally, it came.

"Liam, I'd like to speak with you."

"You're in some serious trouble, young man." Joshua mocked Isaac by imitating his voice and tone. He lit a cigarette. "Don't worry, I'll take care of Tasha while you're talking with Daddy dearest. Maybe I'll have Sissy come back for a visit."

Liam returned Teddy to his sister and gave her a fond kiss on the top of her head. "Enjoy your cartoons, kid."

Entranced by the show, she bobbed her head. One pony had betrayed the other, and her treachery bubbled to the surface.

Isaac pointed to the front door. The two stepped outside and met under the carport.

"She's too young to be exhibiting symptoms." Isaac looked out toward the ocean, unwilling to make eye contact with his stepson.

"Yes, she is," said Liam, "and that's why you've got to lighten up. She's just got an imaginary friend. Lots of kids her age do. It's not her fault she's related to me."

"There are cases, though, aren't there? Of young children being diagnosed with schizophrenia?" Isaac leaned a trembling hand against the carport wall.

A hot, sticky breeze pushed against Liam's back. He awaited a reappearance of psychotic Tasha with dread.

But no white fringe surrounded his stepfather. No glowing halos of misery emerged from his skin.

Liam didn't require any further proof. The medication *had* given him these awful powers.

"There are. But they're also incredibly rare. And I doubt Tasha would laugh at a hallucination. Mine were never funny or nice." Liam tried to convince himself as well as Isaac. Though he didn't want to admit it, the episode had left him rattled as well.

Tasha was healthy and needed to stay that way.

"You can't talk anymore about your hallucinations. It's not healthy for your sister," Isaac said. "She deserves a normal childhood."

"I only slipped up and mentioned Joshua once in front of Tasha. Believe it or not, I want the same life for her that you do. I want her to grow up to be happy and healthy. Besides, I would never wish my condition upon somebody else. Not even you."

His stepfather didn't laugh.

"Whatever you do, don't make a big deal out of it." Liam clapped his hands together and kept them in a prayer pose. "Chances are if you never mention it again, neither will Tasha. Take her out of the house, and go somewhere fun for the morning. You'll both feel better."

Isaac tapped the wall and stared at him.

"Listen, I know you don't think of me as the voice of reason, but alternate perceptions of reality are pretty much right in my wheelhouse," said Liam. "Trust me."

His stepfather took a deep breath. "All right, I'll take her to the beach today. That'll give you some time alone as well."

Stunned Isaac had agreed with him, he scratched his back and thought up a proper response. He didn't have much practice with harmonious decisions.

"Sounds like a plan," he said.

25

Liam wiped sweaty palms on his khaki cargo shorts and stared at his phone like it could grow fangs and bite him. He hadn't called a girl in years. Matter of fact, he wasn't sure he even knew how to hold a phone conversation anymore. But he had to tell Mai their big plan had fallen flat. After a few false starts, he sent her a text message—it demanded less courage than a call.

"Hey, Mai, Liam here. Anonymous tip didn't work. I'm fine," he wrote.

He held his breath and stared at his phone. How long should he wait for a reply? Minutes? Hours? Would she respond at all?

Mere seconds later, his phone lit up with an incoming message. His heart banged against his chest, and he exhaled years of pent-up frustration.

"What?!? How can that be?" she texted.

"Don't know. Maybe I imagined it," he responded.

"No way. It's real. Let's meet."

Liam jumped and pumped his fist in the air. Mai wanted to see him. Today.

"When can you escape?" she texted.

"Anytime."

"Then I'll meet you at the Hog & Claw at noon. Don't be late."

"Hog & Claw?" he said out loud in dismay. He often drove past the dive of a barbecue restaurant located across the bay from the paper plant. If the wind blew the wrong way, the stench of paper production filled his car, not cooked pig. Mai needed to improve her taste in restaurants, and fast.

"See you soon," he texted.

Exhilarated by the successful conversation, albeit a text one, he tossed his phone onto his navy bedspread. He didn't need any freaking pills. Mai proved it. Not only did she like him, she'd asked him out to lunch. All while he was under the influence of nothing but his own mind. She deserved the whole truth. She needed to see evidence of the murder.

He fished through his underwear drawer, looking for the small bag of cocaine he'd taken from the yacht club, but no plastic crinkled under his fingers. His breathing grew increasingly heavy as he sifted through each item of clothing before tossing it to the floor, searching for the little clear bag with the white powder. Soon enough, his drawer lay empty.

The drugs weren't there.

Joshua said, "Mrs. Channer probably took the coke. I bet she's a junkie. It would explain a lot of her behaviors." A rumpled packet of cigarettes crackled as he dug it out of his black leather jacket.

Much as he wanted to believe Joshua, he couldn't ignore the facts. He collapsed onto his bed and rubbed his eyes. "Mrs. Channer didn't do anything. I hallucinated the drugs."

"That's what she wants you to believe. It's all part of the conspiracy. I have to hand it to her, this latest maneuver is pretty effective. Look at you, simpering about your mental health. Why don't you bend over and let her finish the job while you're at it?" Joshua kicked the wall with his steel-toed boots in disgust.

"What am I supposed to tell Mai?" He cradled his head in his hands.

Joshua swatted away his fingers. "You don't owe her an explanation. If she doesn't believe you, who cares?"

"I do."

Joshua spit in his face. Saliva dripped down his cheek and settled on his chin.

"Why do you need her to like you? Aren't I good enough? I'm always on your side. Stop pushing me away. I'm all you need." Joshua pitched his muscled body onto the papasan and pointed at Liam's chin. "Wipe that shit off your face. It disgusts me."

Liam used his sleeve to clean his chin and contemplated his options. He could fess up to hallucinating the drugs, and in all likelihood, the murder too. Mai'd abandon him, then, after she learned the truth. Happened in all of his relationships. Sooner or later, people realized the difficulties of being friends with him outweighed the benefits.

The idea of losing her turned his stomach. Not many people accepted him. Who knew when he'd find another friend, much less one as devastatingly gorgeous as Mai? He'd spent the past few years companionless. The loneliness ached.

He did have one other option. He could play along with his own delusion and see how far Mai followed. At some point, she'd discover her folly, but until then, he'd have more time with her.

"You're some sort of screwed up." Joshua poked a finger in the air. "Can't even tell up from down, can you?"

He avoided Joshua's stare as he put on his socks.

"This Mai woman is going to see right through you. She'll know by the end of today what a fraud you are."

"Maybe. Maybe not." Liam snapped the tight cotton material against his calves.

"There's no maybe about it. She'll know you're lying."

Liam threw on his shoes and tiptoed down the hall into his mother's room. The top dresser drawer, the one where she stashed a small pile of cash, stuck as he tugged on it. He planted his feet wide and pulled harder. With a groaning creak, the drawer gave up its fight and slid open. He plucked out the money, stuffed it in his wallet, and shoved the drawer back in place.

"Stealing from your mom? Bad idea, jackass. Don't give her any more reasons than she already has to institutionalize you," said Joshua.

A bottle of Isaac's cologne sat on the dresser. On impulse, Liam lifted it and squirted it directly in Joshua's eyes. He screamed shrilly and clawed at his face before blinking out of sight.

"I didn't ask for your opinion, *jackass*. Work on your manners." Liam walked through the sinking scented cloud and made his way to the dining room, where Isaac read The Economist.

"May I borrow the car?" he asked.

"I'm taking Tasha to the beach. Remember?" Isaac said.

"Can't you walk there?" He waved at the blue waves visible from the dining room windows.

Isaac's fingers twitched. "It's not as nice as Mexico Beach."

Distracted from her show, Tasha popped up and leaned over the back of the couch. "Daddy, let's invite Ashlyn and her parents! They can drive us."

God bless that girl. She always had his back.

Isaac hedged. After the morning's scare with his daughter's imaginary friend, he probably wanted to take advantage of any opportunities with real friends she could get.

"All right." His cheeks tightened. "Be back by evening."

"Of course." Liam saluted his little sister, who sat in a pile of costume jewelry. Fake emeralds and rubies flashed against her throat. She smiled and waved a bejeweled hand as he walked out the door.

26

Liam arrived at the Hog & Claw ten minutes to twelve. Though a ramshackle and weatherworn building, the turquoise water of St. Andrew Bay glistened behind it. Not a bad setting, so long as you could ignore the large factory on the opposite side of the bay belching dark clouds of stinking pollution into the air.

Mai leaned against a rusted metal door and checked her phone. She wore a black miniskirt with a white tank. Two-inch, strappy heels boosted her height. The humid breeze blew her short hair, and a few strands landed on the high cheekbones of her lightly freckled face. Her warm, brown eyes looked up from her phone and met Liam's through his windshield. Heat washed over his body.

"Are you coming?" she mouthed. She turned her hands over so her palms faced heavenward.

Liam cracked his neck, then stepped out of the car and tried not to look nervous as he walked toward her.

"You look beautiful," he said.

She curtsied. "Why, thank you. You don't look too shabby yourself."

When had somebody last complimented his looks? He honestly couldn't recall. Though he wanted to say more, the words shriveled in his mouth. He mumbled, "Ready?"

She shoved her phone in her purse and ignored his awkwardness.

"This place doesn't look like much, but trust me, it's incredible."

"Incredible like the buffet we ate at the other day?"

She shot him a warning look. "It might look seedy, but the food is all business and perfection."

He'd have to take Mai's word for it because the inside of the restaurant matched the outside. Dim overhead lights flickered above rows of picnic tables lined up closely to one another, each topped with a white paper tablecloth and battered metal napkin dispenser. Classic blues music drifted from speakers hidden in the kitchen. Patrons packed most of the tables, though one had two side-by-side seats open.

"After you." Liam held out one hand.

The bench creaked as Mai and he slid onto it. While careful to leave as much space as possible between their bodies, he still felt the warmth of her skin next to his. He reached for the menu, but she shot out an arm and grabbed hold of his hand, immobilizing him with the electric current she shot through his body.

"No menus. I've got a reputation to uphold here," she said.

A full-figured woman in a white apron approached their table holding an order form. She flipped a page over and, ignoring Liam, set her gaze on Mai.

"The regular?" She jotted down an order before Mai could answer.

"Two of them today, thanks."

The waitress grunted her understanding and bustled away to pick up empty glasses from a vacated table. New diners filled the seats as soon as she cleared it.

"Busy place," said Liam.

"Too busy to talk, I know, but I thought it best to fill our bellies before having serious conversation. Life is always better on a happy stomach."

"It's a solid plan. You don't want to see me hangry," he said.

"Hangry?"

"Yeah, hungry and angry." The corners of his lips turned up in an impish smile. "It gets ugly."

She laughed. He started to join her when the stench of fresh-baked cookies filtered up his nostrils. His hands clenched the edge of the picnic table as he scanned the restaurant and fought to keep from retching.

"They serve dessert here?" he asked.

"Hey, I'm starving, too, but don't rush the good stuff," she joked.

The smell intensified.

Sweat prickled the space between his shoulder blades. "Cookies. Do they serve chocolate chip cookies here?"

"No. They've got banana pudding and pies, but that's about it. Do we need to go back to that buffet and find you a cookie?" She flicked her nails in vexation.

"I'll be right back." Without further explanation, he vaulted out of his seat, pushed open the restaurant's door, and sprinted to the patchy grass next to the parking lot before doubling over. He emptied his stomach of the morning's oatmeal and waited for the malodorous winds of the pulp mill to overwhelm the cookie scent. Hands placed on his knocking knees, he inhaled the mill's sulfuric stench, cleansing his memory's palate of the chocolate chip cookies.

He could keep it together. He had to. He could get by without his medication.

Keenly aware of precious minutes lost with Mai, he nevertheless stayed outside until the faintest whiff of baked goods disappeared. When he returned to his seat, the restaurant smelled like it should, of barbecue and smoke.

Mai patted his back. "You okay?" Concern had replaced the frustration in her eyes.

"Sorry. Had a vision," he lied.

"Here?" she whispered. Her eyes hopped from table to table.

"I'll tell you about it later."

The efficient waitress whisked over with full hands. "Two pulled pork specials." She plunked down Styrofoam plates overflowing with food. A white hamburger bun, loaded with pulled pork and drenched with a vinegar-based sauce, sat nestled next to a lump of coleslaw shaped like an ice-cream scoop. Baked beans oozed a dark molasses sauce next to the sandwich.

A large, iced soda appeared in front of Liam, cementing the perfection of the meal. His stomach rumbled.

"Enjoy," the waitress said.

Mai beamed. "Is this the best plate of food you've ever seen or what?"

"The best." His mouth hadn't watered this much in years.

Lost in the euphoria of a satisfying meal, the two temporarily suspended conversation. Mai finished her sandwich before he was halfway through his and began to work her way through the coleslaw. She pointed to his full plate. "Sign of a noob. There's a science to packing all this scrumptiousness into your belly. Time is of the essence. You can't stall while you're eating, or you'll never make it to the finish line."

"I obviously require more lessons. Have I told you I'm a slow learner? It's gonna take a lot of outings for me to figure this out," he said.

A smile spread across her face. "I like teaching."

"I'm counting on it."

Ten minutes later, Mai's prediction proved accurate. A quarter of his sandwich sat untouched on his plate, taunting him with its tasty perfection.

"Told you." She leaned back in her chair and patted her full stomach.

The waitress slapped down their bill and eyed the growing line by the front door.

"Guess that's our cue to go," Liam said. He picked up the tab and paid with his mother's stolen cash.

"Thanks for a tasty lunch." Mai patted his back and brushed his shoulders with hers.

He inhaled sharply. "Anytime."

Glowing with the satisfaction of a good meal and an even better date, he followed Mai out to the parking lot. He spotted all manner of trucks and small SUVs, but not a single Civic.

"Where's your car?" he asked.

"Thanh dropped me off on her way to work."

"Thanh? I didn't get the impression she liked me much."

Coins clinked in her red purse as she rummaged through it. She dug out a pair of sunglasses and shot him a knowing look before putting them on. "She doesn't. But she also knows you make me smile, so she kept her thoughts to herself. Or at least most of them."

A warm flush crept up his pale neck. "I make you smile?"

"Don't let the compliment make you arrogant. Pancakes and coffee make me smile, too."

"Too late." He lowered his head so Mai couldn't see his goofy grin.

"Let's get out of here." Mai grabbed his hand. "I've got the perfect place for us to discuss your problem."

Her hand fit perfectly in his. Once they neared the Hyundai, she squeezed his palm once and released it before hopping into the car. Instantly he missed the feel of her skin on his, and he wished he owned a self-driving car so he could continue touching her. She rolled down the window as Liam slunk behind the wheel.

"Where to?" he said.

"Hop back onto Business 98 until you hit Cherry Street. Take a right then, and I'll guide you from there."

Mai sank into her seat, kicked off her heals, and placed her petite feet on the dashboard. Her toenails glistened a plum purple. She clicked on the radio and searched for an acceptable song. Eventually she settled on a country station.

Liam sent her a sidelong glance. "This is the music you like?"

"What? An Asian chick can't like country?"

"It's not that... I figured you for more of an alt rock kind of girl."

She twisted her lips to the side. "Some of that's all right, but most of it depresses me."

"Oh, and country is so upbeat? With the cheating, leaving, and crying?"

"Not all of it's sad. A lot of country music is about being happy with what you've got. I know you want to recruit me to the dark side of your angsty music taste, but I like happy songs. Life's wonderful, so why not appreciate it? I try to live in happy Mai land most days, and positive lyrics help me do it."

Liam kept silent, wondering what it felt like to be happy most days. It was hard to imagine.

"So tell me about this imprint you had at Hog & Claw. I'm guessing it trended dark?" She tapped her fingers on her knees.

His mind raced. He'd forgotten all about conjuring up some story she might believe. "Unfortunately so." He worked up what he hoped resembled a regretful expression. "An older man choked to death at the table next to ours."

Not his most inventive tale ever, but hopefully, she'd buy it.

She clucked sympathetically. "Guess he inhaled his food faster than I did."

Shocked she'd make such an insensitive comment, he whipped his head toward her. "Damn, Mai. That's cold!"

She shrugged. "Then why are you laughing?"

Until she'd pointed it out, he hadn't realized that he was.

"In all seriousness, though, I figure these visions must be hard to take. I don't think I could handle seeing all those deaths." She ran her hand through her hair. "Maybe a little dark humor isn't the worst thing in the world. Not to be disrespectful or anything. It's just I don't want you to get overwhelmed."

Her words covered his raw spirit like a carefully wrapped bandage.

"You have no idea how much I appreciate a little bit of levity. Thank you." He dared a quick tap on her knee. She didn't smack away his hand.

"It's this next intersection, don't miss your turn," she said.

The blinking of his turn signal declared his understanding.

She leaned forward in her seat. "Okay, left up there."

The road led to a quaint neighborhood filled with ramblers and one or two split-levels from the early eighties. Carefully manicured yards boasted large magnolia trees shading the street.

"This driveway here." She pointed to a charming brick bi-level. Sunny yellow shutters lined its windows, and a red door proclaimed visitors welcomed.

"Is this your house?"

"Nah. My *bà nội* lives here. Pretty place, isn't it?"

"Beautiful." He held Mai's gaze.

Though she shook her head, she still smiled. "Come on, Mr.

Roundabout Complimenter, let me show you around."

He reached for her arm and dusted it with his fingertips. "Wait. I'm not exactly 'meeting grandma' material. Are you sure you want to do this?"

"First of all, stop talking nonsense. I'd be proud to introduce you to my grandmother. Second, she's not here right now. You can stop having your panic attack."

"I'm not great with parents is all." He lifted his shirt to his mouth and chewed on it.

Hand on the door handle, she looked him up and down. "No, I don't suppose you would be. But I don't mind. I'm sure you've got other skills." She opened the door and stretched out into the muggy afternoon air.

The nape of his neck prickled as he stepped out of the car. Somebody watched them. Who knew what kinds of surveillance devices Mai's grandmother's neighbors employed? There could be a whole pack of Mrs. Channers watching them now, peeping through drawn blinds or hiding behind cars. He made a cursory survey of the street. No nosy neighbors revealed themselves, but that didn't mean they weren't there. It meant they were wily.

"Follow me." Mai laced her fingers through his and led him around the side of the house.

Perfect in a suburban type of way, the backyard reminded him of a mollifying painting well suited for Dr. Jen's office. A long, rectangular pool sparkled under the blazing sun, its brilliant, blue water pristinely clean. A concrete patio spotted with lounge chairs and drink tables enclosed it. Lush grass led from the patio to a dock where a speedboat and jet ski swayed on the small cove's gentle waves. Water darkened from tree shade lapped at the dock.

"What do you think? Nice, right?" she asked.

"Very." Though too tidy for his taste, you couldn't beat the private cove access.

Hands still intertwined, she led him to the dock. He hoped she couldn't feel the slight tremble her ongoing touch sent through his body. The temperature lowered ten degrees as they stepped under the shade. A soft breeze blew across the water and ruffled his shirt as he closed his eyes and concentrated on the warmth from her hand.

"This is perfect," he said.

She said, "It's my favorite spot in the world." She sat down on the dock and tugged on his hand to join her. He did. The low hum of summer insects floated across the cove.

She kicked off her heels and dipped her toes into the bay. Ripples of water danced across the surface as she flicked her feet. "What are we going to do about your situation, Liam? Are you still in danger?"

He copied Mai by taking off his shoes and letting his feet slip into the warm inlet. "I don't think there's much more we can do. I don't have any proof of what I saw."

"But the killer has to know you're the one who called in the tip about the drugs."

"Drugs Security Forces didn't find. Who knows? Maybe I imagined the whole thing?" His face reddened with the half-truth.

She shook her pointer finger. "Don't doubt yourself. He must've moved the cocaine before the police came. Liam, I'm scared for you. What if this guy comes looking for you?"

"I'll be fine. Really. I can take care of myself."

Under the gentle waves, she wrapped her leg around his and used his weight as an anchor to pull herself closer. Bodies linked together, she took off her sunglasses and tossed them to the side. She turned her face toward his and leaned over so her lips skimmed against his.

"You better. I'm getting rather attached to you."

She hung there, waiting for Liam to move a centimeter closer. Unused to close physical contact and terrified of touching her, he stiffened.

Mai waited. She didn't back away; she didn't move forward. She met his eyes and waited.

His heart thumped, his palms sweated, and his body shook, but Liam leaned forward.

Their lips whispered together, the kiss as soft as the flutter of butterfly wings. He trembled as the pressure from Mai's smooth lips intensified against his. She parted her mouth and drew him in closer. Every nerve ending in his body concentrated on her mouth and how she moved it against his. In his stupor, he sat rigid as a boulder, forgetting he could move his hands or arms. Mai pulled back and ran a fingertip up his neck.

"I've fantasized about this for a while," she said.

Unable to formulate a sentence, he nodded. He wanted more. He worked up the courage to raise a shaking hand to her chin and guide it toward his face. Eyes closed in pleasure, her lips met his again.

She tasted like perfection. He ran his hand through her short hair and pulled her closer until the heat from their bodies eclipsed that of the afternoon. Goose bumps rose on her delicate skin as he caressed her back, and a shudder of pleasure rocked through his body. With a ragged breath, he broke away. He placed his hands on Mai's waist and drowned in her brown eyes.

"If this is happy Mai land, I can see why you like to live here. No place can be better."

She giggled. "Maybe troubled, white-boy land ain't all it's cracked up to be. Who's recruiting who?"

"You're cheating with your recruitment methods. Are these kisses approved by the SEC?"

"You're special, Liam Murphy. I'll bend the rules and make an exception for you."

She had no idea how many special exceptions he required.

Tempted to feel the contours of her lips again, especially with her mouth parted in a smile, he bent forward. A female voice put a sudden stop to his progress.

"You're going to ruin her."

The midday heat intensified like an invisible hand had placed a lamp directly above their heads. Liam flinched. Although months had passed since he'd heard from her, he'd never forget that voice. Alexandra.

"What's wrong?" Mai asked. She reached out to touch his face.

"She has no idea, does she?" Alexandra said.

Liam rubbed his temples and backed away. "Uhh, I remembered I have to get back home now. I'm babysitting my sister tonight."

"Oh." Mai pulled away. "Are you sure that's all?"

His stomach plummeted at the absence of her touch. "Yeah. Sorry to be so abrupt. I forgot with all of your lovely distractions."

One corner of her beautiful mouth pulled down. She didn't believe him.

"It'd be best to tell her now who you are. Makes it easier for all involved in the long run," Alexandra said.

He did his best to ignore her. "Where may I drop you off?" he asked Mai.

"I'm staying here for the afternoon and eating dinner with my *bà nội* later."

"Better be careful with your wild living, Mai." He leaned against her. "It'll catch up to you someday."

She pushed back playfully and rubbed her foot against his. "Right. Before you know it, I'll be all wrinkled and toothless from my hardcore partying. Better see me while the getting's good."

"You'd be gorgeous with no teeth at all. Party away with your grandma."

Alexandra gagged. "Are you flirting by talking about her grandma and dentures? No wonder you haven't had a girlfriend since tenth grade. You're horrible at this."

"I mean, I know you don't party with your grandma." He covered his face in embarrassment. "And I don't find grandmas sexy or anything. I mean, umm..."

Mai laughed and cut off his sputtering. "I know what you mean, Mr. Smooth. I'm also beginning to understand why most of your compliments are veiled. Now shut up and kiss me goodbye."

More than happy to submit to her demands, he parted his hands and kissed her.

Though her lips still intoxicated him, his confidence that he knew what to do with them evaporated as Alexandra smacked obscenely in the background, mocking his fumbling attempts at seduction.

27

The rest of the day bled by, time alternately seeming to linger and then sprint forward. Liam knocked around his room, reliving his kisses with Mai on the dock. Even the reappearance of Alexandra, exiled from his mind since Ohio and his last hospital stay, couldn't temper his enthusiasm. Mai liked him. Somebody not legally related to him wanted to be with him. Even better, she'd kissed him.

He peeked between the tightly drawn blinds in his room. The summer sunset painted the sky a deep red. Although Mrs. Channer often walked in the evening, tonight she stayed out of sight. Her counter surveillance methods improved by the day. He resituated the blinds to prevent the replica from spying on him and thumbed through the albums on his audio player. While he toyed with the idea of playing a country album to celebrate his afternoon with Mai, in the end he selected "Surfer Rosa." It'd been his father's favorite Pixies album. Since Tasha wasn't asleep yet, and his mother objected to the language in some of the songs, he plugged in his earphones.

After he'd returned from his date with Mai, the cat had spent the entire afternoon with him. As a result, Joshua and Alexandra had left him alone. Once bedtime hit, though, RP abandoned him to his own devices. The cat always slept in Tasha's room. Liam leaned back in his bed and rubbed his foot over the slight imprint RP had left.

No medicine for more than twenty-four hours, and he'd survived just fine. Liam closed his eyes.

Then the smell hit him.

Freshly baked cookies.

His eyes flashed open, and his breath caught in his throat.

The twins stood next to him.

Fraternal, they still bore a striking resemblance to one another; squinty, solid black eyes, sunken-in cheeks, and thin lips fringed with yellow fangs. The girl, Bridget, wore a white dress with a ragged and mud-stained trim that dwarfed her fragile frame. The boy, Ethan, wore a black suit two sizes too small for him, with sleeves pulling up to his scrawny forearms and pants revealing holey socks. Redheads both, the boy kept his hair chopped in a bowl cut, and the girl twisted hers in a long, ratty braid.

The music from Liam's headphones stopped. He dug his fingernails into his shorts, dreading what he knew came next.

Bridget held out a plate of blackened cookies. Chunks of scorched chocolate poked through the crust of each homemade confection. "Eat one," she demanded. Her high-pitched voice sounded like the unholy offspring of a squealing pig and dying baby bird.

Liam shook his head and tried his best to remember the twins weren't real. "I don't want any." He pushed back until his torso jammed against the wall.

"Eat one," said Ethan. His colorless eyes narrowed into tiny slits of nothingness.

The twins had always been demanding. But they hadn't seen him in months. He'd show them who was in charge.

"No."

Their lips spread into matching pencil-thin smiles. Bridget's fangs grew until they descended well past her jawbone.

"Mother baked these cookies for you. Don't be rude. Take a bite," Ethan said. He picked up a cookie and dropped burnt crumbs onto Liam's bedspread.

"I told you no." Liam blinked ten times.

Go away, go away, go away.

The twins remained.

Ethan brought up his right fist and pounded it into his left hand. "Nobody disrespects Mother."

Bridget shrieked, a shrill, penetrating sound that pierced his eardrums, and she leapt onto his bed. Her filthy braid swatted his face as she pinned down his arms and jammed her knee under his neck.

"You'll do as we say." She lunged at his chin with her fangs, sunk them in, and tore down.

Pain rocketed through his body, and he moaned in agony. "Stop. Please, stop."

Whether or not the twins existed became immaterial. They existed in his reality, and his reality hurt like a son of a bitch.

Ethan leaned over him and tapped him on the nose. "Take your medicine like a good boy."

His willpower was no match for Bridget's. Fangs still embedded in his chin, she yanked backward to open his jaw. Ethan jammed a cookie in his gaping mouth before she jerked it closed again.

"Chew," Ethan said.

As unrelenting as a pit bull, Bridget continued to bite his chin. She tore at his skin until shreds of it dangled from his bone. Tears rolled down his face, and he complied.

The cookie tasted brittle and the chocolate stale. Any bursts of moisture came from wriggling maggots, squirming throughout his mouth.

Bridget finally lessened her death grip on his chin. "Swallow," she said. Her knee lifted enough so Liam could work his gullet.

Though his mouth was dry and his throat burned, he gulped down as much as he could.

The twins backed off and stood in the corner, supervising him.

Bridget stretched her hand toward the plate. "Finish them." Maggots clung to her fingernails and slid off to the floor.

Left with no choice but to comply, he pulled the plate closer. They'd torture him worse if he didn't. The twins stood guard and inspected his every move until he cleaned the plate.

"There now, the cookies didn't taste so bad, did they?" said

Bridget. She patted his cheeks and kissed his forehead. Her lips moved to his earphone, and she pried it loose with her serpentine tongue. She whispered, "We'll be back. Do yourself a favor and cooperate next time."

Liam pulled the cover over his head and counted to ten. When he inched down the blanket, he exhaled in relief. The twins had left.

For the time being, at least.

He tore off his headphones and ran to the bathroom. He vomited until he dry heaved, emptying his stomach of all contents, real and otherwise.

Allison knocked on the bathroom door. "Liam, are you all right? May I help you?"

Exhausted by the attack, he clung to the toilet.

"I've got a stomach bug. I'll be okay." He didn't want his mother to see him like this.

For several minutes, Allison's shadow under the door didn't move. Eventually, though, she left him in peace.

He stood, washed his face, and examined his reflection in the mirror. His chin, and the skin attached to it, looked intact. But looks deceived. The constant ache pulsing from his chin proved Bridget had ravaged it. She must've covered his bone with a false flesh veneer.

Chin nestled into the small of his neck, Liam shuffled back to his room. With an outstretched pointer finger, he poked open his door and prayed he didn't find the twins there with another plate.

Empty darkness greeted him.

He padded in, collapsed onto his bed, and shoved aside his audio player. The twins were an isolated incident. With them gone, he was safe. Sleep overtook him.

28

Liam awoke to the scent of burning flesh. Wisps of steam rose from his chest, and he realized that flesh was his own. He kicked away his navy blanket and gingerly peeled off his shirt. Blisters covered his body. He rubbed one of the boils and groaned.

His room had become an oven. A sooty darkness, thick and pervasive, encased him as he baked like a roast chicken. He rolled to the side in an attempt to ease the agony of his burns. It didn't help. It also exposed his bare skin to the space beside his bed.

Three icy fingertips stroked the small of his back. Liam stiffened. Ragged fingernails sliced through bubbling blisters as they trailed toward his skull. Dread prickled up his spine along with the fingertips, his already frayed nerves set further aflame by their touch.

"I've missed you," Three Fingers said, his voice raspy and deep.

Liam bunched his twisted sheets between his fingers and, with a mighty effort to avoid hyperventilating, forced his lungs to slowly contract and expand. He mentally counted to ten and rolled over.

Three Fingers hadn't changed. He wore a devil mask the color of faded brick. Small horns lined the center of the skull and a grouping of larger horns fringed his ears. Hideous as it was, Liam suspected the mask hid an even more frightening face underneath. A heavy, black cape hung from Three Fingers' shoulders and swept over the linoleum floor, collecting dust at its hems. One of his arms ended in a rusted hook. The other exposed a hand missing two of its fingers and marred by extensive burns. Liam's blood coated its remaining three digits.

"What do you want?"

"I haven't set off a bomb in a while." The mask muffled Three Fingers' voice. "I can't tell you how much I've missed the thrill of an explosion. And this house...well, it's begging to be incinerated."

He pointed to the corner of Liam's room where a menacing contraption rested. It consisted of a complex set of red, green, and black wires encircling a package of C4. Above the crudely made bomb sat a clock with neon green LED letters glowing 1:59. It ticked down to 1:58.

Liam gasped. "You're setting it off in two minutes?"

"Just long enough to clear your house. But you have to act now." Three Fingers' rusty hook traced Liam's eye socket.

Paralyzed with fear, Liam wasted several precious seconds before he swatted away the hook and tumbled off his bed. His boiling skin crackled as he hit the floor.

"Down to a minute and a half. Do you want your family to die?"

He rocked back and forth. "You're not real. You can't blow up my house."

"Is that a risk you're willing to take?" Three Fingers crouched down next to him, and a foul stench of rotten eggs emanated from his cape.

Liam grasped at the smoky tendrils of his sanity dissipating at a rapid rate. "You're nothing but a visualization of my greatest fears. I'm not going to lose my mom and sister like I lost my dad."

"You sound like Dr. Jen's puppet. Think for yourself, man." Three Fingers tapped his mask with his hook.

"I am! You're not here. You. Aren't. Here."

Chased away with rationalization, Three Fingers fluttered in and out of Liam's vision.

"Before I leave, let's talk about this bomb, shall we?" Reasoning be damned, Three Fingers popped back into solid form by the window. "Alas, my days of crafting explosives are long gone. Look at my hands! There's no way they could make such an intricate device. But... there are plenty of folks still capable of creating them."

He pulled up the shades. A bright light from the Channer's porch poured into Liam's room. "Colonel Channer, for instance. He's deployed to Afghanistan and Iraq how many times? He could make an IED in his sleep. Probably taught his wife how to make them also."

Liam flinched as he bit down on his raw lower lip. "They can't get in here. I've built alarms."

"You mean those pathetic alarms I bypassed? They're no match for the Channers. They came and scoffed at your pitiful defenses." Three Fingers scratched his hook down the glass window. "They've planned on killing you since they first saw you. You should have the decency to at least make it a challenge for them."

Sweat poured down Liam's back and stung his pulsating blisters. The timer read thirty-four seconds. His heart raced. He ran to the corner and lifted the bomb, looking for a way to defuse it.

Three Fingers laughed. "Touch one wrong wire and—*BOOM*! Are you ready to die tonight?"

Hundreds of hours of pent-up fear, loathing, and denial bubbled over. Liam screamed.

Footsteps pounded down the hallway, and his door flung open. Isaac stood tall in the doorframe, his eyes darting around the room. They found Liam huddled on the ground, gibbering about a three-fingered man who didn't exist.

Allison raced in behind her husband and pushed by him to reach Liam. She knelt down next to her son and took his hands in hers.

"It's going to blow, Mom! Take cover!" Liam dragged his mother to the ground and threw his body over hers.

Skin slapped against the floor, and she yelled in pain.

"Get off her!" Isaac yelled. He ran toward his stepson and yanked him away from Allison. Blood poured out of her mouth.

Liam pawed at Isaac, frantic to pull his mother to the ground and away from the blast.

Tasha ran into the room, Teddy clutched closely to her side.

3-2-1.

And then the bomb exploded in the form of Isaac's fist ramming into Liam's face, sending him into a carefree slumber.

29

SUNDAY, AUGUST 31st

A **soggy kitchen towel, filled with the remnants of ice** cubes, dampened Liam's pillow. His mother had held it against the angry knot protruding from his temple until he'd asked her to leave. As soon as she'd shut his door, he'd dropped the towel on his bed. A few pieces of ice wouldn't heal what ailed him.

Liam leaned into the sticky, hot breeze blowing through his window screen. Sweat dripped between his shoulder blades and stained his red shirt. The clock hadn't hit 10:00 a.m. yet and already the thermometer threatened to slip above ninety. He'd been right about at least one sensation the night before. The air conditioner was broken. Since maintenance wouldn't fix their unit on a Sunday, the family would have to suffer through at least one full day of humid misery.

Life wasn't completely terrible, though. His blisters had disappeared. So had Three Fingers.

Through his closed door, he heard his mother and stepfather's muffled voices. They fought about him. He hadn't planned on costing his mother two marriages, but then he hadn't planned on much of the past ten years.

"As usual, it's all your fault, dumbass. If you hadn't assaulted me with Isaac's cologne, I would've protected you. Three Fingers is scared of me. He wouldn't have dared to break into the house with me next to you," Joshua said.

Despite the heat, he wore his tattered black leather jacket and jeans. He lay slumped in the papasan and tapped a cigarette against a Marlboro pack, irritation apparent in every move.

A furry paw jutted under the door, followed by a low guttural growl.

"I don't think RP agrees with you," said Liam. If he'd been in a better mood, he'd have a difficult time hiding his smile. But he had nothing to smile about today.

His mother wanted to check him into a psychiatric facility.

"Isaac won't let them take you. He insists you go voluntarily to the hospital, because an involuntary admission will have a 'profound, negative effect' on your probation." Joshua rolled his eyes in mock exaggeration.

A melting ice cube slid out of the towel. Liam grabbed it and chomped down, mulling over the strange turn of recent events. Isaac indeed campaigned to have him stay in the house, albeit strictly supervised, until he decided to admit himself. So far, his stepfather's ideals trumped his mistrust. You had to give the man credit. He stood by his beliefs, convenient or not. Allison, however, no longer concerned herself with concepts as nebulous as ideals. She focused on stark facts and reality.

Even from the back of the house, the reverberations from the front door slamming shut jolted his bed.

His mother rapped on his door.

"May I come in?" she asked.

He picked up the kitchen towel and held it to his head. "It's your home."

Still wrapped in her pink, terrycloth robe, Allison stepped into his room. Her face held the tell-tale signs of ugly crying. Splotchy complexion, blood-shot eyes, and damp cheeks. Her lower lip bore a nasty gash on the right side and swelled to double its normal size.

"I'm sorry about your lip," he said. "I thought I was protecting you. Apparently, I'm a crappy guard."

She waved off his apology and eyed the wet spot on his pillow. "How are you?"

You mean, other than being terrified you're going to institutionalize me?

"I'm fine. The bump on my forehead will go down in a day or two. You're worse off than me."

Allison looked down at her hands and played with her fingertips. "I'm sorry about what Isaac did to you. Scared for my safety, he didn't think before reacting. But I need you to know I'm not okay with him hitting you. Violence in my home is never acceptable."

Jaw taut and eyes slit into small creases, she looked up at him and pointed to her fat lip. "This can't occur again, either. What if it'd been Tasha and not me? You need to check into a hospital."

"I know. It won't happen again. I promise." He brought a hand up to his chin and covered his mouth with his fingers.

"A promise isn't enough." She shook her head. "This is beyond your control. I know you don't want to have these hallucinations. If you could stop them, you would. You need professional help."

"Don't blow a night terror out of proportion. I'm not having any other regression symptoms. Give me another chance, Mom." A swarm of electric eels roiled in his stomach, zapping his intestines with each breath he took. His mother had to believe him.

"So you won't check into the clinic?" She sucked in her upper lip.

"Not today. I don't need to. Trust me, if I suspect I need help, I'll drive myself to the hospital. Last night was an anomaly. I'm fine. Tasha is safe."

"Please?" Allison whispered. She held her hands together, as if in supplication.

Eyes bright with fear and anger, Joshua paced behind her. He jammed a lit cigarette into his cheek and burned a new hole in his pockmarked skin. "You've gotta try harder. She's gonna send you to the nuthouse if you don't convince her otherwise."

Time for the jugular. "Why do you always try to get rid of me? Am I that awful?"

Her shoulders sagged. "You're not awful. But I have a duty as both your mother and Tasha's to help you, even when you don't want me to."

"Can I experience a minor setback without you thinking I've finally lost it? Will my past forever determine my future?" He pulled the towel from his face and dropped it onto the floor. Water droplets flicked across his room.

She stood motionless, her eyes glued to his.

"I know the easiest answer is to send me away. But it's not the right answer. Not now."

Head bowed low, she crossed the room and hugged Liam before sobbing into his shoulder. His desperate maneuver had worked. Though he felt detached, as if watching a scene played out in a movie, he pretended his mother's tears affected him. He raised a halting hand and patted his mother's back.

Eventually, her sobs turned to sniffles. She pulled away from her son and attempted to tidy up her face.

"Will you at least agree to increase your dosage?" she asked.

"Absolutely." The lie came easier the second time around. "I've got an appointment with Dr. Jen tomorrow morning. I'll tell her about the night terrors. We'll get to the bottom of the issue."

Small feet slapped against the linoleum floor and interrupted their conversation. Tasha jumped onto her older brother's bed, expecting him to catch her midair. He did.

"So this is where everybody's hiding." She burrowed her head into Liam's shoulder, damp from Allison's tears and his sweat. "Teddy and I got worried."

Allison ran her fingers over her daughter's ringlets. "Sorry, baby girl. We were having a discussion."

"About last night?" She reached out a small hand to Allison's lip.

The eels in Liam's stomach redoubled their torture efforts. He hated that Tasha had seen him in the throes of a hallucination. And he especially hated she'd seen her father hit him.

Allison choked out an uncomfortable cough. "Yes. We talked about how it's never okay to hurt somebody. Daddy misunderstood Liam last night and tried to protect me. But he shouldn't have hit your brother."

Small lips pursed in consternation, Tasha agreed. “Daddy made a mistake.”

“It’s not going to happen again. We’ve talked it over, and everything’s going to be fine,” Liam said.

Convinced of her brother’s reassurance, Tasha smiled. He grinned back.

Of all the lies he told his family, the ones of hope were the best.

30

Concerned about Liam sweltering in the un-air-conditioned house, Allison had insisted he open his windows for the entire day. Now, anybody who wanted to peek into his room could. One somebody, in particular, took advantage of his weakened defenses.

Joshua peered out the window and pointed across the street to Mrs. Channer. "That bitch has watched you all morning. She's waited months for a chance like this."

Indeed, she had. The replica's back faced Liam's room, and she feigned pulling weeds in her small garden bed. She fancied he didn't know she had invisible eyes on her neck.

Liam licked his lips and paced back and forth. "I'm gonna call Security Forces and get a restraining order on her. Then she'll have to move off base."

"Come on, don't be such a coward. She tried to blow up your family last night! The circumstances call for more aggressive measures." Joshua cocked his hand like a gun.

The bulging contusion on Liam's forehead pulsed in pain. "You're right. But I can't do it now. We have to wait until dark."

"Why? Your family's gone. It's the perfect time." Joshua fetched a baseball bat he hid in the closet. "Teach the replica a lesson she won't forget."

The aluminum bat bore deep scratches from heavy use during Liam's healthy, baseball years. He grabbed it and swung it hard onto his right hand; his fingers stung from the impact.

He marched out of his room and down the hallway, past his family's empty rooms. Though it'd required a monumental amount of makeup, his mother had camouflaged her fat lip and made herself presentable so the family could attend church at the base chapel. No doubt they attempted to gain some peace about the previous night's incident. Liam didn't bother. Peace was only an elusive idea—the grandest delusion of them all.

Bat raised high over his shoulder, he entered the foyer and stared at the front door. A crafty adversary, Mrs. Channer wouldn't go down easy.

"You nervous about doing the deed yourself?" a silky female voice asked.

Alexandra. He'd been waiting for her.

"A little. What if she gets away and then retaliates against Tasha?"

"That's certainly a possibility. You're not as fast as you once were. I, on the other hand, have kept in shape. Mrs. Channer won't get away from me. Nobody does," she said.

"You'll do it?" He attempted not to get his hopes up. Alexandra was temperamental.

"We'll educate her together. You've acquired some new talents. I'm impressed."

He squinted. "You mean seeing the past? How does that help us deal with the replica?"

"Always so clueless, Liam. And desperate to limit your potential. You've had this window open to the past for a while now; it's nothing new. Started back in Ohio."

He frowned and lowered the bat. "What are you talking about?"

"The vision after your father's death."

His heart rate rocketed. "That was a hallucination."

"Was it? Think, Liam. What did you see?"

He didn't have to think hard. The vision haunted his nightmares on a regular basis. He shook his head and tried to fight off the memories threatening to overwhelm him, but they came anyway.

It'd been 9:11 p.m. His father had been late, which never happened. When the doorbell had rung, he'd already known. Nobody came to visit. The uniformed police officer had clinched it. He hadn't even waited for the cop to speak.

"Where'd the accident happen?" he'd asked.

Taken aback, the police officer hadn't spoken for a moment. Fat raindrops had pelted off his peaked cap and spattered on Liam's face. Then, after removing his cap and placing it under his arm, the cop had recovered. He'd said, "On the corner of Lincoln and Maple. It appears your father lost control of his vehicle and slammed into an oncoming sixteen-wheeler. We believe he died instantaneously. My deepest sympathies."

Liam had shut the door in the policeman's face without another word, laced up his shoes, and run out the backdoor. Though the roiling in his gut had told him his father was dead, he'd needed proof. He had wanted to see where it'd happened. The rain had turned hard then, coming down in angry spikes and stinging every inch of his exposed skin. He'd ignored the pain and taken a shortcut through the wooded area that bordered the alleged intersection.

In the darkest part of the woods, his nostrils had flared wide and inhaled air thick with a metallic odor, like raw meat left unrefrigerated. He'd ignored his instincts and continued to run. That'd been his first mistake. He'd then slipped on what he'd initially presumed to be rainwater. But when he'd pushed off the ground to get up, a strobe of lightning had lit up the sky, and he'd seen the liquid wasn't clear at all, but was rather a viscous crimson, smeared all over the grass. His lizard brain had warned him to freeze, and this time, he'd heeded it. Good thing, too. Because next to a large maple tree had stood a man, so pale he'd seemed to glow in the sparse moonlight, spiking a woman's head on a stake. The rest of her appendages hanged from branches, situated so they pointed at their own severed head.

He hadn't dared to breathe. The killer had worked slowly, arranging his victim's long brown hair, stepping back from time to time to appreciate his handiwork. Blood clots had clung to strings of flesh dangling from her neck.

With the skin on the nape of his own neck crawling, Liam had recognized the killer—he worked at the convenience store Dad often stopped at when they wanted a soda.

He'd tiptoed backward and tried his best not to vomit, hoping with all his might the clerk hadn't seen him. Naively, he'd thought luck had favored him. The murderer had been so engrossed with his *mise-en-place* Liam had escaped.

Though he'd managed to avoid being caught by the killer, his second, and biggest, mistake had been believing he could hide from the memory. Even as he'd stumbled home, the murdered woman's hands had clung to him. And, somehow, the appendages had multiplied by the dozens. They'd gripped the back of his shirt, his shoelaces, his hair. He'd batted at the hands but couldn't detach them, and they had cleaved to him well after he'd slammed shut the back door. All thoughts of visiting the place where his father had taken his final breath had vanished. Instead, he'd spent all of his mental energy unsuccessfully fending off bloody limbs and praying the killer didn't find him.

When the sun had risen the next day, he'd made a decision. The appendages attacking him wouldn't stop until he brought the murderer to justice. The task had seemed simple enough. The convenience store wasn't far. He'd tried to ignore the multiple hands squeezed tightly around his neck as he'd walked there, winding his father's hunting knife between his fingers to calm his jittery nerves.

By the time he'd arrived at the store, black, patchy spots darkened his vision, and he'd fought to keep conscious. But the instant his feet had crossed the threshold, the hands had disappeared. He'd needed no other sign to know he did the right thing.

Unfortunately, he hadn't found the killer. Some grandma had worked her shift instead, and his tale had terrified her. She'd pressed the panic button and sounded the silent alarm. The cops had arrived in minutes.

"You know I'm right." Alexandra snapped him back to the present. "What you saw happened."

Isaac's laptop sat atop the living room coffee table. Liam strode over to it and flipped it open, not caring if Isaac checked the search engine's memory. The pursuit of truth overrode his stepfather's delicate sensibilities. He typed in "Cuyahoga County, severed limbs, murder."

A familiar face filled the monitor. Headline after headline reported a string of grisly murders echoing what Liam had seen. The police had caught the killer, one Dale Praden, the previous month. They estimated his killing spree went back five years.

"What'd I tell you? That was no hallucination, Liam. The land doesn't forget. You saw its memory. If the police hadn't stopped you, you could've prevented all these other murders."

Alexandra's words wrapped around his face and caressed him like a lover's touch. He wasn't crazy. He was special.

"How am I able to see these imprints?" he asked.

"You, dear Liam, experienced a potent cocktail of events permanently rewiring your brain. The emotional trauma of your father's sudden death, plus your already unique mental predisposition, plus the chemicals from your meds—well, they all combined at the perfect juncture to alter the synapses and plasticity of your brain. You're now able to reach past the invisible lines that limit everybody else's minds. You've only just begun to see the manifestation of your new skills."

He twirled the bat. "So what else can I do?

"You can move objects with your mind."

The twirling stopped. "What?"

"It's true. Pick an object. Any object. Then move it."

He concentrated on the opaque purple vase on the dining room table. It'd been one of the last gifts his father had given his mother. Now it held a bouquet of yellow tulips Isaac brought home Friday.

"Lift it," commanded Alexandra.

He breathed in and flicked up his pointer finger. The vase convulsed into the air and hovered a few inches above the table.

Alexandra whistled appreciatively. "Not bad. Time for a bigger task. Move the dining room table."

He ground his teeth, channeled his inner poltergeist, and waved his hand. The heavy oak table lurched upward and spun in the air. It collided with the vase with a loud crack. Purple glass shards scattered across the room and water splashed onto the Turkish rug below. The table crashed to the floor, crushing the fallen yellow tulips.

"Let's practice some finesse. Shred the magazine on the coffee table."

Isaac's latest copy of "The Economist" floated in the air. With the powers of his mind, Liam shredded the magazine into hundreds of small pieces until only glossy slivers of paper remained. They fell in a mound on the coffee table.

"So, tell me," Alexandra said, "are you still worried Mrs. Channer will get the better of you?"

The bat clanked to the floor with a metallic thud, and he bared his teeth in a smug smile. "Let's show her what happens when she threatens Tasha."

"There's the Liam I love."

Alexandra opened the front door. He followed. Her footsteps pounded away from him, smacking against the driveway's blacktop.

From the safety of the porch, he peered across the street. In her arrogance, Mrs. Channer remained outside. She stood and placed a gloved hand on the small of her back. With the other hand she wiped her leathery brow and sent a halfhearted wave at Liam.

He didn't wave back.

"Showtime, Liam!" yelled Alexandra.

A pathetic yelp escaped the replica's lips, and she fell to her knees. Like an unseen force strangled her, she pulled at her neck and gasped for breath.

Atta girl, Alexandra.

He concentrated on the orange-handled trowel lying next to Mrs. Channer. It spiraled in the air and darted, pointy end first, into the space between her shoulder blades. Unable to scream with Alexandra's hands crushing her windpipe, Mrs. Channer arched her back and pawed at the tool. He turned the trowel and bumped it upward so its flat edge floated parallel with her head and slammed it against her skull. A sickening crunch floated across the street as her body went rigid, and she fell face first onto her yellowed lawn.

"One last lesson." He aimed the trowel's metal tip at the replica's right elbow and rammed it down, again and again, until her bone had to be pulverized. Blood pooled by her arm and seeped into the dry grass.

He regarded Mrs. Channer's prostrate form and exhaled.

A warm gush of air rushed against his face. "Not too bad for your first telekinetic attack," said Alexandra. Done with her mission, she had returned as silent as a brown recluse awaiting its prey.

"Thanks. How long before she replicates?"

"No telling. She's especially efficient, so a few hours at the most. You'll need to take some extra precautions tonight for Tasha."

Liam scrunched his toes. "What kind of precautions?"

"Get her out of this house. None of the alarms you've set so far have kept the Channers at bay. There is one place, though, where Tasha will be safe."

"Where?"

"The beach. The Channers can't go in the water. It messes up their circuitry. All Tasha and you have to do is spend the night with your feet in the water, and you'll be fine."

Liam rubbed his forehead and winced when he touched the knot on his temple. "What about my mother? And Isaac?"

"For all I care, have them join you as well."

"I won't be able to convince my mother to go to the beach." At least not without her calling the cops to drag him to a psychiatric ward.

"That's a shame, but it doesn't change what you need to do for your sister. Nobody understands the danger facing Tasha better than you. Give her a fighting chance. Bring her to the water. Your mother and Isaac can fend for themselves."

He dug his hands into his pockets and glared at Mrs. Channer. Her foot jerked, and a labored moan escaped her lips.

"Let's go inside. Replication can be ugly," Alexandra said.

With one last malevolent look at Mrs. Channer, he went indoors. The dining room table still lay on its side. He waved his hand at it, and the table jerked upright before settling on four sturdy legs. Next, he concentrated on each tiny purple shard, weaving them back together until the vase looked new. Nobody would ever know it'd been broken. The crushed tulips remained on the wet Turkish rug. Isaac or his mother could clean them.

He plopped down on the couch. "How many times will we have to silence the Channers?"

"As many times as it takes. Eventually, they'll tire of creating new models and leave your family alone. Then, and only then, we can stop this silly charade."

The cellphone in his pocket buzzed. He retrieved it and saw a new text from Mai.

"Thinking about you this morning. Had fun yesterday," it read.

Before he could text back, "Same here," a familiar low rumble radiated from the hallway. A second later, RP jumped onto the coffee table, sending the decimated magazine pages cascading to the floor. The cat sniffed the air, trying to detect where the evasive Alexandra hid.

Forgotten, his cellphone slipped between two couch cushions.

Alexandra grunted as the cat pounced onto Liam's lap and settled there, alert eyes still roaming the living room.

"Since when did that fur ball decide he liked you?" she asked.

He shrugged. "We help each other out."

"Don't forget what I told you. Bring Tasha to the water tonight. Don't let the replica hurt her."

The hot air dissipated, and took with it Alexandra. Task completed, RP wrapped his gray and black tail around his body and purred.

Liam mulled over his options and scratched the cat below his ears. Despicable and slippery as she was, Alexandra was right.

Tasha was in trouble, and only he could rescue her.

31

R**P, dead asleep on Liam's lap, startled when the house** phone rang. Though Liam didn't want to answer the call, he couldn't ignore it. Nobody would call but his mother, and she'd worry if he didn't pick up. He slid the cat off his lap, walked into the kitchen, and pressed the speak button on the cordless.

"Liam?" Allison's voice echoed over the line. Her cell must've been on speakerphone.

"The one and only."

"Tasha wants to eat brunch at the O Club, so we're headed over there. Would you like to join us?" His mother managed to sound sincere even though she couldn't possibly want him to come.

"Nah. I'm not hungry." He didn't mention it somehow felt disloyal to his father's memory to dine at an Officers' Club when so many of his fondest family recollections revolved around brunches at NCO Clubs.

A barely audible sigh of relief whispered through the receiver. "Are you doing okay?"

"Yep. Enjoy your brunch." He clicked off the phone and placed it back in its cradle.

With a mighty yawn, RP sauntered into the kitchen. He threaded between Liam's legs, meowing at the kitchen door.

"Missing your girlfriend?"

RP meowed again.

"I'll take that as a yes. Don't get into too much trouble."

He opened the kitchen door, and RP bolted out, headed for his favorite bush. Green leaves shook as the cat's tail disappeared under the shrub.

As Liam turned to go back inside, the rusted Schwinn caught his eye. The last time he'd ridden it, he'd cowered under Cull's threats. His success putting Mrs. Channer in her place this morning emboldened him to investigate the man now. Nobody threatened him without consequences.

Besides, he had some newfound skills to show off.

Full of good intentions and ingenious solutions, he made a beeline to the family room. Like a favorable omen, Isaac's plastic office access key dangled from the hall tree. Liam clipped it to his shirt and hurried out of the house. He didn't bother to lock the door. The newest Mrs. Channer wasn't a threat yet; the replica wouldn't be fully fabricated until later. He hopped onto his bike and pedaled past her house, disappointed to see the only evidence of their encounter was the bloody path she'd left from her garden to her porch.

He navigated onto the bike path that lined Beacon Beach Road and kept his eyes trained two feet ahead of him. Otherwise, the gray concrete sidewalk resembled more an endless corridor to purgatory than a trail to the base's professional sector.

Ultraviolet rays beat down on his skin, forming new blisters on the back of his hands. The asphalt road beside him morphed into a long snake that undulated under the late summer sun. Screams and shouts echoed through the woods.

The pine trees whispered, "We know who you are, Liam Murphy. You're bad. Bad news, bad man, bad soul."

He snorted. He could handle these voices. What he couldn't handle was witnessing a teenage kid beat his dog to death. Today, he'd already passed the spot where the dreadful incident had occurred with no ill effects other than a bad taste in his mouth.

A sage-green stroller squeaked toward him, powered by a demon disguised as a middle-aged jogger. She deemed her camouflage strong enough to fool him, but he was no noob. A quick glance confirmed his suspicion—not a car dotted the long road before or behind him. The damn demon must've derailed traffic so there'd be no witnesses. He'd succeeded against worse odds, though, so he hunkered down and pedaled harder. His burst of speed caught the fiend by surprise, and a supremely calculated kick to the knees sent her screaming and tumbling to the ground. The stroller careened to the side and teetered on one wheel before toppling on the demon.

Served her right.

The demons, however, decided not to let him off easy. Four more bikes loomed ahead in the distance. He'd be able to handle two of them, but four at once would overwhelm him. He choked back his disgust and veered onto the road, where his bike's tires bumped over the reptilian scales of the monster snake masquerading as a street. Every jolt and swell in the road revealed the multitudes of animals the serpent had devoured.

Vile and horrid as they were, Liam had to credit the demons for their flexibility. Because, shortly after his successful parry and move to the road, they reversed course and decided to use traffic to their advantage. A car zoomed up behind him and blasted its horn. He ignored it. The car honked again. He gasped for breath and flung a weak hand out to wave the vehicle on. His lungs hadn't seen a workout like this since high school. A white sedan pulled beside him, its window rolled down so a squat man could yell, "Get out of the road! You're going to get yourself killed!"

The bikers rode parallel to him now. While playing the innocent altruist, the driver actually conspired with the demons and tried to force him into their midst.

Liam shook his fist and spit at the man. He slowed his pace and dropped behind the sedan. The biker demons, dressed as pre-teens, stared at him open-mouthed.

"Don't get near me!" he screamed.

They shook their heads in unison and rode away in silent terror. Wonderful. They understood he'd grown stronger.

More cars honked as they piled behind him, but he tuned them out.

Nothing mattered but getting to Isaac's office. His calves cramped, but he bit down on his tongue and biked through the pain. His heart fluttered with stress and exertion as he finally neared the Base Support Center. Once he arrived at the building, he threw down his bike and doubled over to catch his breath. The ground stayed still and solid under his feet. He'd escaped the snake.

A hot gust of wind pushed against his back and urged him forward. He climbed up the steps to the entrance and tried the door. It was locked. A small video camera focused on the entrance blinked a red light at him. He bet Mrs. Channer had a live feed of the camera in her house. Too bad the bitch had to replicate. She'd be upset when she discovered she'd missed his investigation.

He waved Isaac's access key in front of a small laser reader. The door clicked open, and the sweet kiss of air-conditioning welcomed him inside. Sweat rolled down his neck as he made a slow circuit around the building. He ducked into cubicles where well-worn cardigans hung over the backs of chairs, stepped into offices showcasing desks lined with neat paper stacks, and investigated the small kitchenette littered with half-finished cans of soda. Though he scrutinized each framed picture or snapshot tacked on the wall, none showed any sign of Cull.

Soon enough, he'd searched everywhere except one last set of cubicles near Isaac's office. He snooped around the stall directly opposite his stepfather's door but found only trite aphorisms printed over pictures of cute kittens. Disappointed he'd struck out yet again, he flung himself onto a black chair positioned in front of the workstation. He stabbed a leg at the ground and pushed off, repeating the process until the chair's squeaky wheels sang a discordant symphony. Then a stench hit his nostrils. He froze. The smell intensified, like potent ammonia with a dash of ground-up worms. He gagged and reached for the wastebasket but snatched his hand away when he saw what lay within it.

A thick coral snake writhed in the trashcan. Its red, yellow, and black scales pulsed against the plastic container. Liam gasped.

Additional movement from above caught his eye. A black mamba wended its way down the fabric cubicle wall, pausing to taste the air with its forked tongue before dropping to the floor. Liam stopped breathing. The mamba had joined a boiling mass of snakes. Boas, rattlers, corn snakes, pythons. They crested each other like hissing, rolling waves, building upon one another until they neared the chair's fake leather cushion.

His fingers tingled with dread as he held out his right hand and closed it into a fist. He commanded the roof to collapse on the snakes and edged backward, preparing to cover his head against the falling debris.

The roof didn't budge.

He relaxed his hand, flicked his pointer finger up to the sky, and ordered his chair to rise. He'd float out of this hellish office.

The only motion from his chair came from the snakes rocking it as they slithered ever closer to him.

Panicked, he stood on the uncooperative chair and stepped onto the desk behind him. He grabbed hold of the cubicle's top cap and jumped, attempting to swing his leg over the partition. The move required more flexibility than he possessed, though, so instead of launching over the panel, his leg hit it with a pathetic thud. The partition careened backward under the burden of his weight and for a heart-pounding moment, came close to toppling. He fought to recover his balance and pushed the panel back upright.

Despite his better judgment, he glanced at the chair on which he'd sat. Snakes engulfed it, their festering movements jerking it back and forth. His knees threatened to give out, but he punched them into a locked position. His hands shook as he gathered all the binders and books he could find on the desk and piled them high. When nothing more remained to make the stack taller, he climbed onto it. The makeshift stepladder teetered and threatened to slide out from under him.

His waist now hit the top of the cubicle. He leaned over, clutching the fabric wall so tightly he cracked a nail, and swung over his right leg. The panel swayed under his weight, and the haphazard stack of books collapsed after he pushed off with his left leg. Once both legs hung from the opposite side of the partition, he dropped onto the desk below.

A quick survey confirmed the snakes hadn't followed him. Yet. He crouched and jumped down but misjudged the distance to the ground and hit it hard. His face banged the corner of a filing cabinet, and a gushing wound opened on his cheek. Heedless of the pain, Liam pulled himself to standing.

Fear so contorted his vision he almost missed it. Then his eyes focused on a photo tacked to the cubicle. Tattered around the edges and full of pin holes, it depicted a smiling man embracing a brunette in front of a sailboat. Pulse already quickened—Liam would recognize the man's face even if it hadn't been turned slightly to the side so that his spider tattoo peeked out—it skyrocketed when he squinted at the picture. Looping cursive letters on the boat's hull declared its name: Freedom.

Finally. The victim really existed, and he'd found him, with physical proof tying him to Cull's boat. A white nameplate adhered to the cubicle named the man "Stuart Laughlin."

A shuffling sound behind him sent chills racing through his body. Liam turned and held his breath. A throng of snakes slithered toward him, their progress slow but relentless. He stifled a cry of terror and took a step toward the front door when it swung open wide.

Stuart Laughlin and Cull stood before him. Deep in conversation, the two men obviously didn't expect to see anybody here on a Sunday morning, and so far remained oblivious to his presence. Liam whipped his head behind the wall and sprinted across the hall to another cubicle. He huddled under its desk, hidden from Stuart and Cull's view.

"Pickup is scheduled for three weeks from today. And take my word for it, Stuart, these guys will count the money. Every single dime needs to be accounted for," Cull said.

"I'm not moving the product as quickly as I'd like. They can't fault me for low demand," Stuart said.

A harsh snicker. "There's always a high demand for our product. Either you're not trying hard enough, or you're skimming off the top."

A cobra slithered across the hallway and peeked its red eyes around the wall at Liam. If a snake ever smiled, this one did. It had found fresh prey. Liam scooted to the other end of the desk. The cobra followed.

"Cull, you know I wouldn't steal from you. I'm not dumb. I'm merely suggesting maybe the guys we went into business with are more trouble than they're worth. They're not the only source for cocaine," Stuart said.

Snakes dropped now from the ceiling and piled up in front of the cubicle where Liam hid, waiting to smother him in their coiling masses. He rocked back and forth.

"Don't strain yourself, Stuart. Leave the supplier to me. I've got it figured out," Cull said.

Keys tinkled against each other, followed by the slight swishing sound of a drawer opening.

"Here's all the cash so far. It's a tidy sum," Stuart said.

Cull chuckled. "I'm impressed. Hiding the cash in the relative open? Ballsy and effective."

The drawer closed, followed by the sound of a key turning a lock.

"You need to be extra careful around Colonel Northman, though. That messed-up stepson of his saw our stash. I bet he's the one who called in the tip to Security Forces," Cull said.

"The kid's not a problem. He's as unreliable a witness as they come. Nobody would believe him," said Stuart.

"True, but I don't want any unnecessary heat. He might have to disappear. Lucky for us, the kid's crazy. Nobody will bother searching for him."

The churning mass of snakes reached Liam's feet. Tens of snakes constricted his legs while others bit his knees and thighs. He struggled to keep from blacking out.

The two men shuffled out to the hallway, taking their leave at a leisurely pace.

The snakes reached Liam's torso now, and his body swayed with the movements of the reptiles. A torturously long boa wrapped around his chest and squeezed his ribs until they cracked.

He strained to hear the door swing shut through the slithering of snakes. Finally, the lock clicked.

Liam cried out and flung his hands into the pool of snakes, trying to part his way through it like Moses did the Red Sea. A massive boa crushed his lungs, and several smaller constrictors pulsed their smooth muscles over his legs and abdomen, impeding his progress. He crawled through the snakes and batted away cobras that sunk venomous fangs into his hands, face, and arms. Black stars danced in his vision. Both his lack of oxygen and searing pain threatened to pull him under the sea of serpents.

A red exit sign loomed impossibly far ahead. A coral snake slithered through his hair and bit his earlobe. Liam vomited from the poison, but he pushed forward, slogging through his own rank bile.

When he reached the exit, he rose to his trembling knees. The door handles hissed at him and wriggled out of his touch when he grasped them.

"No!" He closed his eyes, counted to ten, and reached again with the last of his energy. This time, he grasped solid metal and forced his way out to the open air. The snakes sizzled upon contact with the sun, skin crackling as they burned. Liam flung them off his body and unwound the boa from his chest. With each loop loosened, he found more of his breath. He kicked the serpents off his lower legs until the monsters no longer clung to him.

The gallons of venom injected into his veins stung every inch of his body. He lurched toward his bike. His swollen hands ached when he clenched the handlebars and sat on the Schwinn. Nobody would rescue him. He had to leave before the snakes figured out how to survive in the sun.

With a shaky shove from his left foot, Liam fled from Isaac's office and its nightmares.

32

Liam didn't return home. Instead, he retreated to the live oak grove in the backyard. He climbed up his favorite tree and hovered on the highest knotted branch he could reach. Every balance check he made shot searing pain through his ribs. A thirst like none he'd ever known burned his throat, and the gash in his cheek seeped blood like a bubbling hot spring oozing sulfur.

He'd gone to Isaac's office seeking the truth. The price he'd paid to gain it was immense, and now he didn't even know what he could do with it. Stuart was right; Isaac would never believe him. Nor would any law enforcement officer. Liam questioned the vision himself, especially considering Stuart, the man he saw murdered, was alive and well. That certainly complicated reporting his death.

A wave of intense heat hit Liam. A husky voice spoke from the air. "What are you doing up here?"

Alexandra. Again.

"Recovering."

"You've 'recovered' all day. Your mother's sick with concern. Even Tasha's worried. Not to mention Joshua. He's very upset with you."

Joshua glowered behind the dining room windows, his eyes burrowing into Liam's. Allison stood beside him and gazed out at the beach, unaware her son hid a hundred feet away.

"I had a rough day. You lied to me. I can't move objects with my mind. You're the one with the power. You lifted the table, and you attacked Mrs. Channer. Not me."

"I'm not a liar, Liam. Your powers are connected to me. They don't work unless I'm there."

"Awfully convenient, that." A mosquito buzzed by his ear and landed on his neck. The insect pricked his skin, but he didn't swat it away.

"I don't make the rules," Alexandra said. "Regardless of your petty hurt feelings, you've got to pull your act together for tonight. Do you remember our agreement?"

His grip on the tree branch tightened. "Yes."

"Good. Because Mrs. Channer's replication is one hundred percent complete now, and she's pissed. She's going to attack tonight. Tasha needs to be out of the house when she does."

"I understand," he said. And he did. But he couldn't bring himself to go home quite yet. His mother would suspect he'd lost his fight with schizophrenia once again. If he could wait until dark, he could mask his symptoms better. Plus, Tasha would be asleep and not see him this way.

After hours of insects crawling on his skin and sweat pooling in the small of his back, the grayness of dusk replaced the afternoon light. Time to leave his haven. He skidded down chunks of bark, scraping his hands and knees raw. He walked into the house a matted mess of sweat, dirt, blood, and vomit.

Separated by Tasha's vacant seat, Isaac and Allison sat at the dining room table. They stared at him with wide eyes.

"Honey, what happened to your head? Where've you been?" asked Allison. Her forehead wrinkled as she frowned.

"Here and there. There and here. Like a steer with no fear. I have no peer," said Liam.

Allison cleared her throat. "We're concerned about you. Have you taken your medicine today?"

"Meds, meds, like beds. They're so red."

The table creaked under Allison's weight as she placed her elbows on it and buried her face in her hands. "Liam, you need help. You can decide to check into a hospital tonight, or I'll decide for you."

He thrashed his hands in the air. "No!"

"Take it easy, Liam. It won't be like Ohio," Isaac said. He feigned calmness and rested his hands at his side.

"He's a liar," whispered Alexandra. "It'll be exactly like Ohio. The police will come and beat you, then they'll abandon you in a hospital with insane people for days."

Liam dropped into a tae kwon do defensive stance. "No hospitals."

Allison dropped her hands and looked at Isaac. "We've got to call Security Forces. Liam's a danger to himself and others."

"No cops! They pop and top and don't stop!" He prepared to bolt outside when Isaac, for the first time in their acquaintance, surprised him.

"I won't call Security Forces." Isaac scrubbed his hands over his face before letting out a long sigh. "Liam should make this decision. Not us, and not law enforcement."

"Does he look capable of sound judgment to you? I'm the one who's lived through this before, not you," Allison snapped. She made eye contact with Liam. "We're calling Dr. Jen." She picked up the phone next to her and dialed the psychologist's number.

"Yes, Dr. Jen? This is Allison Northman. Liam is having a breakdown. Will you speak with him?"

"Dr. Jen! Dr. Jen!" Liam pounded at the sky.

Isaac pushed out from the dining room table and moved over to the hallway, where he posed himself between Liam and Tasha's room.

"Yes, he's quite agitated. Thank you." Allison handed the phone to Liam.

Dr. Jen said, "Liam? Are you there?"

"Where? Stare? Hair? Mare?"

"It sounds like you went off your medication. Would you be willing to take two pills right now?"

He stared forward. The new scratches on his hands burned and itched. "Okay."

"I'd also like you to consider checking into a clinic tonight."

"No hospitals!" He stomped his feet in emphasis.

Dead air on the other end of the phone. Then, "Please take your pills. Right now, while we talk."

He left a trail of grime on his way to the kitchen. The smell of tobacco lay heavy in the air, and tendrils of smoke rose from the washing machine. Joshua sat on top of it, nursing a cigarette down to its stub.

"Dr. Jen wants to separate us. She doesn't know I keep you safe. I watch out for you, Liam. I'm your best defender," he said.

Liam lifted his pillbox and rolled it around his fingers. "These make me see things. Bad rings, flings, pings. I don't want to see things."

"Do you remember our conversation about self-sabotage, Liam?" Dr. Jen asked. "You're doing it now. This medicine works for you. Take this step, and regain control over your health. You want control. Remember that."

A dim part of his mind did remember longing for independence. But Joshua made concentrating on this fact exceptionally difficult.

"There's no control apart from me. I help you. Not the medicine," said Joshua. He hopped down from the washing machine and strode over to Liam. He clasped his hand over the prescription bottle. "You don't want to see inside people's heads anymore. How did it feel to see your mother grieving you? While you're still flesh and blood, living under her own roof, she feels as though you're dead. And Isaac? Do you want to see him dreading Tasha's future?"

Liam lowered the pills.

"Liam? Liam!" Dr. Jen said in a stern voice. "Are you listening?"

Of course he listened. There were just so many people speaking. Alexandra, the twins, Joshua, his mother, Isaac, Dr. Jen. They all demanded his attention.

"Take your pills," Dr. Jen said. "You can do it, Liam."

Allison placed a hand on Liam's back. She slipped the bottle out of his hand, unscrewed the top, turned it over, and shook out two pills.

"Please, baby. Come back to me." The little yellow medicine rolled in her palm.

Joshua placed his face directly in front of Liam's so their noses touched, and his foul breath washed over his bloodied cheeks. "Take these pills and I'll hurt you. Tasha, too. You really wanna hear her cry?"

"I can jam those pills somewhere if your mother is so desperate for them to disappear," chimed in Alexandra. "For that matter, so can you, Liam. Stick those pills exactly where you want them. It'd give your mother the surprise of a lifetime."

The twins stood next to Allison, with their heads cocked to opposite sides, inspecting her like a meal.

His chin still ached from their attack the night before. Liam's gut told him the twins wouldn't be as lenient with his mother as they had been with him; he had to knock his pills out of her hands before they attacked. He took a trembling step toward her. A long scratch from the door stopped him midstride.

Allison's eyes followed her son's to the kitchen door. A deep growl sounded from behind it.

"RP," muttered Liam.

"That furry sonuvabitch is staying outdoors where he belongs!" said Joshua. He ran to block the cat.

Allison seized on what she thought was a break in her son's hallucinations and reached through Joshua to open the door.

"Get your filthy hands off me!" Joshua yelled. He hated it when people felt through him.

RP charged into the kitchen. He batted at Joshua, scratching Allison's ankle in the process. The cat disregarded his mother's scream of pain, and he pounced on the twins. For a terrible moment, the three parties bared their fangs at each other before Bridget and Ethan vanished. Not finished with his mission, RP searched for Alexandra and hissed in frustration when he couldn't locate her. His hunt still succeeded in banishing her, though, because the kitchen's temperature cooled a few degrees.

Unable to stay out of the mix any longer, Isaac joined their twisted party in the kitchen. His chest rose and fell in rapid succession.

The phone lay forgotten in Liam's hand until Dr. Jen said, "I'm still here. I'll wait all night if you need. Take your medicine."

He held out his hand toward his mother. Without hesitation, she crossed the room and placed the pills in his palm. Liam tossed them in his mouth. A glass clinked as Isaac took it out of a cabinet. His stepfather filled it with water from the sink, then presented the tumbler to him with extended fingertips. Liam accepted the offering and drank.

Cheeks sucked in and breath held, Allison darted a quick look at her husband, whose dipping Adam's apple exposed his silent swallow.

The countertop hit Liam's lower back as he leaned against it. "I took the pills, what a thrill in the grill."

"Will you think about checking into a hospital tonight?" Dr. Jen asked.

"No."

A slight sigh. "Then come see me at eight tomorrow morning."

Liam grunted in the affirmative and handed the phone back to his mother.

"What options do we have here?" she said into the receiver.

Isaac inched toward his wife until his broad shoulders obstructed her from Liam's view.

"I don't care about HIPAA rules. I care about helping my son!" she sobbed. Tears of frustration rolled down her face, and she flung the phone across the room. RP skittered out of the kitchen.

"Since Liam is an adult, his psychologist can't speak about his condition to us. If we're to learn anything, it's got to come from him. And he's in no shape to tell us." Allison pushed aside her husband. "Liam, I know you don't want to go, but a hospital is the best option for you now."

He shook his head and edged out of the kitchen. He wouldn't go back to an institution. Not no way, not no how. They'd lock him up, and he'd be trapped forever. His tongue itched thinking about all the medication they'd force down his throat.

Isaac and Allison followed him into the living room.

"It's up to you, Liam. You're in charge here, okay?" Isaac held his hands up in a reassuring manner.

"No. Hospitals." Liam made the sign of an X with his arms.

His stepfather nodded. "We'll do it your way. But you have to stay in your room for the rest of the night. I'm going to sit by your door until morning when we leave for Dr. Jen's. Okay?"

"Okay," Liam lied.

Allison paled. "This better be the right call, Isaac. We're not playing a game here. This is Liam's well-being we're discussing, as well as the rest our family's. Are you sure about this?"

Isaac didn't meet his wife's eyes. "Yes."

33

An oscillating fan blew fetid air in Liam's face. Mesmerized by its motion, he didn't dare blink.

Isaac had fallen asleep outside his door half an hour ago. It had to be long enough. Each second Liam delayed put Tasha at greater risk. They needed to leave the house. Now.

The newest Mrs. Channer was coming tonight.

"Cut through the screen and escape through the window," said Alexandra.

Liam rolled out of his bed in slow motion, each movement so precise it pained his muscles, and tiptoed over to the window. A few short hours ago, he'd cursed his mother's insistence that he keep his blinds raised and window open. While it still unnerved him to give Mrs. Channer such a direct view into his room, he now appreciated the broken air conditioner. Without it malfunctioning, he would've had to factor in the metallic blinds clinking together during his breakout.

Maybe life wasn't *always* a bitch. Maybe even she needed to take vacations from time to time. Whatever the case, he appreciated her cooperating with him for once.

He picked up the pair of scissors he'd hidden earlier and sliced through the screen, stopping twice to ascertain if the hushed pinging of the cutting stirred Isaac. It didn't.

The black filth that lined the window ledge smeared on his hands as he gripped it and pushed one leg through the ruined screen. Isaac's snore stopped. So did Liam.

Minutes ticked by with him straddling the window, one leg hanging outside and the other in. When Isaac finally snored again, Liam exhaled and hefted his other leg outside. He crouched down and scuttled around the house, still clutching the scissors. Once outside Tasha's room, he made short work of her window.

"Tasha," he whispered.

His sister lay above her covers, clad in a Princess Tiana nightie. She rubbed her eyes with small fists. Before she could speak, he held his finger to his lips. He whispered, "Shh. We're going to play a game that's the same, a flame, that's my name."

Awakened by the promise of playing with her older brother, Tasha giggled.

He placed his hands below her window and gestured for her to step onto them. She made a show of stretching and then placed her feet in Liam's waiting hands like she descended a royal carriage.

"What now?" she whispered.

"The beach." He squatted down and gestured to his back.

She draped her arms around his neck and jumped onto his back. Though sandburs pierced his bare feet, he jogged through the backyard. He'd deal with the minor inconvenience of pain if it meant getting Tasha to safety. Burdened by his sister's extra weight, his pace slowed as they passed the live oaks, but he didn't stop. They needed to get to the beach.

"You're almost there," said Alexandra. "Tasha is nearly out of Mrs. Channer's reach. Just a bit farther."

"Where are we going?" asked Tasha. She placed her warm cheek next to his.

He patted her foot. "Catching the moon soon."

Exhausted by the day's physical demands, he slowed to a walk and limped forward. He glanced behind, expecting to see Mrs. Channer giving chase. Nothing but darkness followed.

Eventually, the ground transitioned to sugar white sand. The promised moon reflected off the jet-black ocean's waves.

He pointed to the dark water. "For our feet, in the heat, it's so sweet."

"The ocean is our potion for motion!" sang out Tasha, imitating her brother's rhyming. She slid down his back, and Liam reached for her hand. The two waded into the waves, the warm water enveloping their feet and calves.

Alexandra said, "Not far enough."

He waded in until the ocean licked his knees. Tasha followed. The waves lapped at her waist.

"This is fun!" She splashed salt water into the night sky and made a holy racket whooping and hollering. Liam didn't mind. Mrs. Channer couldn't hurt them here.

"Farther," urged Alexandra.

He trudged forward. The water hit Tasha's chest now. A rolling wave bobbed her up and down and forced her away from him. She yelled and held her hands up high like she rode a terrifying roller coaster.

"TASHA!" Isaac's voice rang out from the shore.

Liam turned and saw his stepfather sprint toward him. The moonlight hit the whites of his eyes, enlarged in terror.

"She's safe," said Liam. He turned around to point to his sister, but only the placid waves of the Gulf remained.

Tasha was gone.

34

Isaac raced across the shallow waves, kicking up water that shot into the sky like silvery fireworks.

"Tasha!" He scoured the ocean for his daughter. Her head popped above the surface a disturbing distance from shore. She sputtered for air and raised a hand before disappearing from view again.

The water's increasing depth slowed Isaac's charge to deep lunges, and he dove into the current. Angry bubbles frothed in his wake as he motored out to where he'd last seen his daughter. There, a wave swallowed him whole, like a dark blue monster consuming his victim. A short while later, Isaac fought back to the surface. His hands didn't hold Tasha.

Isaac inhaled a massive gulp of oxygen and dipped under the water again. Seconds trickled by, indifferent to the unfolding drama.

Forty-four, forty-five, forty-six.

The cool evening air caressed Liam's face with a puff of wind, and a sense of serenity filled his soul. Everything would be fine. Alexandra had promised him.

Sixty-one, sixty-two, sixty-three.

The deathly silence shattered into thousands of water beads flung into the sky as Isaac rose out of the ocean with a mighty exhale. He supported his daughter's lolling head above the water.

"Breathe, baby, breathe!" he cried.

Tasha's arms hung lifeless from his grasp and dragged in the water. The current pulled them behind Isaac, unwilling to release her from its salty embrace.

Ragged, hollow shrieks from the shore announced Allison's arrival. She screamed incoherent denials and fell to her knees.

Isaac looked to the sky and prayed. "Please Lord, don't take her. Not yet. Please!" A mixture of salt water and tears streamed down his face, and his biceps bulged with the effort of fighting the Gulf's claim on his daughter.

Terrified Mrs. Channer hid in the darkness, Liam held out a halting hand. "It's not safe to bring her to shore!" he yelled.

Isaac ignored him. He stumbled up the shore and laid his daughter on the slim beach. Allison started CPR while he held Tasha's hand.

A sharp object, perhaps a spiky shell or a shard of plastic trash, grazed Liam's thigh. The minor brush with reality nudged his brain toward admitting the truth.

His sister had drowned because Alexandra had lied. Tasha wasn't safe in the water. She wasn't safe at all. But Mrs. Channer didn't pose the danger. He did.

Liam wailed then, grief and fear and regret rolled up into a ball of despair. He tripped through the water and fell onto the shore next to Tasha's body. "No! Baby girl, no!" He grasped her tiny, motionless foot.

Tasha's chest heaved. Allison turned her daughter's face to the side as Tasha vomited salt water. She coughed and vomited again before jaggedly inhaling.

A tremor of relief rocked Liam's body. He leaned his head into the wet sand next to his sister.

Nobody spoke. All three adults lay a light hand on Tasha's abdomen and anxiously monitored each rise and fall of her chest.

Once Tasha had taken ten breaths, Isaac sobbed and lifted his hands to the heavens. "Thank you, Lord, thank you, thank you."

Tasha coughed again and reached out for her mother's embrace. Tears rolled down Allison's cheeks as she caressed her daughter's face and kissed her forehead. Isaac wrapped his wife and daughter in a protective bear hug.

A swarm of sandflies hovered over Liam's body and feasted on his neck. He stared at his mother and stepfather crying tears of relief. He knew he should feel something, but exactly what, he couldn't comprehend.

Allison sniffed and wiped a still shaking hand on her nose. "We need to get her to the ER, but I don't want to wait for an ambulance. I'll drive, you hold Tasha," she said.

Water dripped from Isaac's drenched clothes as he took Tasha from his wife's arms. He sprinted toward home, and despite his breakneck pace, whispered words of comfort in his daughter's ear. Allison followed close behind.

Never a strong runner and already fatigued, Liam failed to keep up. His family's figures quickly pulled away from him and became ghostly gray shadows in the distance. Even so, he chased after them.

His feet hit the backyard just in time to hear the SUV's engine roar to life in the carport. He dug deep and willed himself forward. The headlights flashed on and caught him stumbling toward the vehicle. Allison opened her door and stuck out her head.

"I hope skipping your medication was worth it, Liam," she called. "You very nearly killed your sister. You're going to the hospital when we get back. Don't even try arguing with me. You're dangerous."

She slammed her door shut and backed down the driveway. The SUV screeched away in the beginnings of dawn, and the mist of the oncoming day hovered over the vehicle like a shroud.

He limped into the carport and crumpled onto the concrete. His lungs burned, but not as brightly as his self-hatred.

What had he done?

His mother's words rolled over and over in his mind.

Killed your sister.

Dangerous.

Hospital.

Dangerous.

He clawed up to his feet and staggered toward the house. He jerked open the kitchen door, left unlocked in the panic to find Tasha, and walked to the craft cupboard his mother kept. Containers of pink glitter and googly eyes wobbled as he opened the cabinet and searched through countless piles of construction paper and foam cut-outs. Squished in between an ancient bottle of glue and a spool of blue ribbon hung a bag of plastic zip ties. Liam fished out a handful before he dropped to the floor and leaned back against the washing machine.

The cool metal on his neck soothed him. Ready for his task, he started at his ankles, wrapping a zip tie around them and tightening it as much as he could. He nodded his head in satisfaction and worked his way up his legs until the zip ties no longer fit. Though his fingers cramped with the effort, he held his hands together and wound a zip tie around his wrists. Then he brought his wrists to his mouth, bit down on the zip tie, and yanked at it until it pulled taut.

Now, his family was safe.

He, on the other hand, became sitting bait for the demons that lived in his mind.

"You're one pathetic bastard. One little mishap and you go and tie yourself up?" Joshua hunched over him and kicked at his ankles with steel-toed boots. "Really, Liam, don't be so dramatic."

He concentrated on the linoleum's repeating concentric design, but Joshua remained. The quick strike of a match followed by the scent of cigarettes confirmed his fears. "Please don't," he pleaded.

"Are you going to quit being an idiot and cut yourself out of this self-created prison?" Joshua asked.

"You know I can't." Liam tried to sway away from Joshua but had done too thorough a job with the zip ties.

"Then I'm forced to punish you. You know the consequences for this type of behavior. It's completely unacceptable."

The burning started on the right side of Liam's neck. The cigarette seared into his skin, sizzling as it met flesh. He howled, but Joshua didn't stop. No, Joshua worked a slow line down his neck and arm, not moving from one burn to the next until a circular welt surfaced on his skin. Joshua licked his lips as he ground the burning tobacco into

Liam's thumb and halted his torture only when a growl sounded from the kitchen doorway.

Joshua worked his jaw and strained his arms against his leather jacket. "One of these days that cat won't be here to help you. I can out-wait him. I'm never leaving you." He disappeared as RP dove for him.

The cat skidded across the kitchen and landed with a thump against Liam. He twitched his whiskers and climbed into Liam's lap to sit guard against any further unpleasant interactions. The one thing the furry bastard couldn't do was stop Liam's self-loathing.

Joshua was right.

He wasn't good. He never had been, and he never would be.

35

Isaac had spent the drive home from the hospital mentally preparing for a number of different scenarios with Liam. None of them readied him for what he saw now.

Slumped on the floor, Liam sat in a puddle of urine. Red welts from zip ties striped his legs, and the bright pink of raw skin encircled his wrists like a macabre bracelet. RP sat on his lap, flicking his tail in irritation.

"How's Tasha?" were the first words Liam said. His medicine must've kicked in. Still far from sane, maybe he could see lucidity on the horizon now.

"They're running tests but think she'll make a full recovery. She'll stay in the hospital overnight for observation." Isaac rubbed sweaty palms on his shorts and resisted the urge to cross the room and strangle his stepson.

"I have to be gone when she comes home," Liam said.

What he didn't know was he would never, ever live under the same roof with his sister again. Isaac would make sure of that.

"You're willing to go to the clinic now?"

He nodded.

Anger and relief flooded Isaac in equal measures. If only Liam had agreed to admission earlier, Tasha would be in bed sleeping and not at the hospital being examined for brain damage. Isaac knew he shouldn't hold him responsible for sins committed while in the throes of a psychotic break, but the distance between shouldn't and would had closed considerably in the past few hours.

"We need to clean you up," Isaac said.

Liam smacked his lips. "No, let's go with the flow and row."

The skin on the back of Isaac's neck crawled. So maybe the horizon stayed distant. Liam didn't realize he sat in his own filth. He also still strung together a chain of nonsensical rhyming words—what the doctors referred to as "word salad." The symptom unsettled him, to say the least.

Isaac reached for a pair of scissors.

"No! I have to stay tied!" Liam sat up straight and waved his bound hands in the air. "I'll hurt somebody."

Thick panic choked his stepson's voice. As much as he wanted to hate Liam, and sometimes did, he couldn't help but sympathize with the man. He was Allison's son. Hidden underneath all the psychosis existed a good person. But that good person had retreated far, far below the surface.

"I can't carry you out to the car. We need to untie you."

Saliva dribbled from the corners of Liam's mouth as he babbled unintelligible sounds.

Isaac had preferred word salad. He held up the shears and met his stepson's terrified gaze. The whites of Liam's eyes eclipsed the cornflower blue of his irises.

"I won't hurt you." *No matter how much I want to.* "I'm here to help you," Isaac said.

Liam blinked. He shook his head at some internal debate, then held up his wrists.

Relieved Liam had consented to his help, he side-stepped the fetid pool of urine and cut the zip ties on his stepson's legs and wrist.

Freed from his self-induced prison, Liam stared at Isaac. A beefy type of muscular, he greatly resembled his father. If he set his mind to it, he'd mow down whomever stood in his path. Despite recent events, though, he didn't tend toward violence. He specialized in unpredictability.

At least that's what Isaac told himself.

Stiff from the extended period of time he'd spent tied up, Liam struggled to stand. He swatted away Isaac's offered hand of help, scooped RP into his arms, and walked forward, slow and halting, like a zombie out of some horror show. Somehow, the cat purred and leaned his head into Liam's armpit. Another aberrant piece of behavior in a day chock full of them.

Eyes locked on his stepson, Isaac walked backward out of the kitchen. "After we get you changed, we'll leave for the hospital."

"You have to tie me up, in a cup like a pup rup." Liam rubbed his raw wrists together.

He'd likely break dozens of laws if he zip tied his stepson, but he doubted any of the legislatures creating said laws had dealt with this particular dilemma. He worried more about trampling his own moral code. No matter what Liam had done, he deserved to be treated with dignity. How to balance dignity and safety turned out to be a challenging proposition, especially when the deepest, darkest part of his soul would like to make Liam suffer.

"All right." He grimaced. "But you have to change first."

His younger self would be ashamed. Twenty-year-old Isaac would've known how to handle Liam with compassion and confidence. But then, twenty-year-old Isaac wouldn't be reeling from the near death of his daughter.

After a walk nearly as long as the Bataan Death March, the two made it to Liam's room. Humid air wafted through the torn screen. The anger coursing through Isaac's veins morphed into a dark and seething undercurrent of permanent resentment.

With a heavy-handed tug, he slid open the dresser drawer. He threw a fresh pair of boxers and shorts onto the bed. Liam tottered toward it and placed the cat down next to the clean clothes. In normal circumstances, he'd never invade Liam's privacy and watch him change. But today's ordeal deviated so far from normal the only rules he'd abide by were the ones leaving both of them alive. Isaac stepped out of the room but remained in the doorway.

After Liam changed, he retrieved a handful of zip ties from the pocket of his soiled shorts. He left the dirty clothes on the ground, stepping on them as he made his way to Isaac.

"Tie me. Now." He held out the zip ties.

Against his better wisdom, Isaac placed the zip tie on Liam's wrists and pulled it closed. To avoid further chafing Liam's skin, he left it loose.

"Tighter," Liam said.

The teeth of the zip tie bit into Liam's skin by the time Isaac released it.

Liam's shoulders relaxed. "Let's go." He pushed past Isaac and walked with purpose to the front door.

Glad Allison wasn't here to see her son's self-flagellation, Isaac followed. Wanting to hurt Liam for what he'd done to Tasha was one thing; having him enlist you in his self-punishment was quite another.

As they neared the foyer, Liam panted and ducked away from some unseen danger. He moaned in pain and shook his head. Isaac reached past him and opened the door.

Terrorized by some hallucination, Liam raced outside and huddled by the Hyundai. He held his bound hands over his eyes and remained stationary until Isaac pulled out his keys and unlocked the car, after which he slid into the backseat and curled into a fetal position.

Isaac sat down and started the long drive to the psychiatric facility in Tallahassee, trying his best not to think about exposing his back to Liam. It would be a long two hours.

36

A **white sign with "Rose Smith Clinic" spelled out in red** letters loomed above the psychiatric facility, a square, innocuous building surrounded by pink impatiens and palm trees. Behind it, the evening sun shot crimson hues through the atmosphere. Isaac darted a look back at Liam.

His stepson leaned against the Hyundai's cheap gray upholstery and stared ahead with glazed eyes. He hadn't said a word since entering the car.

"Are you ready?" Isaac asked.

No answer.

He mentally braced himself for a possible physical confrontation, exited the car, and opened the backseat. Liam didn't move. From his pocket, Isaac retrieved the scissors he'd brought and cut the zip tie, saying a silent prayer of thanks he hadn't needed to use the shears for protection.

"It's time to go," he said.

Liam sat as lifeless as a wax sculpture. A hamburger wrapper skittered across the vacant parking lot and settled at Isaac's feet, leaving a smudge of grease on his big toe. He waited, attempting to match the stillness of the moment. The next few steps were critical. Liam's treatment would work best if he initiated it. Isaac wouldn't risk inadvertently changing his stepson's mind about seeking help by rushing him. He could wait as long as Liam liked. Hopefully.

A gust of warmth slammed against him. Though he'd had the AC on full blast in the car, the scorching temperature seemed to emanate from its interior, like the Hyundai had become a sauna in the ten seconds since he'd turned off the ignition. Liam arched his back like an invisible force stabbed his kidney and gagged. He grasped the headrest in front of him, leaned forward, and trembled.

"Help," he whispered.

Isaac tensed and leaned down. "Let's do this together." He reached into the car and grabbed him under his shoulders.

With a slight nod, Liam slumped over. Isaac breathed through his mouth to avoid the worst of his stepson's stench, dug his heels into the ground, and pulled backward. Like a cork out of a bottle, Liam popped out of the car, collapsed on top of him, and knocked out his breath. Temporarily immobile, his heart raced when Liam scrambled up and sprinted down the sidewalk. He rolled to the side and tried to yell "Stop!" but it came out a whimper.

The overwhelming heat vanished, instantly replaced with the typical Floridian late afternoon mugginess. In shock, he watched as Liam ran *into* the clinic, not away from it. Automatic double doors wheezed open with a pneumatic whoosh as Liam hopped under them. He dashed inside and left Isaac alone in the parking lot.

Dazed, he leaned his head against the warm concrete. A sense of gratitude washed over him. Liam had done it. He'd walked into the clinic on his own volition.

Glittery shards of glass from a long ago broken bottle scraped his elbows as he pushed up and followed his stepson.

Cool yet stagnant air greeted him upon passing through the clinic's threshold, and the overwhelming scent of antiseptic cleanser stung his eyes. Liam stood at the front desk, staring blankly at the attendant.

Isaac joined him. "Liam wants to be admitted to the hospital. He's in the midst of a psychotic break."

The receptionist, an angular white woman who wore Winnie-the-Pooh nursing scrubs and oversized wire-rimmed glasses, squinted at

Isaac. She took a drawn-out look at the milky-pale Liam, and then dragged her gaze to the dark-skinned Isaac, looking him up and down. The only traits the two shared were looking disheveled and reeking of urine and vomit. Liam's red hair was matted and unkempt while Isaac still wore his night undershirt and shorts, wrinkled and salt stained from his dash in the sea.

"What happened to your head?" the receptionist asked Liam.

Isaac's stomach plunged.

The feeling in his gut didn't improve when Liam flipped his wrists toward the receptionist and revealed his raw skin.

"He tied himself up after endangering his sister," Isaac explained.

"I see. And who are you?" the receptionist said. She looked down her nose at Isaac.

"His stepfather."

It was about to get real.

"Stepfather. Right." She sniffed. "And why are you the one transporting him?"

Isaac ran his tongue along the inside of his cheek. He didn't have the time or patience for this bullshit. "Because his mother is with his sister, who almost drowned last night thanks to one of Liam's delusions. Liam also hit his mother recently, so I didn't feel comfortable with the two being alone."

"Seems like an awful lot of violence," the receptionist said. Her eyebrows arched so high they disappeared beneath her bangs.

"You think? Your astute powers of observation are incredible. Must be why you're entrusted with such an important desk job."

The receptionist reared her head back in offense like she was the one who had a right to be angry.

Liam responded to the tension in the air by banging on an invisible wall. "Dangerous, strangerous, contagious!" he yelled.

"How old is your stepson?" A look of disapproval soured the receptionist's pinched face.

"Twenty-five."

She pushed forward a stack of papers. "Take a seat and complete this paperwork. I must remind you that because your stepson is an adult, we will not be allowed to discuss his health with you."

If the night had left even a trace of humor in his bones, Isaac would've laughed at the irony of filling out the very paperwork he wouldn't later be allowed to see.

A middle-aged woman stood up and relocated to the other side of the waiting room when Liam scuttled over to the corner next to her and crouched down, batting at the air in self-defense. Isaac chose a seat facing his stepson, careful to keep his peripheral vision on him as he filled out the myriad of questionnaires. When he completed the reams of paperwork, he dumped them on the front desk.

The receptionist didn't meet his eyes but took the pile from him. She closed the shatterproof glass window separating her from the waiting room and disappeared from view.

Whatever or whoever haunted Liam continued to torture him, causing him to groan and shout on occasion. Isaac brought out his phone and texted Allison.

"At the clinic. Waiting to be admitted," he wrote. "How's Tasha?"

Allison texted, "Tasha is well. All tests confirm she didn't sustain any neurological damage. She's resting now by my side."

Thank you, Lord.

Isaac lifted his chin to the heavens and closed his eyes. The adrenaline sustaining him for the past day drained away, replaced by an exhaustion so deep it seemed to burrow into the marrow of his bones.

The phone's screen dimmed to black. Then:

"How's it gone with Liam? Were you able to get him there without a struggle?"

Isaac's hand tightened over his phone. The two had fought over him bringing Liam to the hospital. Her rebuttal still rang in his ears. "I don't trust your judgment. Your decision to keep Liam home just about cost Tasha her life," she'd said. She'd wanted to call Security Forces and have Liam hauled away. "Don't make the situation worse than it already is."

But he'd avoided calling the police expressly *to* mitigate potential risks. Allison would never fully understand the dangers her son faced every time he had an interaction with the police. Nor, for that matter, could she truly comprehend how it put his own life as a black man at risk. He couldn't protect his family from every danger (especially when it came to his stepson), but he sure as hell wouldn't invite more of it into his home. In one of his least-stellar husband moves, he hadn't waited for her agreement and had instead left after stating his intention to drive Liam to the clinic.

Furthermore, if Liam reentered a psychiatric facility on his own recognizance, it would likely prolong his probation, but an involuntary commitment would negate it. His stepson couldn't continue to live with them, but he shouldn't be jailed for the next ten years, either. He needed help, not imprisonment.

One day, Isaac may face the same decision with Tasha. She'd remember how her parents handled her brother's condition and expect the same treatment. He wouldn't make her fearful of the future.

"He came willingly. No issues," Isaac texted.

He'd tell her about the self-injury later. She had enough to deal with.

The next three hours crawled by without incident. Finally, the white metal door by the front desk whisked open.

"Liam Murphy?" a male nurse called. Light blue scrubs hung loosely over his muscular frame.

Head bowed and hands tapping the carpet, Liam rocked back and forth in his corner.

Isaac stood. "Do you need help?"

"Maybe," the nurse said. He walked near Liam and called his name again.

This time, he looked up.

"Mr. Murphy, I need you to come with me," the nurse said.

"No!" Spittle flew from Liam's mouth as he yelled.

The nurse didn't flinch. "You asked to be admitted. I'm here to help you."

Liam pushed his back into the wall and continued to knock the floor.

"You want to be safe for Tasha, remember?" Isaac said.

The tapping stopped.

Isaac shoved his hands into his pockets and refrained from crossing the room and shaking some sense into him. "You decided to come here. You want help."

Liam placed a hand on the wall and pulled up to shaky legs. The nurse stayed put and pointed toward the door, allowing his patient some personal space.

Fists balled into tight circles, Liam walked toward the door. Before he disappeared behind the white walls, he inhaled deeply. Then, without a backward glance, he entered the clinic.

The nurse shot a last look at Isaac. "We'll take it from here," he said.

The waiting area, now devoid of Liam's various tics, fell quiet.

Isaac knocked on the glass at the receptionist's desk. In full menial-bureaucratic-boss mode, she returned with an angry huff and crossed arms.

"What contact can we expect from the clinic?" Isaac asked.

"Whatever contact Mr. Murphy approves," she said.

So, no contact at all.

This woman tried patience he no longer possessed. He pinched the bridge of his nose. "Will you at least notify us when he's discharged?"

"It's not required." She shrugged apathetically. "It's up to him to notify you."

He placed the palms of his hands on the window in exasperation. "But we need some sort of indication when he gets out. His mother and I need to know where he is."

The receptionist's eyes widened, and she stepped away from the glass like he was some sort of Hulk who could break her window if he pressed too hard. "That's not my problem, sir." She turned her back to him, forestalling any further arguments, and marched behind the white walls.

Left with nothing but the glossy pamphlets lining the front desk, Isaac hung his head. He couldn't control what happened next. He'd done his best to help Liam. Only time would tell if it'd been enough.

37

TUESDAY, SEPTEMBER 2nd

Thirty-six hours after admitting Liam to the Rose Smith Clinic, Isaac looked up from the briefing he reviewed to answer a knock on his office door.

"Colonel Northman, may we speak?" a willowy woman with light tan skin asked. She kept her brown hair cropped short and sported a smart russet-colored pantsuit.

Isaac pushed back from his desk and smiled in greeting. "Of course, Ms. Alvarez. I always welcome Family Advocacy. Do you have a case for me?"

"I'm sorry, but this isn't my typical visit. It's rather…more personal than usual," Camila said. Her eyes fell to the floor as she closed the door.

The smile dropped from Isaac's face. He motioned to the seat opposite his desk. "I see. Please, make yourself comfortable." A bright red light glowed from his telephone as he hit the "do not disturb" function.

The visit from Family Advocacy shouldn't have surprised him considering the suspicion heaped upon him by the white receptionist at the clinic. Nevertheless, it still stung. He didn't enjoy sitting on this side of an interrogation.

Camila retrieved a smartphone, pen, and notepad from a well-worn leather briefcase before placing it on the floor and seating herself. She set the phone on Isaac's desk and opened up a recording app.

"Do I have your permission to record our conversation?" All familiarity from her voice disappeared.

Isaac knew his rights. He didn't have to cooperate with the investigation. But he also knew it'd be better for his career if he did.

"Yes," he said.

Camila pressed record. "Tuesday morning at 0900, Camila Alvarez conducting an interview with Lieutenant Colonel Northman." She cleared her throat. "Colonel Northman, does your stepson, Liam Murphy, reside with you at 9709 Eagle Drive?"

"Yes."

Blue ink flowed from her pen as she began to take notes. "How long has he lived with you?"

"For about six months. He moved in shortly after his father died."

"I understand he faced some legal issues around that time?"

He resisted the urge to crack his knuckles. "After his father passed, Liam suffered a psychotic break that culminated in him brandishing a knife in a convenience store."

Camila tipped her head. "Instead of serving time for the incident, I see from his records a judge placed him on probation and ordered him to stay under a psychologist's care. Another stipulation was he live with family until deemed healthy enough to live independently." She looked up. "Your stepson's legal requirements must have been a difficult development for his mother and you."

Silent, Isaac held her gaze until she looked down again at her notebook. She flipped through it until a heavily marked page stopped her search.

"Are you the person who checked Liam into the Rose Smith Clinic on Sunday night?"

"Affirmative."

Her cheeks tightened. "We received information from the hospital that Liam was admitted with wounds on his arms and legs consistent with being tightly bound. Did you see the wounds in question?"

"Yes." Isaac leaned back in his chair.

"Do you know how he obtained the wounds?"

"He zip-tied himself in an effort to keep from hurting anybody."

"So Mr. Murphy zip-tied his own wrists together?" Camila's pen halted its motion.

"I wondered at his ingenuity myself." Isaac rolled his wedding band with his thumb. "Somehow, yes he did."

She eyed his fidgeting fingers. "An impressive feat for one suffering a breakdown."

He froze his thumb and dropped his hands to the desk. "Liam is a man of unique abilities."

Camila tugged at her suit jacket. While she couldn't have felt as uncomfortable as him, they had worked in the past on a number of cases. Either she investigated a complete hypocrite or an innocent man. Neither scenario made for a fun interview.

"The staff also noted Liam had a significant bruise and knot on his temple, as well as a gash on his cheek. Can you tell me how those wounds happened?"

"I reserve the right to not answer the question." There was no good way to say he'd hit his stepson.

Camila jotted in her notepad. "You have a daughter with Liam's mother?"

He nodded. "Tasha. She's five."

"She recently received treatment at the base hospital for a near-drowning experience?" The words came out of her mouth in a flat monotone, like she read a boring instructional manual and not the details about his daughter's terrifying ordeal.

"Yes, early on Sunday morning." Isaac's jaw tightened with anger at the memory. He could still taste the salty ocean water that had almost killed his daughter.

Camila gazed at his face. "Did the accident occur before or after Liam received his head wound?"

He remained tightlipped.

"All right." She tapped her pen against her notebook and frowned.

"How did Tasha end up on the beach in the early hours of Sunday morning unsupervised?"

His left eye twitched. "Liam sneaked out of the house with her. He had some delusion Tasha was in danger."

"Why does he consider your house dangerous?" She set the notebook on the table and smoothed the exposed page, even though no wrinkles marred its surface.

"There's no telling why Liam thinks half of what he does."

She leaned forward. "Does he have reason to be afraid?"

The aggressive questioning and presumption of abuse put him over the edge. He'd had more than enough. It always came back to the same issue. All he was guilty of was being a black man in an impossible situation.

He placed his face near Camila's. "Why am I the person being investigated here? My white stepson nearly killed my daughter, but his actions aren't your concern. No, it's whether or not his black stepdad is nice to him. My family isn't afraid of me. I'm not the one with the criminal record. They're afraid of Liam. You should be here on Tasha's behalf, not his."

Camila flinched. "Are you accusing me of being racist?" Her eyes narrowed. "You should know me better than that."

"I could say the same." He failed to keep the rising anger out of his voice.

Bright-red spots blossomed on her cheeks. "I don't know whether these allegations will be substantiated, but I thoroughly investigate every report I receive. I do my job, whether the results are painful or not. I can't allow our previous positive interactions to influence my decision, but rest assured your race won't affect it either. Are you officially requesting me to open a file on Tasha?"

"No!" Isaac gritted his teeth. His daughter needed a Family Advocacy case like he needed another stepson. Besides, Liam would never have the opportunity to hurt Tasha again.

"Listen, Liam has had delusions for years now. You may want to consult with his regular psychologist. She can confirm this fact."

"I've spoken with his therapist." She picked up her notepad.

“Colonel Northman, I’ve got a job here and need to make sure your stepson is safe. It’s not personal. Please don’t take it as such.”

The interrogation was entirely personal. Camila came here to judge his moral character. He’d be a lot less stressed if he didn’t question it himself.

“Do you have an update on Liam?” Every passing day brought his stepson’s release closer. Exactly how much closer, he wouldn’t hazard a guess.

“I’m sorry, but I can’t discuss the particulars of his healthcare with you.” She rubbed the back of her neck. “I’ve got a few more questions. Can you tell me where Tasha is now?”

From a framed portrait on his desk, Tasha flashed her adorable smile. She wore her favorite pink glittery dress and hugged her well-loved stuffed bunny. “She’s at her grandparent’s house in Georgia. Since we have no idea when to expect Liam home, we’ve had to relocate her.”

“Is your wife staying with her?”

“Yes.” His chest constricted.

Camila gave him a sharp look. “So when Liam returns, it’ll be only the two of you at home?”

He hesitated. “Yes.”

She tugged at her jacket again. “Then I’m going to request you remove yourself to the barracks until our investigation is completed.”

Unable to hide his disdain, he snorted. “My stepson is still in the hospital. The house will be completely empty if I leave.”

“Can you tell me when he’ll return home?”

The now familiar blend of resentment, anger, and fear boiled in his stomach. “No.”

“Then I must insist, Colonel Northman. If he comes home and something happens…” She shifted in her chair. “I’m sorry for the inconvenience, but it’s merely protocol. I’m sure you understand.”

He didn’t, but nodded all the same. “May I stop by my house and at least replace the window screens Liam ruined while he kidnapped my daughter?” He tried not to hold it against Camila when she didn’t wince at his mention of Tasha’s abduction.

"Call maintenance to fix the screens. You should stop home long enough only to get clothing and essentials."

He found the ridiculousness of his predicament hard to stomach. Liam could live alone in the house. The house Isaac's job paid for, the home Isaac had made with Allison. None of that mattered. Evidently, Liam and his needs trumped all.

Camila stood and clicked off the record button. "I could finish my investigation in a timelier manner if you answered all the questions."

What answers? Does she think there's an actual solution to my problem?

He shot her a disdainful look.

Unlike every other time the two of them had concluded business, she didn't offer a parting handshake. "I'll be in touch." She gathered up her briefcase and left.

A massive headache spread its tentacles across his brain. He pushed back into his chair and opened the top drawer of his desk. A quarter full bottle of ibuprofen rattled next to his pens. He shook out two pills and cracked open a cold soda from his personal fridge. He knocked the pills back with a long pull, then dialed up his wife. The phone rang five times before she answered.

"Allison? How are you and Tasha doing?" he asked.

Silence filled the air. Then, "We're doing fine." Allison didn't ask about his welfare.

"We've got a new issue," he said.

"Does it have a little something to do with Liam baring bondage marks when you admitted him to the hospital?"

The soda churned in his stomach. "How did you—"

She interrupted him. "Family Advocacy interviewed me via telephone this morning. They're concerned Liam is being abused. Do you have something you want to tell me?"

He rolled his neck. "Liam tied himself up while we were at the hospital with Tasha and insisted on being driven to the clinic still bound. I didn't want to worry you and planned to tell you about it later."

"It appears 'later' is now. When I insisted Liam be picked up by Security Forces, I wasn't thinking just about Tasha and him. I was thinking of you, too. I knew getting Liam to leave would be messy. After you punched him the other night, I wanted to keep the potential conflict between you two at a minimum. And what happened when you disregarded my wishes? My son shows up injured, and Family Advocacy begins investigating you. Exactly what I tried to avoid. We don't need this extra stress."

Isaac scrubbed his hair.

"You thought it'd be easier, didn't you? With all your beautiful ideals and theories, you thought you could handle living with Liam. That you could do a better job of it than I could," she said.

Shamed at the truth in his wife's words, he closed his eyes.

"You promised Liam would be safe with us. That we could take better care of him than a mental institution. That our family could stay intact. And, while I'm being totally honest, I have to admit I knew your promises were too pretty to be true. But I wanted them to be true so badly I let myself believe you. I don't anymore." Her voice cracked. "Don't let yourself slip into his illness, Isaac. Even when he makes nonsensical decisions, you have to remain rational. Sean spent the last decade of his life spiraling down the same rabbit hole that captured Liam. It's hard to scratch your way out of it."

If Liam's father, Sean, had constantly worried he never made the right decision for his family, then Isaac felt a certain kinship with the man. And that, even in a life full of increasingly hazy emotions, did not bode well for his marriage.

38

TUESDAY, SEPTEMBER 16th

The stove clicked a staccato beat until a flame sprang up in a circle around the gas burner. Allison set a saucepan on the stovetop and poured enough olive oil in it to coat the surface. She would've liked to make Liam a favorite meal for his homecoming, but food didn't interest him much these days. So she'd decided to make an old standby. Kielbasa sausage, bean, and kale soup. It'd been one of Sean's favorites.

Peeking out of the kitchen, she saw Liam sat where she'd left him: smooshed into the corner of the couch with RP lying in his lap. How and why the family's surly tomcat had taken a sudden liking to Liam mystified her. RP simply didn't like people. He tolerated Tasha and begrudgingly allowed Isaac and Allison to feed him, but he never, ever snuggled up to anybody like he did to Liam now. She sighed. If only the rest of Liam's life could be so charmed.

"Hey, Mom," Liam called.

She walked out of the kitchen and toward her son. "Yes?"

"Who took care of RP when you were in Georgia?"

"The Channers. I gave them a key." She cringed, anticipating his reaction.

His body went rigid. "They have a key?" he whispered.

"Not anymore. I picked it up earlier."

RP rolled over and stretched his legs. In such ecstasy over Liam's return, he hadn't stopped purring since her son had walked through the door. Now his pink tongue stuck out between his fangs, and he nudged Liam's knee, begging to be pet. Liam's shoulders lowered, and his face relaxed as his fingers sank into the cat's fur. "They could've made a copy, though. We need to get our locks changed."

On a normal day, Allison would've ignored his suggestion. She found participating in her son's delusions unwise. Moreover, the Channers couldn't possibly be a menace. Sara had taken a nasty tumble outside her house a few weeks back and suffered numerous injuries. She was in no shape to lurk about. Preoccupied with caretaking and calling his mistress on the side, her husband didn't pose much of a threat either.

Today, though, she looked at Liam, knuckles white from clenching the couch, and caved. "Okay. I'll call up maintenance."

He exhaled and then smiled.

She laced her fingertips above her head and tried to come up with a viable reason for maintenance that didn't make Isaac look guiltier of domestic abuse than he already did. A request for new locks one day after Liam's homecoming didn't look great. But it certainly beat him going off the rails again.

Smoke billowed from the kitchen, followed closely by the fire alarm sounding. She rushed into the kitchen and cursed. The olive oil burned a dark brown semi-circle in the saucepan. She lowered the temperature on the stovetop and waved a towel around to cut the acrid smoke.

Once the alarm subsided, she pulled out the cutting board. Never the fastest chopper in the world, she slogged through dicing the onions and tossed them into the pan. They hissed when they hit the hot surface, and she muttered a prayer they wouldn't set off the alarm again. She dumped in the sausage, beans, and chicken broth without waiting for the onions to turn properly translucent. In a different lifetime, she'd followed recipes meticulously. Now, she had more pressing concerns than cooking the perfect meal.

She left the soup to simmer and scoured the junk cabinet above the washing machine. A sliver of hair escaped from her ponytail and fell onto her cheek as her hand closed over the handle of a screwdriver. She strode out of the kitchen and opened the front door. The screwdriver clinked against the brass lock as she applied all of her weight to it, and she rocked the tool back and forth, hoping it'd be enough to break the lock.

The springs on the couch creaked as Liam rose and ambled over to the door. Like a discerning foreman, he watched her work. RP leaned against his legs and meowed for attention. Even though the door stayed wide open, the cat didn't make a run for it.

Liam nodded in approval. "Good job, Mom."

Her hands froze. She ignored her sixth sense shouting at her to stop and instead took a break. Salt stung her eyes as she leaned against the doorway and rubbed her sweaty face on her shirt. Florida weather in early September rivaled the hottest day of July in most other places. Not that Isaac would ever get stationed to one of those magical locations that didn't feel like the equator. They used to kid their next station would be hell.

Neither of them told that joke anymore.

She shooed Liam back inside the house and closed the door. It shut but then swung back open. The door could no longer close. Perfect. Maintenance would have to fix it today.

She repeated the process on both the kitchen and back doors. Angry, red blisters formed on her thumbs from wielding the screwdriver.

Liam inspected each lock and surveyed whether he deemed the damage severe enough. His eyes met hers in acknowledgment, and he grinned. "Thanks, Mom."

"You're welcome." She didn't ask why the Channers threatened him. For reasons known only to him, he'd long held an obsession with them. She'd already gone too far in enabling his ideas.

The phone call to maintenance got a little hairy, but she didn't hang up until she'd convinced them she needed new locks tonight. Afterward, she and Liam ate at the dining room table. She tried to ignore Tasha's and Isaac's painfully empty seats.

"Got any upcoming sales?" he asked.

An innocent enough question on the surface, it still scratched at her bottled-up resentment. She'd lost the big sale on Hugh Drive. The couple had wanted to take the weekend to decide on the purchase. By that Monday, Tasha was in the hospital for observation and Liam was in a psychiatric ward. Fully occupied by her children's issues, she'd handed the sale back to Lexi.

"Since I went to Georgia with Tasha, I haven't worked much," she said.

"How long will Tasha stay in Georgia?" he asked. "I miss her."

Separated from her daughter for less than a day, Allison already did too.

"She might stay there until Christmas. Grammy doesn't get to see her very often and talked me into it."

Liam's spoon tinkled against his soup bowl. He knew her well enough to know she lied. Tasha wasn't here because he was.

"She's gonna be spoiled rotten when she gets home. Grammy used to give me whatever I liked." He looked off into space, probably lost in the memories of his youth.

Years had passed since he'd even seen his grandmother. Terrified of her own grandson, she'd campaigned long and hard to keep Allison from returning and living alone with him. It'd been difficult to argue with her. Liam behaved unpredictably. He hadn't intentionally hurt Tasha, but he still had. If Isaac hadn't followed his instincts and run to the beach, Tasha would be dead.

At some point, Allison would have to figure out a long-term solution to their living arrangements. Tasha and Liam would never live together again. She didn't intend to miss out on Tasha's childhood, nor did she intend to abandon Liam for a second time. How she'd accomplish both goals was a question for another day.

"What about Isaac? When does he come home?" Liam asked.

"Depends. He may return if and when Family Advocacy deems him innocent and closes his case." She yearned to say, "We don't have to stay here if he returns. We can live wherever you like. If you're not comfortable, then I'm not either. You and Tasha are my main concern." But she wouldn't give Liam false hope. Tasha needed protection from him. And although Allison now doubted Isaac's judgment when it came to Liam, she needed his help dealing with her son.

She stared out the back window. The sight of the ocean glittering in the distance made her nauseous.

Liam said, "Isaac's a decent man. He'll be cleared. Anyway, I'm going to get healthy and move out on my own soon enough. Then I can stop ruining your marriages."

"You don't 'ruin my marriages.' I'm more than capable of doing that on my own."

He dropped his spoon. It sunk to the bottom of his bowl. "You know what I'm saying is true. You and Dad would've never divorced if I hadn't developed schizophrenia. He never stopped loving you. Had pictures of you all over the place."

Her breath caught. Though they'd divorced years before he died, Sean's passing had hit her hard. The two had been high school sweethearts, marrying after graduation when Allison found out she was pregnant with Liam. Love had filled their first fifteen years together.

"Your schizophrenia didn't cause our breakup. It exposed rifts already there. Even if you had never developed it, something else would've sniffed out our issues." Probably, anyway. There were few stressors in life as severe as watching your child descend into mental illness.

"Here's the thing, Mom. Isaac loves you as much as Dad did. He married you, all the while knowing I'll always be a part of your life. Against his better judgment, he allows me to live with you and Tasha, the people he adores most on this planet. And he does all of this because he wants you to be happy." Liam ran his fingers along the grain of the oak table. "Take it from me, happiness is elusive. Don't let me steal yours."

She reached a trembling hand out to hold his. They'd never had a conversation so honest before. So adult. "You don't steal my happiness."

The doorbell rang.

He shrank back. "Maintenance is here." He crossed his arms.

In the span of a heartbeat, her son left again. For a few bright, shining moments they'd connected. This small taste of a real relationship with her son made the absence of it all the more tangible. She stifled a sob.

She battled to keep her emotions in check and answered the door. A maintenance man squatted in front of it, inspecting the lock until Allison swung the door away from him.

"What happened? Looks like somebody tried to break in. They did a real number," he said.

"My adult son came for a visit and didn't have a key. He's seen one too many YouTube videos on how to pick a lock."

The technician eyed her. "All three locks look this way?"

"Pretty much. My son is thorough."

His gaze traveled to her red and blistered hands. She stuffed them in her pockets.

"You don't want to tell me why this really happened?" he asked.

"Though I wish I had a more interesting story, that's the truth." She put on her best lying smile and held her breath.

"If you say so," the man muttered. He grabbed his baseball cap and pulled it down. While he'd certainly heard tall tales before, she doubted he could guess the peculiar truth of her life.

The whisper of footprints turned her head. Liam skulked past her and retreated to his room. He closed his door with an assertive thud.

She rubbed her eyes. This morning, Liam had called to inform her he wanted to leave the clinic. An hour after getting off the phone with him, she'd driven down from Georgia and picked him up. Now, she longed for twelve consecutive hours of sleep.

As she watched the maintenance man install the new lock, black metal that absorbed the porch light instead of reflecting it like the old brass one, she felt a stab of loneliness. No matter how much sleep called to her like a jealous lover, her cold, empty bed didn't tempt her. She'd sleep on the couch tonight.

39

THURSDAY, SEPTEMBER 18th

Liam brushed his fingers over his phone. Over the past two days, he'd spent hours reading and rereading texts Mai had sent him while he was in the hospital. They'd started off flirtatious— "Miss you," turned concerned— "Are you okay? Send me a text. Please!" and then veered into anger— "I deserve to know you're alive."

He hadn't responded yet. What could he say? "Sorry, got caught up in a psychotic break! LOL."

Besides, he didn't trust the texts. Maybe he yearned for Mai to be real so badly his mind conjured them up. For now, he'd allow the texts to comfort him, angry missives and all. He'd decide later if they were real.

With a long sigh, he stuffed his phone into his pocket. Across the oak dining room table sat Camila Alvarez, his Family Advocacy caseworker. Attractive and young, he pegged her age closer to his than Isaac's. She maintained a meticulous appearance, from finely manicured nails to a perfectly fitted skirt suit to shiny, short hair tucked behind her ears. If he didn't know better, he'd say she had it all together.

Except he did know better. Camila was a special case.

Ever since she'd stepped foot through the front door, a trail of white images had followed her. She didn't carry one burden. She carried dozens. They crowded the room. Babies, toddlers, children. Teenagers with haunted expressions and women with blackened eyes. Camila and her entourage downright depressed him.

"Are you ready for our discussion?" she asked.

The high-backed wooden chair pressed against his back. He nodded.

Joshua sat in the chair next to Camila and leaned toward her, black leather jacket crinkling with the movement. "This is the woman who will decide Isaac's entire future? She determines whether or not he's a respectable man?" He placed his nose next to her neck and sniffed. "Smells delectable. That's a good sign. She might be the one to help free us from your stepdad."

She took out her phone, opened up an app, and hit record. "I'm going to tape our conversation," she said.

Joshua hovered mere inches from Camila's face, staring at her.

"Swell." Liam tried to ignore the nervous butterflies in his stomach.

"The staff at the Rose Smith Clinic notified the authorities that you checked in two weeks ago with bondage marks and several contusions to your head. I understand this may be painful, but can you tell me how you acquired those wounds?"

He cocked his head to the side. "You certainly carry the weight of the world around with you."

"Excuse me?" She lifted her eyebrows.

"I'm guessing you don't leave your work at the office."

"I'm here to discuss you, Mr. Murphy. My life is irrelevant." Her demeanor was cool yet professional.

Joshua sat back in his chair and withdrew a pack of Marlboros from his pocket. He tapped out a cigarette. "You're making her uncomfortable, jackass. Quit it."

"Forgive me." Liam flashed Camila a bright smile. "I distract easily. Where were we?"

"Your wounds, Mr. Murphy. How did you receive them?"

"I did them to myself. I know you're here to pin this on Isaac, but it's not his fault. I can be difficult to live with."

She stiffened. "Being difficult to live with doesn't make it okay to hurt you."

"I didn't say it did. But Isaac's doing the best he can. And his best is pretty darn good." Liam's eyes unwillingly wandered to where his mother sat in the living room. Her shoulders hunched upward like they always did when she felt stressed.

A cloud of smoke surrounded Joshua as he pulled on his cigarette. "This isn't what we agreed upon. You're supposed to make the caseworker hate Isaac."

"Sometimes, a person's best isn't enough," Camila said.

"Seems like you know that better than most." Liam leaned forward and placed his hands on the table.

She jerked her head. "What do you mean?"

"The multitudes of people you feel you've failed. You could pack a room with them."

She shifted in her chair.

He tugged on his five o'clock shadow. One of the visions glowed brighter than the rest, so he pressed his advantage and took a chance. "One case, in particular, haunts you. A teen with a penchant for nose rings and gothic makeup. Ring any bells?"

Joshua hit pause on her phone. "You stupid prick. You're making us look crazy. Behave and stick to the plan. Or you'll regret it."

"How do you know about that?" Camila whispered. Her lower lip trembled.

Liam wanted to stop, to avoid making her relive a terrible memory. But the time for mercy had come and gone. "Her father beat her to death, didn't he?"

The case worker's mouth dropped open in horror.

"Did you drag your feet on her case? Or not understand the severity of her abuse?" The overwhelming sorrow flooding her face proved he'd hit the bullseye of her guilt.

She opened her mouth, then shut it, then opened it again. "This isn't funny. Where are you getting your information?"

"Let's just say I've got special abilities that allow me a window into people's souls. As far as superhero powers go, though, it's a crappy one."

"I don't believe you."

"Story of my life." He shrugged.

Joshua jumped out of his seat and paced between the table and windows. "You're not gonna get a better chance than this, Liam. Don't waste it. Let's get rid of Isaac for keeps."

The look on Camila's face teetered between dismay and wariness. She fiddled with one of her earrings and looked at her phone. Her eyes narrowed when she noticed the recording app paused. Lips pinched tight, she hit play again. She squared her shoulders and sat up straight. "Let's stay on track, Mr. Murphy. Are you denying Colonel Northman gave you the aforementioned wounds?"

"Yes. Except for the one head injury. He knocked me out the night before admitting me to the hospital."

Her eyes popped wide.

Joshua raised his elbows and placed his hands behind his head. "Finally. Now we're getting somewhere."

"What? Colonel Northman hit you?"

"Only after I endangered his wife. He made a snap decision, but one I would've made as well in his place."

The squinting of her eyes led Liam to believe he shouldn't have placed Isaac's decision-making prowess in the same ballpark as his.

"Do you feel safe at home?" she continued.

Of course not.

"Yes," he said.

She tapped the dining room table. "Covering up abuse is dangerous, Mr. Murphy. Take it from the girl with the nose rings."

"You've undoubtedly interviewed my stepfather?" He sucked in his upper lip.

She didn't answer.

RP's plaintive meow echoed through the walls. As part of his prep work, Liam had locked him in the bathroom.

"Then you know he's an honorable man. He's in a tough position but doesn't deserve to suffer because I've got issues. Heck, in law school, all kinds of important people lauded Isaac for his efforts toward granting those of us living with mental illness the same civil rights the rest of you enjoy."

"I'm aware of his reputation." Her mouth twitched.

It all clicked into place then.

"Ahh, so you know Isaac. You've worked on cases together, am I correct?"

Her shoulders slumped.

"If you knew Isaac previously, then I'm guessing you held him up on a pedestal of sorts? I wouldn't blame you. Most people do. Isaac is the very definition of bleeding-heart goodness. He believes all people should be given the same opportunities. Or believed, at any rate."

He took a steadying breath. "Life gets complicated when ideals and reality intersect. How can I blame Isaac for not responding appropriately to a difficult situation when sometimes I don't either? I can't expect Isaac to have patience with me if I don't extend it to him."

"Isaac's the problem, not you!" screamed Joshua. He jabbed an angry finger on Camila's phone and paused the recorder once again. "If you won't help yourself, I will."

Her starched dress shirt creased as she crossed her arms. "Isaac never should've hit you."

"You're right. He shouldn't have. He made a bad decision. But believe me, I'm sure Isaac is harder on himself for this mistake than you or I could ever be. So cut the man some slack, and let him be human. He can't be Captain America all the time. Maybe there's one percent of him that's like the rest of us. We've all got some evil in our souls. Isaac, however, has much less than most of us. Wish I could say the same about myself."

She massaged her temple with her right hand. The images behind her intensified and brightened. The teen with nose rings became as vivid as life, tempting him to reach out a hand and tug on the piercings.

"The bondage marks?" she asked. She closed her eyes.

"I tied myself up, afraid of what I'd do when my family returned. I didn't trust my own actions." He didn't mention Isaac reapplying them before they left for Tallahassee.

She ran her hand over her hair and opened her eyes. Her forehead wrinkled in confusion when she checked her phone and found the app paused once again. With a leery expression, she pressed record.

"You admitted Isaac allowed you to injure yourself. Did he object in any matter?"

"I can be persuasive when I want. Tell me, what would you do in his position?"

Joshua hit the pause button, reached across the table, and slapped him. The force of his blow whipped Liam's face to the side.

Startled, Camila reflexively jumped away from him.

A mighty hiss emanated from the bathroom. The door banged against its frame as RP hurled his weight against it.

Allison stood. "Excuse me for the interruption. It seems our cat is trapped and unhappy." She hurried out of the room and toward the bathroom.

"Are you okay, Mr. Murphy?" Camila asked, concern evident in her tone.

"Turn on your recording app again." He pointed to her mobile.

Like she expected her phone to start oozing black, poisonous liquid, she picked it up and held it at a distance. "I don't understand what's happening with this app." She turned the device over in her hands.

Liam worked his jaw. His cheek smarted from the slap. "It's Joshua. He's messing with our interview."

Her hands went still. "Who's Joshua?"

"You could call him an imaginary friend. Occasionally he reaches across the lines of reality." He peered around the room theatrically, praying he didn't overdo this bit. "He doesn't want Isaac to come home."

"Why not?" Her voice, low and quiet, cracked.

He crooked his pointer finger and beckoned her closer. After a heartbeat, she leaned her head toward his.

"Because he likes having Mom and Tasha all to ourselves. Isaac takes up too much space," he whispered.

Camila chewed on her fingernail, ruining her perfect manicure. "Do you want Isaac to come home?"

"I need him to come home. He's what makes this family work. Without him, we'll be a mess. My sister needs her father."

"What about your mother?"

He leaned back. "She's harmless. But it's hard for her to deal with me long term. Few people can." The words stung more than he thought they would, but the truth didn't care about his feelings.

Joshua wrenched Camila's phone out of her fingers and reared his hand back to toss the device across the room. "You stupid sonuvabitch! You can't do anything right! Now I've gotta fix your mistake like I always do."

Freed now from his prison, RP barreled through the hallway and collided against Joshua a snarling mess of fur. Camila lifted her feet to her chest and away from the hissing cat, unaware of Joshua's howling. The phone clanked on the floor as he evaporated.

RP swished his tail irritably and circled the dining room table. Satisfied he'd scared away his prey, he hopped onto Liam's lap and settled down like a sphinx watching guard.

Camila's heels clattered against the oak chair. "What just happened?"

"Joshua." Liam shook his head with a practiced resignation.

Wary of the unpredictable animal, the caseworker climbed down from her perch and retrieved her phone. Beads of sweat formed on her forehead as she stood. "Thank you for your time, Mr. Murphy."

He tried not to smile. "Are you okay, Camila?"

Although kind of a douchey move, unnerving her had been an important aspect of his strategy. She needed to know what it felt like to be around him, what Isaac had to deal with every day. While he'd gambled that Joshua could touch the real world, his plan couldn't have turned out better. Liam still hated Alexandra, but ultimately she deserved credit for his idea. He'd theorized she wasn't his only hallucination now able to cross over into reality. Turned out his theory had been correct. Liam—1. World—9, 581, 361.

She said, "I'm fine." Her pitch rose higher than usual.

"Then may I ask you a question before you leave?"

"Okay." She straightened invisible wrinkles in her skirt with a shaking hand.

"You've spent about fifteen minutes with me. How do you think you'd do for an entire day? How about a week? Or even six months?"

She swallowed.

Liam scratched RP under his chin. "Clear Isaac. We're safer with him."

Allison emerged from the hall. Though she had to have heard his plea for Isaac to return home, she trained her face blank as she escorted Camila, and all of her burdens, to the door.

Joshua would make Liam pay for his betrayal. But if Isaac came home, the pain would be worth it.

40

WEDNESDAY, SEPTEMBER 24th

Liam paced the halls of Isaac's house, trailing his hands along the wall. His fingernail caught on a peeling piece of paint, and he ripped it off. The layer below looked exactly the same. White flakes fluttered to the floor and settled on his bare feet as he continued to dig. What secrets hid within these walls? Would he unleash them upon his mind if he delved deep enough?

"Liam," said Allison. She stood in her room, watching him create a hole in the wall. "The rain's letting up a bit. Why don't you take a walk?"

"I've got a project. I'm gonna discover how many families have lived in this house before us. The paint won't lie. Each layer equals a move."

More paint chips tumbled to the ground.

"I'm sure that's true. But it's also true we're going to have to pay a hefty fee if you destroy the hallway." She raised both arms and tightened her ponytail.

"Sorry. I've got some pent-up energy." He stopped picking at the wall. "I've been confined indoors for three weeks now."

"I know. A little exercise will do you wonders. No more excuses. Go take a walk." She did her best impression of a Miss America wave.

"Right. How about a few dollars so I can swing by the shoppette?"

She made a show of pulling a five-dollar bill out of her pocket. "Don't spend it all in one place."

The cash, water-stained and ancient, threatened to disintegrate under his grip. He mumbled, "Later," and headed out the back door.

A fine mist of rain tickled his face. Sandburs clung to his shoes and lower legs as he walked through the backyard. He avoided looking at the tree he'd climbed the night he almost killed Tasha. Its twisted limbs still called to him, proving he couldn't trust his desires. They harmed him and the people he loved.

He skirted over to the road winding down to both the shoppette and yacht club. Lead-colored clouds gathered in the sky above and promised to turn the sprinkling rain into a deluge. He picked up his pace. While he didn't care whether he got drenched, it would concern his mother.

Upon reaching the shoppette, he clambered up its wooden steps and opened the door. Pop music filtered down from overhead speakers. He shook his head like a wet dog and picked his way toward the candy and drink aisle, where a mother and her two little sons crowded the chocolate bars. The smaller boy, no older than two or three, put his grimy little paws on every piece of candy he could reach.

Cheese puffs it was.

He hemmed and hawed over his chemical-orange options—curls, balls, or puffs?—and in the end went with the classic selection of cheese curls. He snagged a soda from the refrigerator and brought his treats to the checkout counter. When the cashier didn't give his ID a second glance, he let out a breath he hadn't known he held.

"Have a pleasant day," the cashier said.

"Thanks. I think I will."

Junk food clutched to his chest, he leaned against the exit door and pushed it open. Fat raindrops splattered on his head. He raised the cheese curls like an umbrella and trucked forward, unaware of the two men walking up the steps toward him until he crashed into them.

"Watch where you're going, man!" a familiar voice said.

Liam's stomach dropped. He lowered the junk food bag and fought to keep his lips from trembling when his eyes confirmed what his ears knew. Clad in a tight, olive-green T-shirt, Cull glared at him, snub nose flaring with contempt. A very much alive Stuart Laughlin stood next to him, shuffling his feet and darting furtive glances at the shoppette entrance.

"Well, look who the cat dragged outta the psychiatric ward," Cull said. "Just who I wanted to talk to."

Liam tried to back up the stairs, but Cull grabbed his arm. "Let go of me," he said.

Cull snickered. "You're the one giving orders now, is that it? I don't think you understand your position here."

The mother and two sons still inside the shoppette would walk out at any moment. They couldn't slobber over the candy bars forever. He rolled his soda in his hands. "I understand fine. You think you can blackmail me."

"Be careful what you say to me, boy." Cull lowered his voice. "I'm not blackmailing you. I'm merely asking for my dues. You owe me." His fingers pressed hard against Liam's skin.

Teeth bared in a shameful imitation of a smile, Liam stood his ground. "I don't owe you anything. You'll be in jail soon enough for killing Stuart."

With a great guffaw, Cull gestured at Stuart, who pantomimed choking to death. "You mean the guy standing behind me? Or is he a ghost? Those rumors about you being crazy don't even begin to scratch the surface, do they?"

Liam's face flushed with humiliation, and he jerked away his arm. "I don't have your drugs, and I don't have your money. Leave me alone."

Cull rubbed his finger and thumb together. "Crazy or not, the only way I'll leave you alone is if you give me what I'm owed. And what you owe me is $200. You've got until Friday at 1800 hours. Meet me here with the money. Otherwise, there'll be consequences."

To prove his point, he body checked Liam, hitting him so hard his feet lifted off the landing. He tumbled down the stairs. The bag of cheese curls padded his head as it hit the concrete parking lot, popping like a gun upon impact. The soda skittered under a parked car.

"There's no hope for you, is there? You're one pathetic bastard." He clucked and turned his back on Liam. A soft ding sounded as he opened the shoppette door. Stuart sent him a sideways gaze and hesitated before following Cull.

Liam groaned and closed his eyes. He attempted to sort through the maze of lies his mind had created. What was real? The murder had to be a hallucination since Stuart was alive and sneering at him. But what about the rest of it? If Cull and Stuart were real, were the drugs also? The money he owed?

The shoppette door burst open, and Liam cringed, anticipating more threats from Cull. Instead, the woman and her squealing children emerged from the store. Dark-brown smears of chocolate covered both boys' faces. They skipped down the stairs, consumed with the bliss of sugar.

He sat up and leaned against the aged wooden railing.

The woman blinked at him. She said, "May I help you with something, sir?"

"I wish you could, but thanks for the offer."

The woman frowned and eyed him before ordering her children into their car.

He abandoned his crushed cheese curls on the pavement, fought his way to his feet, and followed the red taillights of her vehicle driving up the small hill parallel to Isaac's house. Hallucinations or not, he had no desire to talk with Cull and Stuart again.

Rain soaked his clothes and shoes as he slogged home. The pit in the bottom of his stomach grew with each step. No way could he summon up $200. He had to find the drugs and return them. Cull might not be happy about it, but the little bag of cocaine would have to be enough.

At step 512, he strode through the back door and headed to his room, heedless of the puddles he made. The cocaine had to still be there. He must've misplaced it. He pulled out the drawers of his dresser and dumped them upside down. Rumpled clothing cascaded to the floor. He threw the empty drawers to the side and waded through his clothes. He checked pockets, turned pants inside out, snapped shirts taut.

The packet of cocaine wasn't there.

He could think of only two possible explanations. He'd lost the drugs and was in a world of trouble with Cull, or he'd imagined the entire situation.

Either way, Liam was fucked. That much he knew was true.

41

THURSDAY, SEPTEMBER 25th

Liam pointed at the framed print hanging above Dr. Jen's desk, no bland wall covering as he'd previously thought. Baby loggerhead turtles that marched toward gruesome deaths in the ocean didn't soothe anyone. Not even him. "That's some menacing shit you've got on your wall there," he said.

"What upsets you about this painting?" asked Dr. Jen.

"The turtles are going to die. They think it's safe in the water, but it's not. All kinds of creatures will devour them."

Sunlight streamed through the small window above her desk and revealed dust motes floating in the air. "Did Tasha think the ocean was safe, too?"

"No. I did. Alexandra told me she'd be safe there. She lied to me."

Dr. Jen adjusted her glasses. "Liam, I suggest you stop thinking of the commands the voices in your mind give you as straightforward. Instead, think of them as ways your brain is indirectly communicating with you. Let's take Alexandra, for example."

A pearl of blood dripped from his thumb after he picked too hard at his fingernail.

"Alexandra is your protector. She takes care of incidents and people who scare you. Instead of acting out her commands, think about the deeper reason why you're afraid of these people or circumstances. The neighbor across the street, for example. What, exactly, makes you uncomfortable about her?"

Other than the fact that she was a replica intent on killing him and his family?

"She's rigid, bound by her schedule."

"Are you nervous you'll end up the same way? Do you fear your delusions will keep you captive and prevent you from acting in a free manner?"

He rubbed his ear and chewed his lip.

She placed her pen on her desk and rested her palms upward on her lap. "I know you don't want to discuss what happened with Tasha, but you need to work through it. Why did you really want to bring her out of the house and into the ocean? What's so scary about your home?"

"Me." He shifted in his chair. "I don't want her held back because of my issues. I want to free her."

"While it's healthy to explore your fears, don't let Alexandra dictate how you resolve them. Also, recognize you're not a burden to your family. You can play an active role in Tasha's life and have a positive influence on her."

Try selling that line to Isaac.

She continued, "Since Tasha now lives with your grandparents, do you feel safer at home?"

"Yes." He did feel calmer. But not because of Tasha's absence. RP had become akin to a parasite and followed him wherever he went, keeping away his demons. His to-do list for the day, however, did not include telling Dr. Jen his cat possessed paranormal abilities.

"What about your other visions? Have they disappeared?"

He paused. "No."

The projections had become so intense he struggled at times to discern them from reality. Dr. Jen's had hovered in the air next to her for the entire session. The projection flickered on occasion but otherwise looked as solid as his psychologist. He'd done his best to ignore it.

She cupped her chin with her left hand. "Were these visions present during your stay in the hospital?"

"Not in the beginning. Then I only saw the same type of hallucination I've had for years. But when I started to get better, they came back."

"Usually patients don't present new symptoms while improving in most other areas."

He held his hand out in the air. "I'm not your typical guy, or so they tell me."

A glimmer of amusement danced across her face, but she buried it under a serious expression before her next question. "You believe these 'projections' to be some sort of memory or idea that burdens the people to whom they're attached?"

"They have to be."

"And you think you see these projections due to your medication?"

"It makes sense, doesn't it?" He focused on the popcorn ceiling and ordered his eyes to stop flicking at Dr. Jen's ghost-like companion. "I stopped having them once I went off my meds. They only came back once the prescription established again in my blood stream."

"Why do you feel these projections are worse than your historical hallucinations?"

She could never understand what it felt like to watch his mother grieve him and fantasize about the days when he'd been "normal."

"They make me uncomfortable." He tugged at the frayed edge of his khaki shorts.

"Let's explore the idea of these projections being another conduit to your mind. Why do you think you'd see other people's pain?"

Liam set his lips in a tight line. Dr. Jen wanted a rational reason for his visions, but one didn't exist.

"Do you think you could be attempting to make connections with other people? Knowing everybody has pain, everybody carries burdens? Do you feel more secure having these commonalities?"

The idea made sense, on a logical level. But it didn't explain the librarian's tryst or the murder he'd seen.

"Maybe."

She took off her glasses and rubbed her eyes. "Let's take the projection you saw next to me. The one of the woman with the infinity tattoo."

Adrenaline shot through his body. He'd hoped she had the decency to never mention this topic again. His tongue stuck to the roof of his mouth.

"You described my sister with remarkable precision. I must admit it unnerved me. The last time I saw her alive, she wore a pink and blue striped dress with her hair up in a bun. I often remember her that way." The corners of her lips turned down.

I know.

"But you can't see the inner workings of my mind, Liam." She tapped her glasses against her lap. "You had to have searched the internet and found a picture of the two of us together."

He scuffed his heels on the floor. "Tell me about her tattoo."

She flinched. Her right hand touched the inside of her left wrist, where her sister's tattoo had been, and she shook her head.

"I understand. It's hard to talk about those who have left us," he said.

In a rushed breath, like the words had to escape her mouth before her mind thought better of it, Dr. Jen spilled her secret. "She told me it represented our bond—how we'd always be tied together. We had a tough childhood and sort of raised each other."

A silent tension filled the room. She'd never before discussed her private life. Now that she had, they'd crossed some indefinable bridge. He didn't know how to feel about it.

Apparently, she didn't either. She glanced at her clock and rubbed her cheek. Five minutes left in the session.

She cleared her throat. "Have you heard from your stepfather?"

He laced his fingers together and flipped them over. The knuckles on his hands dimpled as he flexed them. "No. He's living in the barracks until the Family Advocacy case is settled. I'm not sure when he'll get home."

Ever the professional, she returned to form and pretended nothing abnormal had occurred. "If he returns, how do you plan on interacting with him?"

By keeping to myself.

"We'll be civil to one another. For Tasha and Mom's sakes."

"It would be natural for Isaac to bear some feelings of resentment about what happened to your sister. Are you prepared to discuss the subject with him?"

He swallowed. "My stepfather won't talk with me about his emotions. He keeps his distance."

"What if you confided in him first? If you trust him with your feelings, would the gates of communication swing open?"

A disbelieving snort shot out of his nose. "Most definitely not."

She shrugged. "You'll never know until you try. You've made remarkable steps in the past week, Liam. You should be proud of your progress."

He raised both hands in the air, clapped them together, and mimicked an Olympian's victory pump. "When do I get my trophy for 'Most Improved Psychotic Patient?'"

She actually smiled. "Are you keeping up with your meds?"

"Yes." While he'd taken twenty steps backward on his trip to independence, he still yearned to live on his own. If "sane" life included troubling memories and projections, then so be it. It was better than the alternative.

"I'll see you on Monday. Call me if you need me before then."

For a sentimental moment, Liam considered telling Dr. Jen what a positive impact she'd had on his life. That he'd made more progress with her in six months than years with other psychologists. That she should let go of whatever guilt she carried about her sister because some burdens weren't meant to be carried forever. That she'd more than made up for whatever sins she'd committed.

Instead, he said, "See you on the flipside."

42

On the drive home from Liam's appointment, Allison flipped through radio stations, discontent with her options until she landed on a country channel playing a Sam Hunt song. She tapped her fingers in time on the steering wheel and stared out at the long road ahead of them.

Liam shut his eyes and leaned back in his chair, thinking of Mai and wondering if she liked the song. It'd be nice to ask her in person, but he still hadn't called her since returning home. If he reached out and discovered she was another figment of his imagination, some of his best memories ever—like the touch of her soft lips against his, or the feel of her warm skin, or even the way her southern accent made his name sound sexy and special—were hallucinations.

His eyes flashed open as Allison stomped on the brakes. The Hyundai hummed an inch behind a golden Cadillac. The gray-haired woman driving it turned around and gave his mother an ugly glare.

"Come on, sweetheart. A yellow light doesn't mean stop, you old snowbird," Allison muttered.

He turned his face and concealed a smile. To his mother, yellow meant floor the gas. Her speedster tendencies had earned her a well-deserved ticket or two.

A small brick building to the right caught his attention. Flat-roofed and humble, a neon sign hanging from the window read, "Parker Florist." Tacked to the front door, a hastily written poster board proclaimed "Homecoming Specials!" An orange tabby cat snuggled tight by the entrance, lying by an empty water dish.

He pointed to the sign. "Huh. Must be homecoming this weekend," he said.

"How can you tell?" Allison leaned over his seat.

"On the doorway over there, right where the orange cat is. No doubt some poor sucker is gonna buy his boutonniere there." He'd missed much during his later adolescent years, but he didn't regret having to skip school dances. Those seemed to be exercises in torture set to pop music.

"I don't see—" the sudden urgent blare of a horn from the intersection ahead cut off whatever she said next. A Town Car blazed through it and crashed into an SUV crossing from the other direction. The SUV spun out of control, aiming directly toward the Cadillac in front of them.

"Duck!" He threw his arm across his mother and braced for impact.

Five seconds passed, and the Hyundai's constant loud hum didn't so much as hiccup. Country music continued to stream from its speakers. He blinked.

No Town Car smoked in the middle of the intersection, and the Cadillac in front of them remained fully intact. The woman inside adjusted her old lady helmet in the mirror.

Allison kept stock-still, her flaring nostrils the only sign of her discomfort.

"I thought I saw a car about to crash into us," he said. "My mistake." He craned his neck to the side, looking over the entire intersection. Not even a single skid mark stained the road.

She rubbed the dark circles of her eyes. "So you hallucinated an accident? Is that a normal occurrence for you?"

He doubted his definition of "normal" matched hers.

"No. Don't worry about it." Despite his denial, he could see from his mother's face she most definitely would.

The light ahead turned green. As they passed through the intersection, he scanned the road for proof of the accident, hoping to find a spare lug nut or strip of rubber. Nothing but heat-baked asphalt appeared. He'd imagined it. Like he'd imagined Alexandra, the twins, the sexy librarian, the murder at the yacht club, and probably even Mai.

Would it really kill his schizophrenia to give him a few weeks' rest?

His mother had the grace not to grill him on the episode, and the two rode in an uncomfortable silence. The tap of his right foot on the floor mat counted the seconds until he returned home and spent the rest of his afternoon in solitude.

Solitude, however, did not await him. Instead, Isaac and his suitcase sat on the front porch. He waved in greeting as they pulled up the driveway.

"Family Advocacy must've cleared him," Liam said.

His mother bit her lip. She'd had a long couple of weeks. Separated from her daughter and husband, monitoring him had become her primary job. And this particular job boasted the benefits of exhaustion and thanklessness.

Isaac opened Allison's car door and bent down to give her a kiss. She moved her face to the right in a deflection maneuver.

"Are you home for good?" she asked.

Romantic efforts rebuffed, Isaac removed his long fingers from the door and backed away from his wife. "Until I'm told otherwise."

Allison stepped out of the car and held her purse in front of her like a faux-leather shield while she made a beeline for the front door.

Damn. She usually reserves that sort of treatment for me. Isaac has some peacock-sized feathers to unruffle.

Liam sent a quick nod in Isaac's direction after closing the passenger door. "Nice to see you back," he said. If his mother wouldn't extend an olive branch, he could at least offer a trite welcome.

"Thanks. I'm happy to be home. I would've waited for you in the house, but I didn't have the new key." He gestured toward the new black hardware. "When did you change the locks?"

Allison ignored the question and pushed open the door. "Your key is on the nightstand in our bedroom. I figured you'd call before coming home so I could make sure to be here."

Isaac grabbed her hand. "You're right. I should've called. These last few weeks have challenged all of us. Let's make tonight enjoyable. We've earned it."

The two locked eyes. Liam studied his shoes in discomfort and pushed past them.

RP galloped toward him and rubbed against his legs in greeting. Grateful for the distraction, he petted the cat's head then made his way to the living room. He sank into the cool leather of the couch and grabbed the TV remote. More than ready for some mindless entertainment, he flipped on the television and allowed RP to settle in his lap. He tuned out Isaac and Allison's conversation near the dining room table.

Nothing interested him, so he settled for the local news. The segment featured a feel-good piece about a Rutherford High School football player's full scholarship to the University of Florida. The kid beamed in his interview, excited about the prospects of his future. Liam tried to remember the feeling.

A blinking red ticker flashed "BREAKING NEWS!" across the screen. The news anchor tapped paperwork on her desk. She said, "Channel Six brings you an exclusive, developing story about a gruesome discovery for some boaters this morning out at Shell Island. A family in search of some relaxing beach time instead found a man's body hidden in the dunes."

He looked over his shoulder at the windows facing the beach. He could see Shell Island from where he sat. It'd be a quick trip from the yacht club to dispose of a body there.

The newscaster continued, "Police have identified the deceased individual as one—"

"Stuart Laughlin." He matched the reporter's words verbatim.

The conversation behind him stopped abruptly. Voice strained, Isaac said, "What? Stuart is dead? How'd you know that, Liam?"

He fought off a wave of nausea. “I heard it on the news earlier,” he lied. The TV blinked to black as he turned it off. He’d heard enough already.

Allison’s shoes clicked across the linoleum. She placed a hand on his shoulder. “You knew the victim?” Her brow furrowed so hard she looked like an eighty-year-old.

“Nah. I remember his name from the news story.” He tried not to fidget.

“I knew him,” Isaac said. He rubbed his close-cropped head with an unsteady hand and joined Allison. “Remember that civilian paralegal I told you about? The guy acting erratically and missing work? His name is Stuart Laughlin.”

Isaac fixed a rock-hard glare at Liam.

Tick, tick, boom.

43

I'm so sorry, Isaac. What terrible news." Allison squeezed Liam's clavicle. "When did you hear about it, honey?"

With the exception of his appointment, they'd been together all day.

"It came on the radio between songs. Don't you remember?"

She blanched. Of course she didn't remember. It hadn't actually occurred.

Isaac didn't take his eyes off Liam. "Stuart missed work today. I rang his cell but never got a call back. I figured he'd come into work tomorrow with some lame excuse, and I'd have to fire him."

"Do you know more about this than you're saying, Liam?" Allison fingered the seam on the couch's shoulder.

"No. How would I?"

She bobbed her head as if agreeing with some internal voice.

Liam's shirt's collar seemed to constrict. He yanked it away from his skin. "I'm going to take a walk, get some fresh air."

"Don't be gone too long," she murmured. She turned and leaned against the mahogany buffet, knocking over his framed tae kwon do portrait. It lay face down on the buffet. She didn't right it.

Cheeks burning with anger, he fled out the front door and jogged to the sidewalk that snaked along Eagle Drive.

The early evening sun beat down on yellow ramblers that lined either side of the street. Brown placards placed in the front lawns declared the inhabitant's rank and name. Once upon a time, he'd known most of his neighbors, on a base not dissimilar to this one. As a child, he'd roam the neighborhood with a pack of kids, hopping from house to house in search of entertainment. He'd loved the constant access to tens of playmates and had considered it the best part of living on base.

Now, he didn't know a single neighbor. Except for the Channers.

Them he knew rather too well.

About half a mile down the road, the sidewalk led to a small parking lot next to a beach access point. By the time he arrived there, his hair had curled into tight red ringlets and perspiration marked his armpits and lower back. He kicked off his flip-flops and walked onto the snowy white beach and inhaled the salty air.

Across the blue waves of the Gulf stood the small barrier island where the unlucky family had found Stuart's body. Shell Island was a lonely place, uninhabited and isolated. While Cull would've been smarter to toss Stuart's body into the ocean, it lacked the panache a Shell Island discovery offered. It also meant Cull wanted Stuart's body found. Why commit a murder if you couldn't flaunt it?

A sailboat crossed the horizon, its sails blackened by the setting sun. Liam reached out to it and squashed the miniature boat between his thumb and forefinger. He waded into the water and drove his toes deep into the sand. From somewhere deep within his mind, Alexandra urged him farther. Although caged by incredibly high doses of medicine, she hid in the folds and conduits of his brain. He resisted her entreaties.

A flock of birds swarmed above him in the dimming light. They dove down to the sea and skimmed above its surface before ascending once again to the sky. A wave crested, speckling the hem of his khaki shorts with sea spray. He bent over and trailed his fingers over the warm water, tickling its surface. The water pulled and swayed under his touch.

He knelt down and plunged his hands into the sand, and he flexed his knuckles in an effort to dig deeper. Though seawater drenched his shirt and shorts, the soothing tug of the current reminded him of his

father, who'd been as steady as the tide, strong and predictable.

Liam flashed back to a favorite childhood memory. They'd attended a Christmas parade, his father, mother, and he. His dad had carried him on his shoulders. A clumsy six-year-old, he'd sloshed a cup of hot chocolate onto his father's uncovered head. Terrified he'd hurt his dad and would get in trouble, his father had surprised him with a slow, rumbling laugh. He'd said, "Thanks for keeping me warm!" and then grasped Liam's mittened hand.

The recollection, and others like it, was all that remained of his father. If he succumbed to schizophrenia, would it disappear? Or would imprints remain of it, like the ones he saw? Would somebody in another time or place see his treasured memories? Were they strong enough to remain after his mind abandoned him?

A wave slapped his face. Salt water stung his eyes and ran down his cheekbones. His body went rigid as understanding blossomed through his mind. He'd been thinking of the memory imprints all wrong, like linear occurrences. But memories weren't linear or orderly. They evolved over time, changing as much as the person who carried them. Memories wove themselves into an endless cycle, where knowing when one moment stopped and the next began was sometimes impossible.

Not all of the imprints Liam had seen were from the past. Some were visions from the future.

He'd seen the murder at the yacht club before it occurred. No sign of a struggle appeared when he'd checked previously because Stuart had been still alive. Blood had yet to be spilled.

The day before, the heavens had unleashed a torrential downpour in the late afternoon. Just like in his vision.

He looked across the waves toward the marina. The evidence would be there now.

There was only one way to find the truth.

He needed to go back.

44

Compacted sand absorbed Liam's footfalls as he ran toward the marina. Dusk wrapped its increasingly heavy cloak over the water and surrounding beach. He had to hurry, or there'd be no light to help him investigate. Before long, Liam's thighs itched with exertion, and his lungs begged for air.

As he neared the dock, he hoped for the first time the yacht club would be busy. A retiree tying up her speedboat or a couple sharing drinks on the club's deck would do the trick.

No such luck. Not a soul joined him at the marina.

He was on his own.

A severe stitch slowed his run to a walk as he traveled the familiar trail to the jetty he once considered a safe place. Instead of following it to its end, he stepped out onto the dock where his vision had occurred.

Cull's sailboat, Freedom, rested in its slip, fifty paces from where he stood. Gently swaying waves slapped its hull.

The oncoming night darkened the weather-beaten dock and hampered his. examination of its surface. But he knew where to look—his memory of the murder hadn't faded one smidge.

A rusty brown spot discolored the wood where Stuart's head had lain after Cull beat him. It formed an abstract hourglass figure, outlining the contours of his face and bashed skull. Liam squatted

down and ran his fingers across the splintering slats.

Cull had really killed Stuart here.

Liam scooted over to the piling and held on as he leaned over the dock. Below it appeared massive, dark stains where rainwater hadn't washed off the blood.

Shuffling from Freedom's deck sent goose bumps racing up his spine.

He swung his head up and jumped to a squat. Fear seared his nerves. He expected to see Cull aboard Freedom, pointing a gun at his head. Dusk, however, skippered the sailboat alone tonight.

His heart beat again as he rose to his feet and tiptoed toward Freedom. Its deck glistened white. He leaned over and sniffed the hull where he'd seen Cull throw Stuart's body. The strong scent of bleach made him cough.

"Can't leave well enough alone, can you, boy?" Cull asked from below deck.

He froze.

From the depths of the sailboat, Cull said, "This is all your fault. Stuart's death. The drop in sales because of increased law enforcement attention. All of it."

A terrible mixture of fear and rage took hold of Liam. His hands shuddered as he inched backward. "You're not real!" he yelled. Cull, and all of the blood, so much blood, was too horrible to be real.

"There's one way to find out. Why don't you join me below deck for a little drink? Let's see how real I am."

Liam swallowed. He placed a hand on the sailboat.

"Keep coming, son. Don't be scared."

"You don't have to play along with your hallucinations, Liam. Make your own decisions," Dr. Jen had advised him.

He ground his teeth, removed his hand, and took two bounding steps away.

"This ain't the right decision. It's gonna cost you. And your family," Cull said.

Liam shivered and ran back to the yacht club, ignoring the stabbing

pain in his side. He spared a final glance at the sailboat once his feet hit the parking lot. Freedom rocked on the waves, her deck devoid of any signs of life.

Five hundred and twelve steps to go and then he'd be home.

Isaac scrutinized Liam as he slouched through the living room. Oblivious of the trail of sand he left in his wake, his stepson shuffled through the house in bare feet. He'd come home without shoes, unaware he'd lost them at some point. His shorts, dark with salt water, clung to his thighs.

Liam's long jaunt to the beach after hearing the news report had been no coincidence. Somehow, he was involved with Stuart's death. Allison knew it too, though she did her best to deny it. She'd put on forties band music in a desperate bid to lift her spirits and busied herself in the kitchen. But no amount of distractions could conceal the truth. Schizophrenia had finally won. They'd lost Liam to his illness.

Though he should've called Security Forces with his suspicions, Isaac didn't. He refused to invite the police into their lives. And as much as he'd like Liam out of his house, he'd hoped for a more positive departure.

The authorities would piece together the evidence soon enough. They didn't need a head start. He gave Liam three or four days before a legal system increasingly terrified of people like him buried him alive. Any hope for a semi-independent future had vanished.

He had failed Liam.

45

FRIDAY, SEPTEMBER 26th

Liam felt like a total creeper, people-watching for hours on end in Isaac's SUV. Despite the sticky heat that long before had forced him to roll down the windows, he wore a black hoodie, slouching under its protection. Sweat dripped down his temples.

Not allowed to drive since the "incident" with Tasha, he'd sneaked out of the house in the early morning hours and taken Isaac's vehicle. He hated to inconvenience his mother, but he'd needed to leave. He'd spent a sleepless night debating whether he'd seen a premonition of Stuart's murder or merely created a complex delusion he alone could resolve. The latter option reflected textbook schizophrenic behavior. The former was difficult to believe, even for him.

If he had any hope of untangling his mind, he needed to bounce his new theory off somebody who wouldn't immediately chalk up his visions to mental illness. His diagnosis colored everybody's perception of him. Everybody, that is, except for one person.

Mai.

So here he sat, waiting by the community college library, watching fresh-faced students parading in and out of its silver doors. Mai hadn't showed. A number of reasons could explain her absence. Maybe she felt sick. Maybe she avoided the library because it reminded her of his freaky visions. Maybe she'd already come and gone.

Or, maybe she'd never existed in the first place.

Liam slumped over the steering wheel and glanced at his watch. Ten-fifty a.m.

A group of women walked up the sidewalk to the library. They wore the typical Florida student uniform, tank tops and indecently short shorts with flip-flops. He craned his neck to get a better view.

None of them was Mai.

The late morning heat roasted the car's interior. He pushed back in his seat and placed the key in the ignition. Time to leave. It'd been a fool's errand, coming here and thinking Mai existed. He turned the key and placed his hand on the gearshift when a harsh knock on the car door startled him. Yelping, he hopped up an inch and raised both hands to his chest in a defensive posture.

"Not a very manly sound, Liam. I'd even classify it as a little girl scream," Mai said. She leaned into the car, and her arms rested on the open window. Her typically bright eyes had lost their gleam. Dark bags lined her eye sockets.

"You know this is weird, even for troubled white boys, right?" She nodded at his sweat drenched black hoodie.

His breath caught, and the world stopped for one beautiful second. Mai was real. When he could manage forming words, he said, "I sort of specialize in weird."

"That you do." She reached down, unlocked the passenger side door, and opened it. Then she hopped into the SUV and pumped the A/C to high. The vents blasted mildew-tinged cold air through her short hair.

"This your stepdad's car?" she asked. She looked at the dashboard and not him.

"Yeah. I borrowed it for the day." The SUV started quieter than the Hyundai and wouldn't awaken his family.

"So where have you holed up these past few weeks?" She shot him a look from the corner of her eye one could almost interpret as hurt. "You had me worried, what with a murderer chasing after you and all. I haven't slept through the night since you went missing."

"I had some family issues to sort through."

She barked out a laugh. "We've all got family issues. But most of us still call our friends and attend, or at least pretend to attend, classes while we work our way through them."

He reached out a tentative hand toward her and placed it lightly on her forearm.

"You're right. I'm sorry. I should've called or texted. I got so wrapped up in my own mind I lost touch for a while." He tried to keep a straight face. He didn't exactly lie. More like told the understatement of the year.

She held his gaze for a long moment before breaking it. She folded her arms tightly, and pulling away from his touch, stared out the open window.

"Don't do it again, okay? Thanh would kill me if she knew I was even speaking with you."

He gulped back any further excuses and nodded.

"So why did you come back?" She continued to avoid eye contact.

"Other than to see you?"

She rolled her eyes, but the corners of her mouth tugged up slightly.

"I'm in over my head with this whole imprint thing. I need your help."

Her head whipped around to face his. He had her attention now. "Did you see a new one?" she asked.

"Did you watch the news yesterday?"

Her eyes widened. "The man found on Shell Island?"

"He's the man I saw murdered." The hoodie's strings tangled in his fingers.

"But isn't this what we wanted? The police have a body now. They'll have to believe you." She sat up straight and tapped the dashboard with her pointer finger.

"Not likely. I still don't have any proof. There's also the little problem of elapsed time between my vision and Stuart's death."

"What do you mean?"

"I saw Cull kill Stuart a month ago. He just went missing from work yesterday."

Her finger stopped tapping. "So what're you saying? You couldn't have seen the murder?"

He rubbed the steering wheel. "I'm saying I saw the murder before it happened."

"What? You saw the future?" Mai's eyebrows knit together so closely they almost formed a unibrow.

"I know it's hard to believe, but nothing else makes sense." He tugged on his hair, still damp with perspiration.

She slumped in her seat. "Well… that puts a new spin on the situation."

"There's more. The murderer knows I know. He also knows where I live. I think he might be coming after me." Liam sucked in his breath after this latest revelation. Would she see through it and know how insane he was?

She did not.

"Then you need to get him arrested. You've got to contact the police," she said.

"We've discussed this. They won't believe me."

"Ugh! Why does this have to be hard?" She pounded her fist on the armrest. "The only option left is to run."

Liam clutched his stomach as a spasm of pain ricocheted through it. Deep down, he agreed with her. He had to leave Florida. His absence would be better for everybody. For his mother, for Tasha, for Mai. Much as he hated to leave any of them, the idea of losing his psychologist terrified him. He'd never find another therapist as perfect as Dr. Jen. She tethered him to reality and helped keep him sane.

Mai concentrated on her perfectly pedicured feet. "I'll help you. We can leave tonight. I'll stay with you for a few weeks until you get situated."

His breath hitched. "You believe me so much you'd pause your whole life and run away with me? You don't think I'm living in a fantasy world?"

"Of course not." She looked up. "You're my friend, and I promised I wouldn't abandon you. I keep my promises."

He fought to keep from blinking. If he did, Mai might disappear. He'd scarcely allowed himself to believe she was real, much less that she'd sacrifice her happy and organized life to be with him.

Grateful didn't seem a large enough word to encapsulate his emotions. His pulse raced and his arms shook as he leaned toward her face. Would her lips still feel the way he remembered?

A harsh snicker threw cold water on their heat, and his lips froze mere centimeters from hers.

"So you thought you'd show up and pretend like the last few weeks didn't happen, huh?" His car window framed a daffodil-yellow sundress suspended off bony shoulders.

Thanh had found them. She raised tortoise-shell sunglasses to give him a better look at the scorn in her eyes.

His face dropped. "I'm sorry. I told Mai I'm sorry, too. I messed up."

Thanh ignored him and glowered at Mai. "How can you forgive him for dropping you like a bad habit? All the texts and calls he ignored? You worried about him for weeks. He doesn't deserve you."

"I make my own decisions." Mai tilted up her chin. "I don't need you bullying me about who I choose to see."

Thanh's face reddened. She stepped away from the car and flung her hands in the air. "You'll see soon enough, Mai. Liam is bad for you. He'll only bring you misery. I can't support your choice to be with him. I'll be waiting for you when he screws up again. I suspect that'll be sooner rather than later." Her long, black hair swung as she turned and stomped away.

Liam and Mai sat in silence before he extended his hand toward her face, stopping short of caressing her lips.

"Thanh's right. No good will come of this. You can't throw away your life for me." He bit the inside of his lip, hoping he didn't convince her of her stupidity.

"So now you're going to tell me what I can do?" Her eyes blazed with anger.

"I wouldn't dream of it. It's just... you don't know the whole story. Some sides of me can be tough to handle."

"This is news how?"

He swallowed hard. "My condition is more serious than it looks."

She clasped his hand and pulled it to her cheek. Her soft skin rested in his palm.

"I think I've got an elementary understanding of what I'm getting myself into. And don't get ahead of yourself. Remember, I'm just going with you for a couple of weeks. I'm coming back to finish up my degree."

He knew better than to accept her offer. She had no idea how much life could change in a short period of time, nor did she understand the difficulties facing them. What she probably considered "quirks" would devolve into full-blown obsessions once she understood their depths. But by the time she discovered what kind of man he really was, it would be too late. She'd be fully committed.

"Don't say I didn't warn you," he said.

She smiled, sorrow and hope and love all wrapped up into one expression. She closed the space between them and kissed him. His lips trembled with hesitation, but Mai traced his jawline with her fingertips, and his uncertainty melted under the heat of anticipation. Wishing he could lose his mind to Mai's wiles and not mental illness, he pulled away.

"Take the day to get your stuff together. We'll meet tonight at 4:00 a.m. in the parking lot of the buffet restaurant off Magnolia Avenue. I trust you know the place?"

"You know I do." She winked at him and reached for the door handle. "You're worth it, Liam Murphy."

Guilt consumed him as she walked away. She couldn't nurse him back to health with affection and positive thinking. Others had tried and failed.

She didn't know it yet, but she'd just taken her future and massacred it.

46

On the drive back to Tyndall, Liam focused on the positives. This time tomorrow morning, he'd be out of Isaac's house and independent again. No longer would Tasha and his mother be held captive to his mental state. Most importantly, the vision he'd had of Cull strangling Tasha wouldn't happen now. With him gone, Cull would have no reason to hurt her.

Sunlight glinted off the silver trunk of the car in front of him, blinding him with its glare. He rummaged around the console for his sunglasses and shoved them on. Ten-dollar specials from a gas station, he'd scratched up the lens the day after buying them. He'd meant to replace them a hundred times but never remembered their flaws until he placed them on his face. They'd have to do. Cheap shades or not, they'd keep him from squinting for the next hour.

Sun-drenched shopping centers filled with generic box stores flashed by as he settled into his drive. In twelve short hours, he'd be gone.

If he'd paid closer attention, and hadn't thought about Mai or Cull or how to keep his medication refilled while on the run, he would've noticed that just before the upcoming intersection sat a florist shop with an orange cat curled by its front door. In its door hung a sign proclaiming, "Homecoming Specials!"

Instead, he drove through the intersection obsessing about a particularly conspicuous scratch on his sunglasses, totally unprepared for the savage punch that jerked his head to the left. The seatbelt bit into his chest as his car twisted through the intersection and smashed into a Jeep waiting at a red light.

Save for his rapid heartbeat, sound disappeared. Liam stared straight ahead, shock slowing his reaction time. The absurd idea that a giant had stepped down and clipped the car, smashing all its parts and pieces to shrapnel, flittered across his brain. Then his senses returned, and he realized he'd been in an accident. Isaac's ruined SUV faced the middle of the intersection, where smoke rose from a Town Car's crumpled hood in alarming black tendrils.

He turned, head and neck aching from whiplash, and inspected the rear of his car. A mess of metal, shattered glass, and upholstery had replaced the backseat. Only the driver's seat had escaped unscathed.

Damn.

47

The young policeman tipped his stiff trooper hat in agitation. He wore a scraggly mustache that Liam's neglected stubble put to shame. His golden nametag "King" shined with exquisite care. The initial swarm of police cruisers, ambulances, and fire trucks responding to the accident had now died down to Officer King's sedan. The other emergency vehicles had trickled away once they discovered there'd been no significant injuries in the accident.

"You're sure you didn't run the light, sir?" Officer King asked.

"Positive," said Liam.

He wasn't, really. The seconds preceding the accident blurred into fuzzy and indistinct memories. Besides his preoccupation with the sunglasses, he'd been on autopilot, thinking more about 4:00 a.m. than the road in front of him.

But it helped he'd seen the accident, albeit a day prior and from a different vantage point. An elderly woman had run her Lincoln Town Car through a red light and crashed into the side of Isaac's SUV, which had spun out of control and into a Jeep.

The policeman shifted from foot to foot. Long ago, he'd excused the other drivers from their interviews. Liam bet neither one of them had a felony charge on their records for attempted armed robbery.

Officer King wanted to pin the accident on him. He could sense something off about Liam. But disappointment visits everybody, and today it called on the officer.

"May I leave? My mother's waited over an hour for me." Liam pointed to a beige sports car. Unfortunately, it belonged to Mrs. Channer. Allison sat inside with the windows rolled down and her left arm hanging out.

Officer King flipped through his notebook and scrutinized each account, looking for a deviation that would allow him to place the blame on Liam. He clicked his boot heel on the pavement and snapped the notebook shut. "You're free to go. However, we'll contact you if and when any new evidence comes to light."

I'm sure you will.

Liam smiled broadly at the policeman. Officer King's mouth tightened, but he didn't care. He'd be gone in less than a day. Let the cop hate him as much as he liked.

The door to Mrs. Channer's car burned his fingertips as he swung it open. His mother had parked under direct sunlight while waiting for him in the miserably hot afternoon.

He poked his head in the stifling automobile. "Why are you driving Mrs. Channer's car?"

"Why were you driving Isaac's?" Allison countered, her tone hard and angry.

The smell of baby powder wafted in Liam's face as he lowered into the passenger's seat. A scented car freshener in the shape of a tree dangled from the rearview mirror. He flicked it with his fingers. "I'm sorry. I wanted to visit a friend."

She shifted the gear into drive and rolled out of the parking lot. "Does this 'friend' have anything to do with Stuart Laughlin?"

Shamed by his mother's suspicions, he jutted out his jaw. "No."

She rubbed bloodshot eyes and sighed. "Why did you have to pick today, of all days, to sneak out and wreck the car, Liam? Why isn't life ever easy with you? Can't I get one bit of bad news at a time?"

His heart skipped a beat. "What happened? Is Tasha okay?"

Tears ran down her face. "Tasha's fine, but Grandpa had a stroke last night. Your sister has to come home. Grammy can't take care of her since she'll be spending all her time at the hospital." Silent sobs shook her shoulders.

He'd loved his grandparents once. Part of him still did. But the intervening years and their neglect had watered down the emotion.

He struggled to find the proper response and settled for a lame, "I'm sorry."

A car full of teenage guys drove parallel to them, staring at Allison with faces full of genuine dismay at her sorrow. One shot Liam the stink eye, assuming he'd caused her grief. Most of the time, the kid would be right. But not today. At least, not completely. Liam flipped him off.

After a few miles, Allison got ahold of herself. She wiped away her tears and sniffed. "Don't think Grandpa's illness gets you out of trouble. What was the hold up back there? Why did the policeman repeatedly interview you?"

He ran a hand through his hair, slicing his fingers on tiny shards of glass still embedded in his red curls. "Because he had access to my records. He looked for a reason, any reason, to put me behind bars again."

"Are you telling me the truth?"

"What do you mean?"

She kept her eyes on the road in front of her. "Did you really think I wouldn't remember you hallucinated about a car accident at that exact intersection yesterday?"

A flutter of hope surged in his chest. His mother was beginning to understand.

She said, "At first, I wanted to know how you set up the accident. Then I wanted to know why. To fulfill some sick vision you had? You put other people's lives in danger to explain away your fantasies?" An expression of revulsion crossed her face.

The flutter died, replaced with a thud.

"Are you kidding me?" He turned his head to look at her and immediately regretted it. His neck muscles and ligaments, tender because of the accident, screamed at him. "You think I made an accident happen to justify a delusion?"

She shut off the radio with a quick jab of her thumb. "What other explanation is there, Liam? It's too much of a coincidence."

"You wouldn't believe me if I told you."

"Try me."

He kept his mouth shut. No matter what she might say, she'd never give him the benefit of the doubt. Besides, he didn't feel comfortable discussing his secret skill in Mrs. Channer's car. She probably had it bugged. For all he knew, the tacky tree air freshener could be where she'd hidden her recording device.

Allison, though, held no qualms about discussing family matters in the Channer's car. "If you worked as hard on real-life issues as you do with your delusions, you'd be the most successful man on the planet. Instead, you've totaled Isaac's car, leaving us with one vehicle. Since Isaac drove to pick up Tasha, I had to borrow Sara's car to pick you up."

Love you, too, Mom.

Despite her patronizing and infuriating comment, he took advantage of the turn in the conversation. "When are Isaac and Tasha getting home?"

"Early this evening." She tugged on her ponytail.

He designed imaginary patterns on his shorts and tried not to look relieved. He could still escape tonight. The Hyundai would be back in plenty of time for his exit. He'd face a challenge guarding Tasha against Cull for the rest of the day, but he could do it. He had to. And once he left the house, his family would be safe. "I know you're worried about me living in the same house as Tasha, but you won't need to for much longer."

"Don't I, though? You just proved I can't trust you. How am I supposed to let you near your sister?"

"I told you. It's not going to be an issue."

She narrowed her eyes. "What do you mean? What are you planning?"

"You're not the only family I've got." He twiddled his thumbs. "I can live with other relatives. Like Dad's brother, Pete."

Her mouth dropped open. "What?"

"Yeah, after Dad died, Uncle Pete said I could stay with him if I ever needed to."

Doubt and relief dueled for dominance on her face. "How come you never mentioned this?"

Because he hadn't actually talked to his Uncle Pete in years. The man hated him more than Isaac did. He correctly blamed Liam for ruining his father's life and driving his health into the ground.

"I didn't think I needed to. I thought our arrangement would work." He tapped his foot on the floorboard.

They drove the next few miles without speaking. If Liam knew his mother, she was weighing all of her options. She didn't know how to live with both Tasha and him under the same roof. He didn't blame her. He'd yet to figure that out either.

The car shuddered over a pothole. She placed a light hand on his knee. "You know I love you, right? I want you to be in my life. You're not a burden. You're my son."

He leaned his head against the window. "Easy to say when I offered you a chance to ship me away. When you'll be free of me. Like before Dad died."

Her voice cracked. "You think I don't want you near me?"

"Don't lie. You want a normal life. 'Normal' doesn't happen with me." The words burned his tongue like acid.

"I need you to really hear me, Liam. Are you listening?" She thumped his knee for emphasis.

"All the time."

"I'm sorry. For many, many mistakes. But mostly for making you feel unwanted. I never wanted to spend a day apart from you. But your father and I had very different ideas of how to treat your illness." She paused. "Do you remember how he used to play along with your hallucinations?"

Liam remembered.

"Sean thought he could bring you back to reality if he lived in the same world you did. I didn't think that strategy helped either of you. At some point, your father came to the same conclusion. But, by then, we didn't trust each other." She moved her hand from his knee and flexed it before gripping the steering wheel. "Your dad claimed you'd be happier with him and wouldn't hear of me retaining custody. And despite whatever mistakes he made in the beginning, I can't deny Sean was always the better parent. No matter how hard I tried, I never had the connection you two did. So I let you go."

The dark water of Bonita Bay swirled below as they crossed DuPont Bridge. Liam's throat ached with an unreleased sob. "I understand. It's difficult to be around me."

"Having schizophrenia doesn't give you a monopoly on being difficult. All proper Murphys are challenging." She gave him a half smile. "You're my son. I'll always love you. No matter what you've done." Her smile withered.

His hand tightened around the passenger seat. The foul stench of unneeded forgiveness flooded his nostrils. He hadn't purposefully caused any accidents, nor had he killed anyone.

"So you agree I need to leave?" he said.

She sent him a sidelong glance. "Are you sure you want to live with your uncle?"

"Absolutely."

"We'll have to talk with your probation officer and see if this is even an option." Allison sighed. "I wish it didn't have to be this way."

"You and me both."

48

Mrs. Channer hid behind the pink hibiscus bush she fretted over daily and lifted her left hand in a mechanical wave as Allison pulled into her driveway. Her meticulously flattened hair defied all laws of humidity and descended down her skull without a single strand springing out of place. A flesh-colored sling covered her right arm.

"What happened to her?" Liam asked.

"A few weeks back she had a freak accident while gardening. Apparently, she fainted in the afternoon heat. She fractured her elbow and got a concussion from the fall."

"Huh."

His mother shot him a concerned look. "Don't mention her injuries. The whole episode really upset her."

I bet.

The door to Mrs. Channer's sports car opened without a sound. She kept the hinges well-oiled.

Allison said, "Sara, thank you so much for letting me borrow your car. Sorry it took longer than I expected." The keys swung from her hands, clanging against each other like wind chimes.

"I'm always happy to help," Mrs. Channer said. She clasped both the keys and his mother's hand. Bright red lipstick bled past her lips into the tiny cracks and wrinkles around her mouth. The corners of

Allison's mouth started to pull down like gravity had suddenly become too hard to fight. Then she matched Mrs. Channer's fake smile with one of her own.

Liam kept his eyes on Mrs. Channer as he edged out of the car and crossed the street, trudging up the slight incline of Isaac's driveway. Though he now intellectually understood the woman wasn't a replica, he still distrusted her. Old habits were murder to kick.

The scent of pot roast filled the house. His mother must've thrown it in the crockpot this morning. No minor crisis would catch her off guard.

Cheerful meows resonated from the hallway, followed by a blur of dark fur. RP wrapped his tail around Liam's calf and rubbed against him.

"I'm gonna miss you." Liam scratched RP under his ears. He'd love to squirrel the animal away with him tonight, but he couldn't think of a practical, quiet way to do so.

"You could've thanked Sara," Allison said. She clicked the door shut and leaned against it.

"I could've. But let's not talk about Mrs. Channer right now. I've got a crazy idea instead."

Allison arched her eyebrows. "I'm all ears."

"For one evening, let's pretend we're happy. No calling probation officers, no arguing. We'll return to our routine in the morning. Tonight, let's be a regular family. For Tasha."

"No." His mother shook her head. "Not just for Tasha. For all of us." She circled the air with her pointer finger.

He rested against the wall. "Dinner followed by a board game?"

A white halo appeared around Allison, who stared at him with an unreadable expression. He cringed, anticipating seeing his younger, saner self.

But this time was different.

The white shield surrounding her grew and grew until it became larger than any other projection he'd seen. It morphed into four separate images; Isaac, Tasha, his mother, and him. They sat around a table, laughing and talking like a healthy family would.

So she did love him. Or at least a fantasized version of him. If his mother longed for one stress-free evening with her family, he'd give it to her. She deserved a night of happiness before he fled.

A menacing growl from RP scattered Allison's projection. The cat hunched down and lurked toward the back door, hissing all the while. Liam stiffened, expecting the air to warm with Alexandra's return, but the temperature stayed at its relegated seventy-eight degrees. Joshua didn't appear, either.

Concerned less by RP hunting prey than by the fact he couldn't see the prey, Liam walked hesitantly toward the door. Had Cull already come for him?

Allison smirked at the gray and black demon pawing at the door. "Our cat has issues."

Hand outstretched and ready to turn the doorknob, Liam froze. His fears could wait their turn. Tonight, his family came first. He pulled his hand back and jammed it in his pocket. "Yeah, he fits right in."

Allison pursed her lips and then burst into laughter, howling so hard she had to hang on to a dining room chair to keep from falling. Unsure whether he should be amused or insulted, he stood silent.

"Sorry. That wasn't even funny," Allison said. After she patted her eyes dry, she covered her mouth and unsuccessfully fought another round of giggles.

He pivoted to amused. He'd had enough serious to fill a few lifetimes. "Oh, I've seen funny. It's not all it's cracked up to be." He tapped his head.

She sank to her knees, cackling like a possessed woman. After weeks of unrelenting solemnity, his mother's release of pent-up emotions was contagious. He let a small chuckle escape from his lips. He'd forgotten about moments like this; moments where all his concerns and worries didn't matter. Moments where he could actually laugh at himself. It somehow made his problems more bearable. He let his emotional wall down with an abandon he didn't know possible and soon laughed louder than his mother. Unaccustomed to such a workout, the muscles in his lower abdomen ached, and he collapsed onto the coach. The pair roared so loud they didn't hear the car pull into the driveway or the voices outside until the front door creaked open.

Isaac stood at the threshold, eyes hidden behind heavily tinted aviator sunglasses. He held his hand over Tasha's face and shielded her. "Allison?" His shoulders leaned forward, ready to bolt across the room if needed.

"Momma!" Tasha yelled. She shoved aside Isaac's protective arm and sprinted full force toward her mother. She ran into Allison's open arms, and the two hugged.

"Baby girl, I'm so happy you're home!" Allison ran her fingers over Tasha's soft cheeks.

"Me, too. What'd I miss? What's so funny?"

"I am," said Liam. He popped up from the couch.

"Liam!" Tasha screamed with delight. She plowed into her older brother and sank her head into his chest. "I've missed you so, so much!"

"Missed you, too." He wished he had longer than one afternoon to share with her.

"Where's my SUV?" Isaac asked. A muscle in his jaw twitched.

"I got T-boned by another vehicle. I'm sorry, but your SUV is a goner." Liam shrugged and pretended like he hadn't stolen the car.

Isaac's boots squeaked on the linoleum floor as he shuffled his feet. One eyebrow shot up his forehead, arched like a cat preparing for battle.

"Mom and I had a productive conversation on the way home. We've got a plan in place," Liam said.

"Does this plan include you buying me a new car?" Isaac's fists tensed. If the SUV had been a person, it'd have fallen third in line for people he loved most in this world.

Cheeks still red from laughing, Allison walked over to Isaac and laid her hand on his arm. "Let's talk about it in the morning, okay?"

His features softened. "Okay."

Liam didn't have to tap into his paranormal abilities to predict that their morning conversation would suck. If one stolen car angered Isaac this much, he'd be livid when the second one disappeared. Thankfully,

Liam would be long gone by then. And even if Allison and Isaac didn't fully appreciate his scheme tomorrow, at some point they would.

He would take their car, but give them freedom.

49

Tasha bounded around the house the rest of the afternoon, overjoyed to be home. Clad in a lavender leotard and pale pink tutu, she pointed a glittery baton at furniture in the living room and pretended to turn each piece into a unicorn or Pegasus or some other equally sparkly creature.

"You must have an entire stable at this point, Tasha. What are you going to do with all these animals?" Liam asked. He wore an aged and cracking crown that at one point colorful plastic rhinestones had adorned. Now only faded glue spots remained. Tasha had dubbed him "Prince Liam of Tyndall."

Fingers placed to her lips, she tiptoed near the kitchen and cocked her ear to the side. The murmur of her parents deep in conversation floated across the air. She skipped back over to Liam. She whispered, "Sissy likes animals. I like to keep her happy."

Ice gripped his soul.

"Did Sissy go with you to Grammy and Grandpa's?" he asked.

"Yep. Lucky for me. Grammy and Grandpa are nice, but they are ooold and boring. Sissy is never boring. See, she's riding a unicorn right now. She's gonna run into the table!" Tasha giggled.

He tried not to vomit.

Sissy was a perfectly rational response to Tasha's situation. Forced to leave her parents and move someplace new, his sister had taken along an imaginary friend. Lots of kids her age would react the same way. It didn't mean she'd develop a mental illness.

RP batted a paw at the dining room table and growled. He arched his back and hissed as the smell of leather and cigarette smoke wafted through the air.

"Well, this is certainly a turn for the worse," Joshua said. He placed his elbow on Liam's shoulder and leaned on him. "Seems you've rubbed off on your sister more than strictly necessary."

He shook off Joshua's touch.

"Easy there, killer. We haven't chatted in a while. You could be more civil."

RP set his green feline eyes on Joshua and swished his tail.

Joshua lowered the cigarette from his mouth, and he blew smoke circles that expanded until they surrounded Liam's head like a hazy halo. "I do have to thank Tasha for bringing in a distraction. That little devil hasn't let me rest in weeks." He pointed his right hand at the cat and cocked it like a gun. "Boom."

Hackles raised, RP crouched.

The tips of Joshua's scraggly fingernails grabbed Liam's cheek and pinched hard, piercing his skin. "I'm glad you're leaving this house. I'll be free to roam wherever you settle next without him constantly harassing me."

RP sprang forward one second too late—Joshua had already evaporated. Miffed he'd missed his prey, the cat prowled around Liam's feet and sniffed the air.

Knuckles pressed over his injured cheek, Liam reconsidered his earlier resolve to stay indoors. The probability that Cull skulked nearby frightened him to the core. He'd wanted to keep Tasha as far as possible from the murderer. Now, though, he had to also consider Joshua. Ever since the incident with Camila, Joshua'd become more ballsy. He wouldn't harm Tasha, but he'd do his best to ruin the evening. And Liam *would* give his family a good memory. Besides, with Isaac watching him closer than an overanxious helicopter parent, Cull wouldn't dare show.

"Wanna go outside?" Liam asked Tasha. "I hear hundreds of

unicorns stomping around the backyard."

She jumped up with a squeal. "Yes!" Her tutu fluttered against her short legs as she ran into the kitchen and tugged on Allison's shirt. "Liam and I are going to play in the backyard."

Isaac raised a hand to object, but Allison placed her palm on his chest and shook her head.

"Okay. But stay where I can see you," she said.

Disapproval oozed out of Isaac's pores as Tasha ran out the back door. "Is this really a wise decision?" he asked.

I certainly hope so.

"You can watch us the whole time out the window. She'll be fine," said Liam.

"If she so much as trips and skins her knee, you'll regret it." Isaac's lips closed tighter than a bank vault.

"Roger that," Liam said. He flung open the screen door and pranced over to his sister like he rode a horse and tried to remember Isaac's distrust would keep Tasha safe.

"They're everywhere, Liam! Great idea!" Tasha skipped around the yard, pigtails bobbing up and down with each step, swinging her baton like a band director.

The yacht club's bell tolled in the distance, and a burst of wind rocked the empty porch swing. Liam played along with Tasha, ignoring the itch on the back of his neck, and collided with imaginary unicorns until he couldn't catch his breath. Panting, he settled on the swing. He called out, "His Royal Highness requires a nap."

"I'll gather up the animals!" she shouted.

He smiled at her joy. He'd made the right call coming out here. If Cull watched from afar, then he saw Isaac's overbearing presence behind the windows, scrutinizing every step his daughter took. No way would he risk showing his ugly face. Nor would Liam worry over whether Tasha acted out the ideas of an imaginative child or displayed early-onset symptoms. She was happy. Nothing else mattered.

The hunt for mythical creatures led Tasha so far into the backyard she soon danced in the grove of live oaks. She leaned against the thick trunk of a tree that resembled an ogre with six massive arms webbing into thinner branches as they reached the sky. It cradled Tasha in its monstrous, magical embrace and would've made the perfect memory snapshot if not for the hand above her head.

Liam sat up bolt straight and rubbed his eyes. The hand, so taut he could see its blue, bulging veins even from where he sat, remained. Except now it moved closer to her small head.

He'd been dead wrong. Cull was here, Isaac as sentinel or not. Cull had promised to harm Liam if he talked to anybody. And harming Tasha would bring him the worst pain imaginable. The swing rocked violently as he leapt out of it.

"Tasha!" Blood thrummed in his ears as he sprinted forward.

She thought it all part of the game and clapped her hands together in delight. "Are you coming to rescue me?"

"Yes! But you have to run to me!"

Cull's hand inched closer to her. A few more centimeters and his fingers could grasp the spiral curls of her pigtails.

"Nope," she said, "you come to me." She patted down her tutu and readied herself to be rescued.

Cull's hand slid farther down the tree to behind her ear. It reached for her neck.

He wouldn't make it in time. Cull's hand would crush his sister's fragile neck.

The back door swung open behind him. Isaac yelled, "Tasha!"

All pleasure on her face trickled away at the tone of her father's voice.

In a blink, Cull's hand vanished. Liam didn't slow his pace until he reached her.

"What's the matter?" Her lower lip trembled.

He raced behind the tree, but nothing other than the heavy evening air greeted him.

Isaac sped across the backyard and made his way to the tree in half the amount of time it'd taken Liam. He pulled Tasha close and shot Liam a murderous look. "What were you doing?"

"Rescuing Tasha." He crossed his arms across his heaving chest.

"We were playing, Daddy," she said. "Don't worry. I'm not really in danger."

"Of course you're not. I'll never let anything bad happen to you again." Isaac's eyes bored into Liam's. "Time to go inside and eat. Mom's made a feast." He hoisted Tasha above his shoulders.

Belly full of giggles once again, Tasha commanded her father forward with a wave of her baton. Left alone by the tree, Liam ran his hand up and down the bark, looking for any signs that proved Cull had been there.

None existed. No footprints other than Tasha's and his, no cigarette stubs. Nothing but his imagination.

50

The atmosphere during dinner fell far short of Allison's projection. Though she and Tasha smiled and laughed, both men stayed on edge. Isaac sat rigid and quiet while Liam stewed about the near miss with Tasha. His desire to leave his family with a happy memory had trumped his sister's safety. He'd never make that mistake again. So what if Cull hadn't actually been there? He *could* have been. And that's what mattered. The lapse in judgment added one more brick of evidence to an already tall tower of mistakes proving he needed to leave.

Between bouts of mentally berating himself, he obsessed over the imaginary hand and what it meant. If he doubted the hand's existence, other, more troubling questions arose. Was Cull even real? Or was he about to ruin the next few weeks of Mai's life because of a dark fantasy?

"Thank you for a 'licious dinner!" Tasha rubbed her stomach and wiped her mouth with a napkin. Traces of ketchup stained her cheeks. "Time for some more fun. I'll pick out our board game!"

She squeezed Liam's neck in a tight embrace, then disappeared into the guest room. Without her presence, the underlying tension in the dining room rose to the surface like an inflamed blister. Untouched peas and carrots rolled together on Liam's plate as he picked it up and cleared the table, anxious to put some space between him and his stepfather.

His plan fell flat as Isaac pushed out from the table. He said, "I'll help you."

"Super. I hoped you'd offer."

"Fantastic. Because you and I are going to be attached at the hip all night. Wherever you go, so do I." Condensation from Isaac's clear glass dripped onto the table as he lifted it and gestured toward the kitchen. "After you."

Allison touched Liam's arm. "I'm sure you understand our concern. It's not that we don't trust you, it's just..."

"You don't trust me. I may have a hard time with reality, but that's one concept I understand with perfect clarity. It's why I'm moving in with Uncle Pete, remember?"

Liam kicked in his chair and walked into the kitchen. True to his word, Isaac followed close on his heels. The men bumped shoulders as they rinsed off their dishes and placed them in the dishwasher.

Tasha skipped into the room with a crisp, new box of Trouble and shoved it into Liam's hands.

"Ready to get beat up?" she asked. She held up a small fist and pumped it menacingly.

"It's just 'get beat'," Isaac corrected. Silverware clinked in his hands as he rinsed the dishes Allison had brought him.

Tasha shrugged as if to say, "What does the old man know?"

A smile inched up Liam's face, and he snapped a dish towel in the air. "You think you're gonna win this game? I'm the king of Trouble."

"Nah-uh. Mommy will be on my team. She always wins."

Allison flexed her biceps and acted like the past two minutes hadn't occurred. "Tasha's right. I play a mean board game. Girls versus boys," she said. She winked at her daughter.

Isaac slammed shut a cupboard, rattling the glasses inside.

"Umm, let's have three teams," said Liam. Up until the little flap about Isaac following him everywhere, the evening had gone relatively well. He had no intention of further tarnishing it by arguing with his stepdad about a game.

"Scared?" Tasha taunted. She placed a small hand on her hip, burying it in her fluffy tutu.

All the time.

"You asked for it," he said.

Once he and Isaac finished the dishes, the family sat again at the table. In all the months he'd lived here, the four had never before come together for an activity other than a meal. A casual observer might think it represented a new beginning. He knew better. Allison allowed the moment because she didn't have to repeat it.

Pretending for one night was easy.

The game of Trouble commenced with Tasha popping a six on the die. She hooted with excitement and moved her yellow piece onto the board. She popped the die again and got another six. Her small foot stomped his under the table, and she sneaked a surreptitious glance at him. "Sissy," she mouthed. Her eyes darted to the right.

Before he could suggest letting his mother pop the die, Tasha slammed it again. Another six.

"Girl's got the magic touch," said Isaac. He grinned, most likely relieved to be rushing through the game.

Tasha popped four more sixes.

The wrinkles on Isaac's forehead deepened with each successive six. His relief must've morphed into the same uneasiness Liam felt.

Join the fun, daddy-o.

"The popper must be broken," said Allison. She tapped it with her fingernail like she could unjinx the game with a mere touch.

Liam had to hand it to Sissy—she'd certainly introduced herself to the family in a blaze of glory. Brazen bitch. Although Allison and Isaac couldn't consciously understand their discomfort, he'd wager the same prickles running down his spine also ran down theirs. For the first time ever, he wished he could see a hallucination. Then maybe he could scare her away.

Delighted, Tasha continued to pop sixes until she'd ushered the last of her pieces into the safe zone. She said, "It's a Trouble miracle!"

Indeed. She'd run the board in a single turn. In celebration of her achievement, she hopped off her chair and twirled around the family room.

Liam stared at the board game like it might start levitating. On impulse, he popped the die. It spun on its side and landed with a single dot facing up.

Isaac picked up the board and shoved it back in its box.

The setting sun framed Allison's silhouette a russet red as she leaned back. "What an incredible game. We should have a rematch to see if Tasha can continue her streak," she said.

Isaac looked as though Allison had said he'd won a year's worth of cyanide.

"Maybe tomorrow," Liam said.

She tilted her head a fraction to the right in disappointment. Her slight movement allowed him to see who hid by the live oaks.

A tall man stood in front of the ogre tree Tasha had leaned against earlier in the day. His shoulders stooped, and abnormally long, muscular arms hung from his side. Cull.

He really was coming for them. Tonight.

Heart lodged in his throat, Liam raced to the back door and cut on the porch floodlight. Moths swarmed around it and concealed Cull as he slinked back into the inky night.

Isaac joined Liam at the doorway and scrutinized him more than the backyard. "What has you so jittery?"

"Heard a noise," he mumbled. Though he didn't like being the only one on guard against the killer, Isaac would never believe him. Drained from the day's emotions, he sat back down at the dining room table and resisted the urge to hunt for Cull in the backyard.

"Time to get ready for bed, baby girl," said Isaac.

"Race you to the bathroom. Last one there's a rotten egg!" Tasha ran flat out to the hallway, determined to beat her father there.

With a flick of his wrist, Isaac shut off the porch light. "Want to help me put Tasha to bed?" he asked Allison.

"Of course." She rose and took her husband's hand.

"You'll be okay out here?" Isaac asked Liam. It was less a question than a command.

Liam grunted in the affirmative.

Alone in the dining room, he listened to his family giggle their way through their nighttime routine. If he hadn't also fallen under his sister's delightful spell, he'd doubt brushing teeth and flossing could be so fun. But he understood. His sister exuded the magic of joy.

Once the family moved into Tasha's room, RP crawled out from under the table and stretched his hind legs. The lazy bugger had slept through Sissy's coming-out party. He meowed, padded over to Liam, and weaved between his legs. Warm fur covered Liam's fingers as he picked up the cat. He'd use the fur ball as an excuse to say goodnight to his sister.

Tucked snug under her pink and white polka dotted comforter, Tasha patted the space beside her. "Come listen while Mommy reads a book," she said.

RP didn't wait for a second invitation. He launched out of Liam's arms and circled out a nesting spot next to Tasha. Saddened he couldn't copy the cat's confidence, Liam eased onto the foot of the bed and listened as his mother read, "Don't Let the Pigeon Drive the Bus."

Allison had her faults as a mother, but she'd always excelled as a storyteller. Her voice, pitched an octave higher than normal, kept both Tasha and Liam captive. His little sister slipped her hand into his, and she squeezed three times—their silent code for "I love you." He squeezed back four times, adding a "too" to the end of their code, and wished every night ended this way.

As soon as Allison closed the book, Isaac cleared his throat from the doorway. He'd determined Liam had spent enough time with his daughter.

"Sweet dreams." Liam kissed the tip of Tasha's nose. "Don't you ever change. You're perfect."

"So are you, Liam. Love you." She brushed his cheek and then pulled up her covers and yawned.

An imaginary dagger twisted his guts. He'd miss Tasha every day for the rest of his life. But whether or not Cull and his threats existed, she was better off with him gone. She'd be safe then.

"I'm exhausted. Think I'll relax in my room," Liam said. He bumped against Isaac and stepped on his foot on the way out of Tasha's room.

"Wish I could knock off for the night, too, but I've had trouble sleeping lately," said Isaac. He jerked his foot out from under Liam's. "Bet I'll be up all night."

"Don't wear yourself out."

Isaac opened his mouth to speak, but before he could, Allison placed her hand in his and leaned against him.

"Try to get a full night's sleep, Liam. Think over your plan and let me know in the morning if it's really what you want." She took her free hand and tucked an unruly wave of hair behind his ear.

"Will do." What he really wanted to say was, "love you," but he didn't. She'd suspect the worst and check on him throughout the night.

Half afraid another hand waited to haunt him in his room, he breathed a sigh of relief when he pushed open his bedroom door and saw nothing but the generic decorations of his room. Only white walls and stark reality accompanied him tonight. Not even Joshua awaited him; he must be biding his time until they moved to a new home. Yet another misjudgment on Liam's part.

He flopped onto his bed and looked at his clock—8:16. In under six hours, he'd leave Isaac's house forever. He'd be independent, and Tasha would be safe.

He'd come up with his best plan yet.

51

Six hours passed slowly. Too slowly. Liam spent most of it picking fuzz off his comforter and devising ways of eluding Isaac. It wouldn't be easy. Fooling his stepfather once was impressive; twice would be miraculous.

One unavoidable constant reared its head in each of his escape scenarios. He needed the Hyundai's keys, but after stealing the SUV that morning, he doubted they'd be dangling from the hall tree waiting for him.

Still, he had to check. At 10:01 he stumbled down the hallway, pretending to stretch his arms and yawn. Isaac sat in the doorway to the living room with a direct view of Tasha's room.

"Need something?" he asked. A half-empty mug of coffee sat to his side.

"A glass of water."

"I'll get it for you." Isaac stood and waited for Liam to pass. Their shoulders brushed in the narrow hallway.

Curled up in a corner of the couch, Allison gripped the remote and watched some superhero show. Police sirens blared from the television. No doubt the cops chased a chiseled millionaire who wore tight leather pants.

"Everything all right?" she asked. Her eyes traveled from Isaac to Liam.

"Helping your son stay refreshed. Nothing to worry about. You didn't have any other reason for coming out here, did you, Liam?" Isaac trailed his fingers along the hall tree as they passed it, the keys conspicuously absent from their normal hanging place.

"None at all."

The two marched into the kitchen, and Liam feigned patience as Isaac filled a glass with tap water and handed it to him. "Thanks, Dad."

Isaac's eyes narrowed. Good thing he'd already handed Liam the glass. Otherwise, it might've shattered under the pressure of his hands.

Liam mumbled, "See you in the morning."

His stepfather resumed his position in the hallway and watched Liam walk back to his bedroom.

The escape plan's difficulty level jumped from yellow to red. Unless he could figure out how to hot wire a car in the next few hours, he'd have to sniff out where Isaac had hidden the keys. No matter how much coffee he consumed, the man would have to fall asleep at some point. Liam could out-wait him.

He switched off his nightstand lamp and paced in the pitch black. He faced a difficult, but not impossible, task in finding the keys. He'd prevailed in worse binds. Besides, hadn't his mother asked him to apply himself to real-life issues? This was a puzzle he could, and would, solve.

First, he had to pack. He popped on a headlamp and stuffed all of his necessities, including the paltry stash of bills he'd stolen for his escape, into his backpack. The bag rattled with the sound of his anti-psychotic medication as he tossed it on his bed. Thankfully, his mother had recently switched to mail order prescriptions, so he had a three-month supply of his meds. He'd have an issue when they ran out, but he'd worry about that later.

He crouched on the floor and peered under his bed. The headlamp revealed mounds of crumpled paper and long-lost socks. Buried under a fine layer of dust lay Mai's portrait. He pulled it out and blew a puff of air at it, sneezing loudly at the resulting dust cloud. As if she knew he thought of her, his phone dinged with an incoming text. He rested the canvas on his bag and picked up his phone.

"Still on for tonight?" Mai texted.

Uncertainty over the Cull situation ate at him. He ran his tongue over his teeth and inhaled. Could he really ask Mai to drop everything for a possible delusion?

"Yes. See you soon," he texted.

With nothing left to do but wait, he hopped onto the papasan and threw on his headphones, playing every Pearl Jam, Pixies, and Smashing Pumpkins album he owned. On impulse, he pulled out his oils and painted a unicorn scene on his last blank canvas. The unicorn's swirling horn resembled a jagged knife a mite more than necessary, but hey, for balancing the canvas on his unsteady knees and working by the light of a headlamp, it didn't turn out half-bad. Tasha would love it.

Eventually, he ran out of distractions and resorted to staring at his walls, even briefly flirting with the idea of calling for Joshua to keep him company. One touch to his cheek, which still stung from where Joshua had pinched it earlier, brought him back to his senses.

After an excruciating wait, and a house devoid of noise, 2:00 a.m. arrived. Liam grabbed his backpack and Mai's portrait and turned his doorknob. The hallway loomed empty. Time to find those keys.

He slinked down the hall and glanced at his mother's closed bedroom as he passed.

Fingernails blackened with dirt crept out from underneath her doorway and extended out to grab him. The filthy hand snapped shut an inch from his ankle. He barely kept back the bloodcurdling scream dying to rush from his lips, and he jumped backward, banging into the wall with his backpack. He blinked. The hand disappeared.

A protracted two minutes had passed before he moved again. Hopefully, he hadn't awakened Isaac with his racket.

The next ten feet were critical. If Isaac still sat by Tasha's doorway, he'd have to conjure up some ninja-like moves to sneak by without waking him. He crept up to the l-shaped corner that led to his sister's room, slowly poked his head out, and peered to the left. Relief flooded his body.

His stepfather had given up his guard post.

Liam skulked down the hallway and into the living room, where moonlight filtered through the curtains. Maybe Isaac had placed the keys on the hall tree after he went to bed. His hand clamped down on an empty hook.

A light clicked on in the living room.

Keys swung from Isaac's long fingers. He sat on the loveseat, coffee mug still close by. "Looking for these?"

Liam's stomach sunk. Game over. Nothing but the cold truth could save him now.

"I've got to leave."

Isaac shook his head. "If you leave now, you'll break probation. Then they'll ship you off to God knows where. And that will make your mother unhappy. Not acceptable."

He flexed his hands over Mai's portrait. "I can't live here with Tasha. You know that."

Face partially obscured by shadows, Isaac exhaled loudly through his nose. "There's no plan with your uncle, is there?"

The clock hanging on the living room wall ticked away silent seconds before he found the courage to answer.

"No. I wanted Mom to feel safe tonight and not worry about Tasha. I dangled a carrot."

Isaac placed his keys in his pocket. "And leaving this way won't worry your mother?"

"It will." He shifted his weight. "But in the long run, it's best for us all."

"There are other options. I appreciate your concern for Tasha. I really do. But you've got to think of your life here. Your future doesn't have to be a disaster."

Doesn't it, though?

Isaac leaned forward and gripped his knees. "I haven't always done right by you, Liam. But I'm trying. And I want us all to figure out the next, best step. I don't have the answer now, but leaving like this isn't it."

"Since when did you become my buddy?" Liam barked out a cynical laugh. "Don't you want me gone? Besides, I'm a danger to everybody here. Somebody's looking for me."

Isaac rolled his lips. "Are they looking for you because of Stuart's death?"

The lump in his throat became too big to swallow. "Yes."

"You've got to tell me now what you know about his murder. I can help only if you let me. Mistakes, even terrible ones, happen," Isaac whispered.

A vein in Liam's forehead popped out. "At least now we're back in familiar territory." He threw his backpack on the ground and tossed the portrait on top of it. "I didn't hurt Stuart."

Isaac rubbed his head and leaned back into the couch. "You seem to have knowledge about the crime that isn't public. What other explanation is there?"

"Why do you always think the worst of me?" He pounded his right hand against his left fist and raised his voice. "Isn't it possible I could be simply a witness? You're a lawyer. Have some imagination."

"Then tell me what your connection is." Isaac grunted in frustration. "I can't help you if you won't let me."

He gambled on the truth. "I see visions."

A long-suffering expression crossed Isaac's face. "We've known that for a while now, Liam."

"No, they're not like the normal hallucinations. These visions are real. They really happen," he said in an embarrassingly pleading tone.

Isaac sucked in his cheeks and ran his fingers around the edge of his coffee mug. "So what did you see?"

He looked at the floor and focused on a long, black scuff. "Cull beating Stuart to death."

After a drawn-out silence, Isaac asked, "Who's Cull?"

A voice filtered out from the hallway behind him.

"I am," it said.

52

Liam stumbled away from Cull's voice and clawed at the hall tree for items he could use as defense weapons. His fingers ran over his mother's silk scarf and closed over it.

"Liam? Are you okay?" asked Isaac.

Prickles of fear stabbed every nerve in his spine. "No! Didn't you hear him?"

Isaac pinched the bridge of his nose. "The two of us are the only ones in this room."

A dark crimson stain blossomed on the wall behind Isaac, expanding into an uneven oval. Long trails of viscous dark red fluid dripped down the wall and pooled onto the aged linoleum. Liam blinked. The blood remained.

"Focus on what's real. And what's real is the two of us." Isaac pointed at his chest and then Liam's.

Bile rose in his throat as he backed into the corner, legs trembling. "It's too late. He's coming."

"It's never too late. You can beat this."

But it *was* too late. Because in the next instant, the back door's glass shattered. Pieces large and small sparkled to the floor as a veiny hand reached in and unlocked it.

"He's here!" Liam yelled. He sprinted toward Tasha's room. He wouldn't be able to delay Cull for long, but maybe long enough to let her escape.

Isaac skidded into Tasha's room after him. With shocking efficiency, he yanked Liam's arms together behind his back and held them. "Don't even think about touching her," he growled.

Tasha sat up in her bed and rubbed her eyes. "Is it morning?"

"Not yet, baby girl. Go back to sleep," Isaac said. His grip intensified.

In a desperate bid to break free, Liam stomped on his stepfather's foot. Unmovable as a redwood tree, Isaac didn't flinch.

They wasted precious time. Cull had arrived.

Liam howled in frustration. "How can you just stand there, Isaac? You're gonna let Cull break in and kill us?"

Tasha's eyes widened.

"There's nobody here. It's all in your head." Isaac's tone sounded much calmer than his body language suggested.

Liam's knees weakened. "You're lying. I saw him."

"Go look." Isaac released his arms and stepped in front of Tasha.

Not sure which alternative he feared most—finding Cull or an intact door—he crept back through the hallway and into the living room. Silence blanketed the night. The back door stood in one piece, and the wall remained blood-free.

Footsteps whispered behind him. In a small and tired voice, Allison said, "Honey? What's going on?" She tied her pink terrycloth bathrobe and placed a hand on his back.

He shook his head. "I don't understand." Cull had been there a second ago.

Hadn't he?

Isaac joined his wife and placed an arm around her waist. "I think you do, Liam. But it's hard for you to admit it."

"Admit what?" His fingers twitched uncontrollably.

"The murder of Stuart Laughlin."

Allison gasped. "You're sure about this?"

Isaac nodded curtly.

Liam held a hand to his spinning head. "I didn't kill him!"

"Yes, you did. I know about the drugs," Isaac said.

He sucked in his breath. "How?"

"I found some a few weeks ago in your sock drawer. You asked me earlier to use my imagination... How's this? You bought cocaine from Stuart. Then the two of you had a falling out. Maybe you threatened to tell me about his extracurricular activities. Maybe you didn't pay him on time. Maybe you stole from him. Whatever the case, the two of you argued, and you killed him. Am I getting warm?"

He licked his lips. "Ice cold."

"Then what did happen?" Allison asked. Her face had turned ghostly pale.

"Cull killed him." His words came out slow and stilted like a child uttering some profound lie he knew nobody believed.

Don't let them confuse you. Stay focused.

Isaac crossed his arms. "You keep talking about this Cull. Cull who?"

"I don't know his last name." Liam walked in a tight circle and wagged his pointer finger. "But he works at your office."

"There are no 'Culls' at my office. But what my office does have is a surveillance camera." Isaac flicked on the living room light and edged closer to him. "And it caught you there the day before you checked into the clinic, pawing around Stuart's desk. Did you steal money or drugs?"

Liam shielded his eyes against the bright light. "Neither! I just investigated Stuart. I knew he'd been killed, but I needed to know more about him."

Isaac sniffed. "Stuart was still alive and well then."

The room seemed to shrink and close in on him. He rolled his shoulder blades and stopped pacing. He said, "I saw the murder before it happened. Sometimes I see the future."

Tears flowed down Allison's face. She wiped her cheek on her robe.

He'd lost her. Again.

"Look at your surveillance footage." His voice trembled with either rage or fear; he couldn't distinguish between the two anymore. "You'll find Stuart there with another man. The other man is Cull, the killer."

A look of pity crossed Isaac's face. "The only images our camera caught were you lurking about the office and then vomiting down the hallway. Our security team showed the footage to me out of courtesy.

They didn't seek any charges against you when I told them you'd sought professional help."

For a few awful moments, only the sound of Allison's sobs punctured the tense silence.

Isaac said, "It's you, Liam. You're the killer. I wish you weren't. I wanted, more than anything, to believe I connected dots where I shouldn't. But you can't see the future, Liam. You can only see what you did."

"It's not true!" Liam closed the distance between his stepfather and him and poked his thick chest. "Don't discredit me because of my illness. Open your mind."

Please!

"Don't make this worse than it already is," Isaac warned.

Rage boiled in his stomach, and hatred shot through his body. His precarious grip on reality wavered enough without Isaac scrambling his brains. Liam reared his skull back to headbutt the man when a small voice caused him to stiffen.

"Liam?" Bleary eyed and bewildered, Tasha leaned against the hall doorway. She clung her stuffed bunny to her chest. "Why are you so upset?" She twisted her bunny's ears.

He stepped away from Isaac. "We're having a little misunderstanding,"

"'Bout what?"

"About what I'm capable of doing."

Her chin quivered. "Did you listen to your voices again?" she whispered.

Like she'd placed a vacuum in his body and switched it on, all oxygen in his lungs vanished in an instant. He struggled to breathe.

How could he deny the possibility when Tasha asked the question? She who'd suffered most because of his voices?

"I tried not to." He hung his head in humiliation. Exhaustion won the contest it'd waged with his anger. He crossed the room, pulled out a dining room chair, and collapsed into it. "I tried so hard."

Tasha brushed aside her mother's hand and stepped forward. The moonlight hit her lilac nightgown, setting it aglow like an ethereal angel's wings. Isaac stepped toward her, but she stalled his progress with a raised hand. "I know. You fought good, Liam. I could tell."

His heart shattered into more pieces than his fractured mind.

She said, "I love you. So does Mommy. Daddy, too, even if he doesn't say so."

Smiling, she joined him at the dining room table and rubbed his unwashed red hair. If only love would fix him like Tasha imagined. It would help him, certainly, but never change what lived in his core—an unpredictable and selfish monster.

The leap from monster to killer wasn't a great one. Dr. Jen always prompted him to analyze his hallucinations and why they scared him. Of all the threats in the world, he feared himself most; the dreadful sins he might commit, the danger he posed to his family, the risks he created for Mai.

Much as he longed to deny it, his stepfather's theory explained the events of the past few months. He'd constructed a complex delusion that had culminated in Stuart's death.

He was a murderer.

Tears brimmed in his eyes as he hugged Tasha. "No matter who you might become one day, remember you're my baby sister, and I love you. Always."

"I know, silly." She met his eyes with maturity beyond her years. She must know he referred to Sissy and the possibility she could become like him. The thought didn't appear to scare her. It should've.

He stood and gestured at Isaac. "I guess we contact the authorities now?"

Allison buried her face in her hands. Unable to take the pain he caused his mother, he turned away toward the back window where, once again, Cull watched over them.

53

Cull's presence didn't scare Liam. The pit of his stomach didn't turn cold, nor did the back of his neck crawl. Instead, a paralyzing sadness filled him. His hallucinations had finally done him in.

When the back door's glass exploded into the family room, he simply watched, entranced as his hallucination repeated itself.

Tasha's screams finally snapped him out of his stupor. She pointed a shaking finger to the backdoor and the lock being opened by a stranger's hand. His pulse quickened.

It skyrocketed when Isaac yelled, "Run!"

Tasha sped toward Allison, who grabbed her by the shoulders and turned to escape down the hallway. Isaac placed his body in front of theirs and ran toward the intruder.

"One more step from anybody and I shoot," Cull said. He swung open the door and aimed his revolver at Isaac, who stopped four feet away from him.

"Michael? What are you doing?" Isaac yelled. His arms shook with anger.

This can't be happening. Right?

Liam stared openmouthed at Cull and blinked ten times. He remained. "Is he really here?" he asked.

Cull snorted. "Appears so." His feet crunched over broken glass as he walked into the house. After slamming the door shut, he flicked his gun at Liam. "You have no idea what a blessing you are. When the unfortunate incident with Stuart happened, I didn't panic. I knew it'd be easy to frame you for his murder. Everybody knows schizos are dangerous."

Eyes widened in horror, Isaac gulped. "Are you admitting to murdering Stuart?"

Liam's mouth went dry. "You see him?"

"Of course I see him," Isaac snapped.

"That's Cull," Liam said. "He's the man who killed Stuart."

Cull chuckled. "You should see your face, Colonel. It's almost worth all the trouble your boy put me through. I gather your stepson hasn't kept his mouth shut and told you about what he found?"

Isaac gaped at Cull in disbelief. "Cull is short for Michael?"

"For a select few. My closest friends."

"Do you kill all of your close friends?" Liam asked. Despite the circumstances, it felt liberating to know, for a fact, Cull existed.

Cull narrowed his eyes. "You're the reason he's dead. You put the idea in my mind."

"Go ahead and try to deflect your guilt," said Liam. His lips curled down in contempt. "But you can't blame other people for your own bad actions. Even I know that."

Gun still aimed at Isaac, Cull stepped to the side so he had a clear view of Allison and Tasha. "Shut up. It's your fault, and you're the one who's gonna pay for it."

"What are you going to do, Michael?" Isaac asked. Not the sort to cower before a tough fight, he placed his left foot forward and inched toward him.

Cull cocked his revolver. "I'll tell you once you've stopped moving. One more centimeter, Colonel, and I kill you."

Isaac ground his teeth and held his stance.

"Good decision, Colonel. I haven't made many of those myself since I first saw your stepson. You know, after all this trouble, I've decided it's time to turn over a new leaf. But I can't move forward without your family's help." He pointed his gun at Tasha. "Bring her to me."

"No," Isaac and Allison said in unison. The muscles in Isaac's jaws bulged, and Allison ushered Tasha behind her.

"Did that sound like a request?" He angled his head to the side, a look of irritated incredulity plastered across his face. "In case you didn't notice, I've got the gun. And it's aimed straight at your wife and daughter. Bring the girl to me."

Allison planted her feet shoulder width apart and splayed her fingers on her hips. "No," she repeated.

Cull sighed. "Don't say I didn't warn you."

The report of his revolver echoed through the living room. Allison groaned in agony and grabbed her shoulder. Blood seeped through a blackened hole in her robe and trickled out of her sleeve and onto Tasha's head, who peeked out to see what had happened.

"Mommy!" she screamed.

"No, no, no, no!" Isaac raced to his wife's side and placed his hands on her wound to stanch the bleeding. A slick, crimson fluid covered his fingers in a disarmingly short period of time. "Hang on, baby. You're going to be okay."

The scene eclipsed Liam's worst nightmares. And then it hit him. This was all a complex hallucination that would end if he didn't engage it. He only had to imagine it away.

You're making this up, dude. Pull yourself together. Wake up, wake up, wake up!

Face white with shock, Allison crumpled to the floor. Isaac knelt with her as Tasha threw herself at her mother's knee and sobbed. Teeth bared in a rage-filled snarl, Isaac turned toward Cull. He said, "Leave my family alone. They've done nothing to you."

"It's like you're not even listening to me, Colonel." Cull huffed and rolled his eyes. "You know what Liam did to me. Besides, for my plan to work, I've got to stage this crime just right. That means your wife needs to bleed to death. I do, however, have a contingency plan. If you make any more trouble, I'll be forced to resort to it. And it involves a bullet in her pretty head."

"Don't worry about me. Protect Tasha," Allison whispered.

Nostrils flared with anger, Isaac kissed her good shoulder.

Cull said, "Now, I don't wanna mislead you. Everybody here has to die. But I think we can agree some deaths are worse than others." He shrugged. "Like yours, Colonel. There's no getting around it. See, Liam here is gonna beat you silly. All his bottled up anger is going to boil out in a terrible way tonight. Your wife will catch him in the act, so he'll shoot her before turning the gun on himself."

Tasha stopped sniffling long enough to glare at Cull. She said, "Liam would never hurt Mommy or Daddy. You're a liar."

"The naivety of children. Usually such a beautiful thing. Tell me, sweetheart, how are you gonna die?" said Cull.

"Shut your mouth!" yelled Isaac. The cords on his neck stuck out as he kept his hand pressed to Allison's shoulder. He turned toward Tasha. "You're going to be fine, baby girl. Remember what I promised you?"

"Yes, Daddy."

Cull clucked. "Aww, so touching. I hate to break it up, but it's time. Liam—you want first dibs?"

Anytime now, self. Shut this shit down. Wish away Cull and this nightmare.

"You ain't gonna say boo, are you, boy? Must've run through all your words at the shoppette." Cull waved the gun and whistled. "Don't you want a shot at the Colonel? You know what he does to your mother, right?"

"Leave my brother alone!" Tasha screeched. She jumped up and tore across the room to Cull.

"No, Tasha!" Isaac lifted his hand from Allison's shoulder and sprang after his daughter. He dove between Cull and Tasha just in time to catch the full force of Cull bringing his gun down to crack her skull. His eyes rolled back, and his body went rigid. With a sickening thud, he fell to the floor.

Cull reached over Isaac's inert body and grabbed Tasha by the hair.

An anguished scream spilled from Allison's mouth. She placed her hands on the wall and tried unsuccessfully to pull up. Blood dripped down from her red palm prints and puddled on the floor.

"I wish you all would've cooperated. It has to get messy now." Cull wrapped his muscular arms around Tasha's throat in a chokehold.

Her eyes bulged, and her feet slapped against the floor as she kicked out her legs.

"Do something, Liam!" Allison cried.

Tasha opened her mouth in a silent struggle for air.

This is real! Help your sister!

The emotional chokehold doubt lorded over Liam finally broke. Cull was real. And if Liam didn't do something, his family would die. Blood roared through his veins as he took a step forward.

Cull laughed. "Gonna be a hero, boy? Because however this all ends, the police will blame you. They'll decide your family became afraid of you, so they locked you out. But a little bolted door couldn't keep you out. No, sir. You broke in and killed them in a psychotic rage. Happens in the news all the time. Your family will be another unfortunate example of murder-suicide."

The silk scarf in his pocket spread like liquid between his fingers. "I'm not killing anybody but you tonight," Liam said.

"Please. Do you know how pathetic you sound? Like a snot-nosed schoolboy taunting a professional boxer."

A familiar rumble sounded from the hallway. Cull's eyes darted toward the sound. "You've got a dog?"

"No. Just one helluva mean cat," said Liam.

A hissing, growling ball of irate fur barreled over Allison's blood-soaked robe. Cull shot at the racing form but missed, the bullet lodging instead in the linoleum. Liam crept close as the cat hopped over Isaac and thrashed Cull's leg with his claws and sank his fangs deep into the murderer's skin. Another shot reverberated.

Liam kicked hard at Cull's hand. The gun flew out of his hold and spun across the room, landing on the corner of the couch. Liam put all of his weight behind a palm strike and aimed straight at Cull's nose. Bone crunched, and blood shot out like they were in a scene from a Quentin Tarantino movie. Cull dropped Tasha and grabbed his ruined face.

Tasha fought to inhale and writhed on the floor next to her father.

A crimson trail followed Allison as she whimpered and crawled over to her family.

"Does hurting little girls make you feel like a big man?" Liam asked. He twisted to the side and kicked Cull's stomach, driving him backward into the wall with a loud smack. His mother's favorite mirror, a large rectangle framed with mahogany wood, shuddered with the impact and came crashing down. Glass shattered into thousands of pieces, the sound so deafening he could barely hear Cull gagging as he doubled over.

"Not breathing sucks, doesn't it?" Liam checked Tasha, whose chest rose and fell in a steady rhythm now. Bruises darkened the delicate skin around her neck, and tears wet her cheeks. He'd make Cull pay for each and every mark on her body.

The silk scarf caught on a hangnail as his hands clenched over it. Time to put it to use. He roped it around Cull's neck and twisted. But before he could tighten the scarf, Cull's shocked expression changed to one of rage. He was ready to fight now. And he was much, much stronger than Liam.

54

C**ull ripped off the scarf and slammed his fist into** Liam's temple. The world went black for a precious second before another punch to his chin sent him sailing onto the couch. The revolver lay a few feet to his left. He stretched for it, but Cull's knee landed hard on his elbow and trapped him. Coarse hands covered his neck and squeezed.

"Change of plans. You won't be here when the cops arrive. They'll think you've run. But you're gonna meet the same end Stuart did. Except Shell Island is too good of a final resting place for you. I'm dumping you into the ocean, where nobody will find you."

Liam jabbed Cull with his free hand, but the man didn't flinch. His vision blurred, then turned red. In desperation he kicked out with his feet but met only empty space.

Moments away from passing out, the red haze of his vision morphed into a projection attached to Cull—the same image he'd seen of himself at Isaac's office. In it, he stared ahead with glassy, bloodshot eyes.

A sense of disembodiment overtook Liam as he pawed at Cull's face. His soul slowly seeped away from his body and joined the projection, like dew evaporating under the morning sun.

Three gunshots interrupted his death.

Cull's head fractured in spectacular fashion. The top of his skull spun up toward the ceiling while his cheekbone splintered and sprayed to the side. He collapsed to the floor and revealed a large oval of blood on the wall behind him.

Liam grabbed his neck and coughed. While he still gulped for air, he turned and looked at the shooter.

The revolver hung from Joshua's hands. A limp cigarette stuck to his lips. "Nobody gets to take you away from me." He dropped the weapon to the floor and pushed his chin up toward Liam. "You owe me one."

Soft sobs tore Liam's eyes from Joshua. Covered in her mother's blood, Tasha stooped next to her parents, with one hand on each. Facedown on the floor, Isaac didn't move. RP rested a few inches away. Though the pool of blood next to him grew, he lay still. Lifeless.

"Liam?" Tasha croaked. The strangling had turned her voice deep and scratchy.

He stumbled to her. "Are you okay?" The words stuck in his mouth with fear.

She nodded. "My throat hurts. But I can breathe. Mommy and Daddy need help."

"I'll be okay, baby girl. Go grab the phone," Allison whispered.

Tasha ran into the kitchen to fetch the phone.

Tears streaked down Allison's cheeks as she melted onto the cold floor and patted her unconscious husband. "Is he...?" She closed her eyes.

Liam girded himself for the worst and felt for Isaac's pulse.

It beat steady and strong.

He gently shook his stepfather. Isaac moaned and opened his eyes. A nasty bump marked the spot where Cull had pistol-whipped him, and blood trickled down the back of his head.

The mechanical beeping of Allison dialing 9-1-1 filled the room. "I need some ambulances. Please hurry. An intruder attacked my family." Her voice weakened as she spoke.

Isaac looked across the living room. His Turkish rug boasted crimson circles where none had been before, and bits of brain matter clung to the leather couch. Although the furniture hid most of Cull's body, his feet stuck out, and they swam in his own blood. Balance still off-kilter, Isaac attempted to stand. It didn't work. He slumped over Liam. "What happened? How's Tasha?"

"Tasha will recover. And we took care of Cull. He can't harm anybody again," Liam said.

Smoke from Joshua's cigarette funneled down to his stepfather's head like a miniature tornado. He squatted next to Liam and thumped him on the back. "Isaac's tougher to kill than a bad case of gonorrhea. At least he looks like shit."

"Sorry to leave you with such a mess, but I've got to split before the authorities arrive," Liam said.

"You can't go. You'll look guilty." The string of small sentences took Isaac a while to form.

"I already look guilty. You thought yourself I killed Stuart. Now his partner is dead at our house. How will Security Forces read that?"

Sweat rolled down Isaac's forehead. "We'll explain. You won't get in trouble."

"Always the dreamer, Isaac. We both know I've already got too many strikes against me in the legal system to come out of this free. Yesterday, a police officer itched for a reason to lock me away after a simple car accident. There's plenty more for them to work with today."

"I wanted to help you."

"I know." Despite their endless tension, Liam heard the truth in Isaac's words. Warmth spread across his chest. "And I'll remember your support for the rest of my life. My mother and sister are blessed to have you."

The keys in Isaac's pocket jangled as his wobbly hand retrieved them. "Hurry. Ditch the car. Don't go anywhere predictable."

Liam's fingers curled around the keys.

"Got a cousin in Milwaukee." Isaac made another Herculean effort to steady himself. He placed his elbows on the floor, wincing from the effort. "Name's Taraji Lowery. She's a psychiatrist. She'll help you."

Gratitude filled Liam. "Thank you."

"Go," said Isaac. He placed his hand over Allison's wound, and she pinched herself to stay conscious.

Liam scooped up RP's body and held it close to his torso. Warm and sticky blood matted the cat's fur.

"I'm sorry, pal. I wish it didn't have to end this way." He brushed his lips across the top of RP's limp head and ran his fingers over the cat's pointy ears.

Heart heavy with sorrow, and throat aching both from Cull's attack and grief, he walked through the kitchen door and made his way to the cat's favorite shrub. He pushed aside prickly branches and leaves. RP's dark fur rippled in the night air as Liam laid him in his hiding place.

"Wherever you are, I hope they've got an endless supply of anoles. Enjoy the afterlife." He ripped off a leaf and placed it like a laurel on RP's head.

Goodbyes were the worst. He couldn't repeat the process with his mother and sister. It would only distract them from surviving. Anyway, he'd never find the words to express what he felt for them. They already knew.

He crept back into the house and picked up his backpack and Mai's portrait from where he'd dropped them earlier. Before leaving, he shot one last look at his family. Tasha fretted over their mother, and Allison focused all her energy on not dying. Isaac alone met his gaze.

The look he gave Liam, the same one he typically reserved for Tasha, almost made him stay. It held no enmity, no suspicion. One might even call it love.

Liam closed the door.

55

The bottom of Mai's flip-flop smacked the parking lot surface. She popped her gum, stale now, and tapped the hood of her car. Liam was late. Very, very late.

A warm breeze whistled through the parking lot, bringing with it the scent of day-old seafood. Liam hated these types of place. The restaurant's name, "I Sea Food," flickered above the boxy building in neon letters.

She checked her phone for the hundredth time. It glowed 4:43. Dread crawled through her gut. Something was wrong. She'd debated for the past half hour if she should call the police and report him missing. But what if he'd simply changed his mind and slept in his bed? She doubted he'd appreciate a police check in the middle of the night after ditching his girlfriend.

She texted him again. "Where are you?"

Like the other eight texts she'd sent, she received no response. With an aggravated sigh she threw her phone into her purse.

A piece of paper fluttering in the corner of the parking lot caught her attention.

It's just trash.

Still, she backed away from her car and walked toward the scratch paper, jammed into a crack in the concrete and held in place by a piece of crumbling rock. She lifted the rock and slid out the paper.

Her heart banged up to her throat as she unraveled the note. Liam wrote in small, precise script.

"Mai,

You can never know what you mean to me. I lived the last few years in darkness. Then I met you, and the light came back, blinding me with its brilliance. You reminded me what love can be. More importantly, you reminded me what I want it to be.

Sorry for bailing on you, but I have to disappear for a bit. Please know that I'm safe, and that I've conquered at least one of my many demons.

Thank you for believing in me. Your undying support is just one of the many ways in which you are far from normal. That's right. I hate to tell you, but you will never, ever achieve mediocrity. Might as well face up to it now. Accept that one-way ticket to success. Once you get there, though, save some room for an Average Joe like me.

I'll be checking on you. And one day soon, let's try this again. I wish you all the best, Mai.

You deserve it.

Love, Liam."

Mai stood in the parking lot reading and rereading the letter until the words bled together and her fingers stung with unanswered anticipation.

Okay, so going with Liam would've been a risky move. But he deserved more than what life had given him. He deserved somebody who believed in him, who wouldn't abandon him despite his challenges. He deserved love.

She folded the letter into a neat square and slipped it in her purse. After a final glance at her dark phone screen, she bent into her car, slammed the door shut, and sobbed. For a chance lost. For a future that might not include Liam. For wishing she'd helped him more.

He had better stay safe. When he finally deigned to contact her again, she'd give him a piece of her mind. She could wait. Even if it took a long time.

56

Hunkered down behind the dumpster, Liam watched Mai's taillights long after she drove away from the parking lot. The farther she drove from him, the more his chest constricted. But he wouldn't drag her into his problems. Hopefully someday they could be together, but not yet.

His hiding place reeked of rotten fish and grease. It also concealed his phone, which he'd turned off and pitched into the mounds of trash. Phones could be tracked, and the authorities would be after him. He didn't intend to make it easy for them to find him.

He snuck out from behind the dumpster and picked up the rock that had anchored his note, tracing the crumbly indentations where Mai's fingertips had touched. It'd taken her so long to find his note he'd feared she wouldn't see it.

Much as he hated saying goodbye, he'd wanted to tell her in person. But that had carried risks. Risks such as Mai begging to come along, beautiful lips quivering, or, even worse, seeing the relief on her face when he told her he had to go alone. He'd hidden near the note in the hope she'd look up and see him. She hadn't.

He dropped the rock and headed for his ride. He'd abandoned the Hyundai somewhere in Callaway, a small town between Tyndall AFB and Panama City. It'd taken a while, but after knocking around several neighborhoods, he'd found an unlocked vehicle with its keys stashed above the sun visor. He understood why the owner didn't bother with security. The 19-ancient Ford Pinto, paint job faded a nice shade of hideous, had seen much better days.

The Pinto's engine hiccupped and burped its way to life. The clunker would have to do until he got farther north. In another day or two, he'd sink the car in a pond or lake someplace and hop onto a Greyhound bus. Where exactly he'd end up, he didn't know. Isaac had told him to be unpredictable. Finally, an order from his stepfather he could follow.

He settled in for a long drive and fumbled with the radio until he found an alternative rock station, a relative rarity in the Panhandle. Eddie Vedder's voice sang out "Just Breathe" from the crackly radio. Liam took his advice and inhaled.

Allison would recover. He was sure of it. And though the evening must have traumatized Tasha, she'd be all right, especially since she had Isaac for a father. No matter how tough it got, he'd support her.

The start of a new adventure began today. Life could only get better from here on out. True, the adventure would be a lot better if Dr. Jen came with him. He'd never replace her. But he'd take what she'd taught him and apply it to his life. Her influence wouldn't stop because he couldn't see her anymore.

He ran his fingers over the portrait of Mai in the passenger seat. As much as he already missed her, they would meet again. Someday.

Until then, Joshua would find him wherever he settled and keep him company.

Dr. Jen unlocked her office and stepped inside, her stomach a boiling pit of regret and guilt. She'd lost Liam.

The same tears that had overwhelmed her all weekend threatened to make a reappearance. She turned on her computer and mentally steeled herself.

It had started with a simple phone call. "Dr. Jen Garciela?" a voice had said. She'd come to know and dread the particular officious tone of callers like that. It meant, "You've lost another one."

"This is Sergeant Adams from Tyndall AFB. I'm calling to gather information about one Liam Murphy."

Though she'd known better, she'd asked, "Is he okay?"

"He's missing. His family claims an intruder attacked them early Saturday morning and killed Mr. Murphy."

"What? Liam's dead?" Her legs had given out, and she'd crumpled onto her living room floor.

"Well, ma'am, we haven't recovered his body, so I can neither confirm nor deny his family's statement. His mother states she shot the intruder after he attacked her husband and daughter. However, we're not convinced events unfolded the way the family claims. Forensic evidence suggests another person's presence in the home during the attack."

She'd held her throbbing head in her hands, knowing what the sergeant would say next.

"We theorize Liam pulled the trigger, not his mother. Given Mr. Murphy's mental history, we haven't ruled out the idea he attacked his family and the so-called intruder unprovoked. We also suspect he escaped the scene and still lives."

She'd wanted to hang up then, but she'd gathered her courage and stayed on the line. "Do you know the intruder's name?"

Sergeant Adams had paused. "Yes, ma'am. We've identified Michael deSanto as the deceased."

She'd repeated the name in her mind. Michael. My-Cull. Her hands had begun shaking then. The rest of their conversation had blurred by, obscured by her overwhelming guilt.

The computer monitor buzzed to life. Dr. Jen typed in her password and prepared to write the report about Liam requested by Sergeant Adams. She opened up a word processing application and stared at an empty, white screen. Her fingers grazed the keyboard but refused to type her analysis of Liam.

Yes, he'd displayed violent tendencies in the past and still fought voices urging him to harm others. She couldn't deny those uncomfortable truths.

But propensities didn't make him a killer. Liam was a good man, and his mental health had improved. He'd learned to interpret his hallucinations. Sometimes his medicine and therapy even banished the voices for short periods of time. He'd had a promising future. Or at least the possibility of one.

The paranoia he'd displayed in his last days had been justified. While she'd disregarded his concerns of being hunted as merely a symptom of schizophrenia, he'd fought for his life.

What would Sergeant Adams think if she wrote up the projections Liam had claimed to see? Would he react the way she initially had, unwilling to consider the possibility Liam told the truth? Even after his dead-on description of Alicia, she hadn't believed him. No matter how extensively she searched, however, she'd never found a photo matching Liam's description of her sister. As far as she knew, no such photo existed. The only place that image of her sister remained was within her own mind.

She pushed back in her chair and stared out of her window. Sunlight glinted off a round, metallic object taped to it. She sat up and leaned toward it. A silver bracelet with a dangling charm hung from the glass. The hair on the nape of her neck stood straight out as she pressed her fingertips to the window. The familiar shape of an infinity symbol, the same size as the tattoo on her sister's wrist, dangled in the morning air. Dr. Jen's breath caught.

She returned to her chair and started typing.

Shout Outs

I owe the inspiration of this novel to my grandmother, Jane Towne Albright. A vibrant woman who loved life, her positive energy charged the atmosphere of every room she entered. She was also a woman of secrets, treasuring them and storing them away where only she knew they existed. The last of her generation in our family, I can't fathom that these secrets simply vanished when she passed. Perhaps, somehow, they are strong enough to linger with us. Nana, I hope that your memories float in the breeze, occasionally buffeted by the wings of birds on their journey to infinity. Love and miss you.

Thanks to all the incredible folks at Curiosity Quills Press. In particular, I'd like to thank Michael Cristiano for seeing the potential of my manuscript. Also, a huge thanks to my editor, Sharon Pickrel, for her insights and revisions that brought Bleed Through to the next level. Thank you to the talented Eugene Teplitsky for my incredible cover. Thanks also to Tanya Yakimenko, Nikki Tetreault, and Clare Dugmore.

Mom and Dad—thank you for a lifetime of love and support. A girl couldn't have asked for better parents. Thanks also for your incisive feedback. You both continue to be my fount of grammar knowledge.

To Lindsay, the best big sister in the world, I can only hope to one day attain your courage, strength, and intellect. Thanks for answering my never-ending requests for instant help with grace and wisdom.

Thank you to Deborah Nichols, Maria Scholz, and Norelli A. Reverón for the hours you spent reading, critiquing, and talking about my book. Because of you, Bleed Through is richer and better. More importantly, though, my life is fuller because of your friendship.

Jami and K.T. at Chimera Editing—thank you for helping me whip the first few chapters into decent shape during my earlier drafts. I carried your constructive critiques throughout the rest of the novel, and know it's better because of them.

To my children—thank you for the being the wonderful people you are. You are my sunlight and heart. I love you.

And for my husband, Benjamin. Thank you for your endless support and for giving me the ability to chase my dreams. Love you. Always. Only time will tell just how many memory imprints we've left upon the land.

About the Author

Born to an Air Force JAG father and an artist mother, **Adriana Arrington** learned from an early age there are at least two sides to every story, and each deserves to be told. After a nomadic upbringing, she married a southern charmer and settled down permanently in his home state of Virginia. To satisfy her enduring wanderlust, she transports herself to the sometimes scary, sometimes beautiful, but always interesting worlds of beautifully crafted novels. Formerly an IT consultant to the DoD, she now writes the stories banging around in her head.

THANK YOU FOR READING

http://adrianaarrington.com

Please visit http://curiosityquills.com/reader-survey to share your reading experience with the author of this book!

Muddy Waters, by Sara O. Thompson

Convicted for murdering her family, and locked up in a psych ward, a Witch makes a deal with the FBI to be their newest Supernormal Investigator--freedom has a price, though it's one she's willing to pay if it means she can track down who set her up for the fall. Solving crimes, doing magic, drinking bourbon. It's dirty work, but somebody has to do it.

Strange Truths, by S.D. Wasley

On track for a spectacular swimming career in the last months of his senior year at school, Mikey's life seems ideal. Until Alice England. The friendless undertaker's daughter starts stalking him at school. Curious, Mikey lets Alice in—just for a moment—and before he knows what's happening she's wedged her foot in the door and busted his world wide open.

67532839R00170

Made in the USA
Charleston, SC
15 February 2017